HONEST WORDS

"It wouldn't be fair to saddle you with my problems," she said.

"What problems do you refer to?"

"My health problems."

"I'm not worried about money. And if you have days you don't feel well, I'll help you."

"You'd soon get tired of that."

"That's not the way it works, Malinda. If two people take vows, it's for all time—in sickness and in health."

"Vows?" Her voice squeaked. She gave a little cough. "You don't know how bad it can get."

"I know it was bad enough to land you in the hospital. I don't want you to be sick, Malinda, but your condition doesn't scare me off. I want to help you, to take care of you."

"No man wants to take on extra household duties with his own chores and work. It would definitely be a burden."

"Why don't you let me decide that?"

Books by Susan Lantz Simpson

THE PROMISE

THE MENDING

Published by Kensington Publishing Corporation

The MENDING

Susan Lantz Simpson

ZEBRA BOOKS
KENSINGTON PUBLISHING CORP.
http://www.kensingtonbooks.com

ZEBRA BOOKS are published by

Kensington Publishing Corp.
119 West 40th Street
New York, NY 10018

First Printing: September 2018
ISBN-13: 978-1-4201-4662-2
ISBN-10: 1-4201-4662-9

eISBN-13: 978-1-4201-4663-9
eISBN-10: 1-4201-4663-7

10 9 8 7 6 5 4 3 2 1

Printed in the United States of America

In memory of my wonderful mother,
Ruth Lantz

ACKNOWLEDGMENTS

Thank you to my family and friends for your continuous love and support.

Thank you to my daughters, Rachel and Holly, for believing in me and dreaming along with me.

(Rachel, you patiently listened to my ideas and ramblings, and Holly, I couldn't have done any of the tech work without your skills!)

Thank you to my mother, who encouraged me from the time I was able to write. I know you are rejoicing in heaven.

Thank you to my Mennonite friends, Greta Martin and Ida Gehman, for all your information.

Thank you to my friends at Mt. Zion United Methodist Church for all your support and encouragement. You ladies are awesome!

Thank you to my wonderful agent, Julie Gwinn, for believing in me from the beginning and for all your tireless work.

Thank you to John Scognamiglio, editor in chief, and the entire staff at Kensington Publishing for all your efforts in turning my dream into reality.

Thank you most of all to God, giver of dreams and abilities and bestower of all blessings.

Prologue

She sensed someone had entered the room, even though she'd been dozing and hadn't heard the whoosh of the door opening or the squeak of athletic shoes on the tile floor. Her eyes felt glued shut. Sleep, a precious commodity, had been in short supply for a long, long time. She probably didn't even need to open her eyes. More than likely the visitor was the nurse, ready to review her discharge instructions with her. With eyes still closed, she freed a hand from under the stiff sheet and thin blanket to poke an errant strand of hair beneath her *kapp*.

"You look as lovely as always, Malinda."

Her eyes flew open. The deep voice certainly did not belong to the nurse. Quickly she pushed herself to a sitting position and yanked the covers up as high as she could get them. "D-Dr. McWilliams."

"Todd. Remember, I've told you on many occasions you can call me Todd."

Malinda nodded. "*Jah*, I remember." It didn't seem natural or right to call an unfamiliar man—especially an *Englisch* man, and a doctor, to boot—by his first name. Her *mamm* would be horrified.

Todd McWilliams wasn't a complete stranger. He'd been

her doctor ever since she had arrived in Ohio to stay with an aunt back in the spring. She'd seen him every day since she had been admitted to the hospital. He'd always been friendly; maybe a wee bit too friendly. She couldn't help but feel flattered that this tall, handsome, smart, important doctor seemed to take an interest in an ordinary Plain girl. Perhaps he treated all his patients as if they were the most special people in the world.

Malinda sucked in a sharp breath at the touch of the young doctor's hand. *Relax. He's probably checking your pulse, like everyone else who enters the room does—that is, if they aren't poking or prodding you for some reason.* But he didn't press his fingers to her wrist. That was a *gut* thing, or he'd feel her wildly galloping heartbeat. Instead, he laced his fingers with hers.

"You don't have to leave Ohio, Malinda. You could stay here with your aunt. That way I could still see you."

"I have a doctor back home who can monitor me. After all, Dr. Nelson referred me here when Aenti Mary called home after I got sick."

"I'm not talking about seeing you strictly as a patient, Malinda. Don't you feel there's something more between us than that?"

"I-I'm Amish. You're *Englisch*." Malinda tried to pull her hand free, but the doctor's grip, though not painful, was too tight for her to extract her hand from his. The warm, tingly feeling coursing through her veins surprised and frightened her.

"You could become '*Englisch*.'"

"*Nee*." She wiggled her fingers but still couldn't free them. "Being Amish is all I know. I've never had any desire to be anything else."

"It's always good to learn new things, to broaden your horizons."

Malinda shook her head, sending her *kapp* strings into a little dance.

"I could become Amish."

Malinda burst out laughing at the very thought of this highly educated, technologically dependent man shucking his medical degree, cell phone, and computer. She clapped her free hand over her mouth to muffle her giggles.

"What's so funny?"

"Th-the c-comment you just made," Malinda gasped, trying to choke back more laughter. She drew in a deep breath. "Do you honestly think you could give up all this?" She waved her hand at her surroundings. "You studied long and hard to become a doctor. Could you throw that away? Could you abandon your life, your car, your phone, and your gadgets?"

"The Amish need doctors, don't they?"

"Of course we *need* them. We just don't *become* them."

"Then it seems the best solution is for you to stay here. We have Mennonite churches around. You could join one, and I'll even join."

"*Nee*. My home is in Maryland. I came here to help my *aenti* after her surgery but ended up in the hospital after a flare-up of my condition. It's time to go home."

"Please, just think about—"

A sound at the door distracted the doctor enough that Malinda could slide her hand out of his grip. She adjusted her sheet and blanket and tucked both hands beneath them, out of reach of the doctor.

"I'm back, Malinda," the voice singsonged before the person fully entered the room. "Oh, Dr. McWilliams. I didn't know you were in here." The nurse skidded to an abrupt stop.

Her purple stethoscope swung around her neck. "I've got Malinda's discharge instructions. I can come back later."

"That's okay," Malinda answered before the doctor could tell Nurse Trudy to come back another time. She surprised herself by speaking up today when she usually was quite docile by nature, especially around authority figures. Todd McWilliams's conversation disturbed her more than she cared to admit. She needed to call it to a halt immediately. "Thank you, Dr. McWilliams, for everything. I'm feeling ever so much better now."

Malinda peeked at Nurse Trudy, who ran the hand not clutching a clipboard through her short, curly, blonde hair. The same hand then tugged down the tight-fitting flowered scrub top. The nurse's gaze flitted from doctor to patient. Malinda took in the frown puckering Trudy's forehead and the momentary anger clouding her wide green eyes. As quickly as they had appeared, the frown lines smoothed and the gaze softened. Trudy marched across the room and laid a possessive hand on the doctor's arm. "We're sure glad to hear that, aren't we, Todd, uh, Dr. McWilliams?"

Todd McWilliams shook his arm free. Malinda noted the brief look of disgust he aimed at the young nurse before he turned a smile on Malinda. "We certainly are." He patted Malinda's shoulder. "You take care now. And remember everything I said." He winked one brown eye, swiped at a lock of sandy hair that had drooped over his forehead, and backed away from the bed. "Do your thing, Nurse Trudy." He smiled once more at Malinda and then turned to stride from the small, private hospital room. He left the door open behind him.

"Okay, sweetie, let me go over your instructions with you. Then you can get out of the lovely hospital gown and put on your own clothes. How does that sound?"

"It sounds great." Malinda would be ever so glad to take off the less-than-modest blue and white gown she'd been compelled to don. The thing had short sleeves and barely came to her knees. And the back of it tied in only two places, leaving wide gaps of exposed flesh. That was the very reason she wore two of the shapeless gowns, one turned frontward and one turned backward. Putting on her own black stockings and long blue dress would be a blessing for sure.

Trudy dragged a padded, straight-backed chair closer to the bed and plopped down. “Whew! It’s good to get off my feet for a minute. I don’t know what Dr. McWilliams told you . . .” She paused and raised her thin, overplucked eyebrows as if waiting for some juicy tidbit of gossip. When Malinda merely shrugged, the nurse continued with her discharge spiel. She ran one long index finger down the top sheet of paper attached to the clipboard on her lap. “You are to continue with all your medications . . .”

Chapter One

Malinda leaned her head against the cool window of the big white van that was transporting her home. She had hugged Aenti Mary and apologized for getting sick when she'd come to help her *aenti*—as if she could control when a flare-up of her Crohn's disease would occur. And this had been a particularly nasty flare-up that had necessitated hospitalization. She still felt tired, weak, and sickly thin, but she was relieved to be out of the hospital and on her way home. She would have to endure Mamm's clucking over her like a mother hen and pushing all kinds of gooey goodies at her to fatten her up. The very thought of food made Malinda's stomach turn inside out, but the idea of climbing into her own comfortable, familiar bed soon settled her gut down a bit.

Malinda closed her eyes to stop the dizziness caused by the trees zooming past the window. Maybe she could sleep the whole nine-hour ride away. She didn't want to appear rude to the other passengers, who would disembark at various towns along the way, but she wasn't up to holding lengthy conversations. If she looked half as sick as she felt, they'd probably all steer clear of her anyway. Her head bumped against the window as the van chugged along. Lest a pounding headache ensue, Malinda slid down as much as the seat belt would allow and leaned her head against the back of the high seat. Conversations, some in Pennsylvania Dutch and others in *Englisch*, swirled around her, but she finally tuned them out. If only she could tune out the voices in her own head.

Had she given Todd McWilliams any indication she was even remotely interested in him as anything other than her health care provider? Why would he assume she could just up and jump the fence? She'd never had any desire to leave her community. Sure, some aspects of the *Englisch* life might be appealing, but not so appealing that she'd sacrifice her beliefs, her family, and her *freinden* for the luxury of turning on an electric light or jumping into a car for a quick ten-minute drive to the grocery store.

And what was with Nurse Trudy? For a brief moment, the nurse's eyes had shot daggers at her from across the room before she assumed her professional nurse expression. It seemed almost as if the young nurse, who was probably only a few years older than Malinda, had feared Malinda was stealing her man. She needn't have worried. Malinda had been a little flattered, but mostly confused and frightened. She was glad Trudy had entered the room when she did to save Malinda from being alone with the doctor any longer. *Ach*! It was too much to think about now. Ohio would soon be behind her.

The hum of rubber tires on the pavement and the steady drone of voices lulled Malinda to sleep. She only vaguely noticed any stops the van made until they reached the mountains of western Maryland. Somewhere near Oakland, the van lurched to a stop.

"*Ach*! Sorry, dear." The blonde, fortyish woman who had been sitting beside Malinda with her knitting needles clacking the whole way spoke softly. Her elbow poked Malinda as she gathered up her purse and small knitting bag in preparation to climb from the van. "Oops. Sorry."

Malinda turned bleary eyes in the woman's direction. "That's okay." With her throat as dry as dust, Malinda's voice came out as a croak. She cleared her throat and sat up straighter to look out the window. "Do you live here?"

"*Jah*. There are several Amish and Mennonite communities here." The woman smiled. If she'd told Malinda her name earlier, Malinda couldn't recall it now.

"It's beautiful." Malinda stared in awe at the surrounding mountains, all green with summer vegetation. She must have dozed through this region on the way out to Ohio. "It must be amazing in the winter, all snow-covered."

"*Jah*. We certainly get our share of snow most winters. It's *gut* for business. We get tourists all year round with the ski resorts in winter and the campers and hikers in summer."

"It must be very nice here."

"Very nice, but it can be very cold in winter. A little thing like you would surely freeze."

"Probably." Some winters in Southern Maryland were so cold and snowy, Malinda wanted to do nothing more than huddle beside the woodstove with one of Mamm's thickest quilts wrapped snugly around her.

Of course, she rarely had that luxury. There were always chores to complete, which Malinda often did with chattering teeth. Being the only girl in a family with five *bruders* meant plenty of cooking, cleaning, washing, and mending needed to get done. Mamm needed her help. She hoped Mamm hadn't worked too hard in her absence. They hadn't planned on her being gone so long.

"It's quite lovely here in summer," the woman continued. "It doesn't get unbearably hot, and there is usually at least a small mountain breeze to give you a breath of air."

"It sounds *wunderbaar*."

"*Kumm* visit us some time. Just ask for Nora Kinsinger.

Most folks around here know me. I have a sewing and stitching store."

"I may just do that one day."

"You'd be most *wilkom*. Enjoy the rest of your trip, Malinda." With that, Nora Kinsinger jumped from the van and followed the driver to the back to retrieve her larger traveling bag.

Malinda must have told Nora her name when they'd first found themselves strapped in next to each other, but her brain was still too fuzzy to conjure up any memory of that. She didn't know about enjoying the rest of the trip, though. Her backside already felt numb, and she had several more hours of bouncing along in one of the middle seats of the extended van to endure. She'd be ever so glad to reach St. Mary's County.

She managed to stay awake as the van twisted and turned on the narrow mountain roads. Malinda found herself whispering prayers on some of the steeper descents. The runaway truck ramps for big rigs that couldn't slow down gave her some cause for concern. She turned slightly and craned her neck to peek out the back window to assure herself that no eighteen-wheelers were rumbling down the mountain behind the van. Towering peaks kissing the cloudless blue sky and dark and light green patchwork valleys provided breathtaking views, but Malinda still heaved a sigh of relief when the highway leveled off and the mountain roads were behind them.

Malinda dozed off and on as the van zipped along the interstate and only fully awoke when it made a left turn right after they crossed the line into Charles County. Depending on traffic, and how fast the driver pushed them, she might be home in St. Mary's County in twenty to thirty minutes. The *Englischer* who usually drove her family or neighbors places too far to travel by buggy was a very cautious driver who strictly obeyed speed limits and road signs. The Ohio man behind the wheel of this van was totally unfamiliar to Malinda and seemed to be a bit more of a risk taker. Malinda knew they had only barely squeaked through several yellow traffic lights, and she felt pretty sure they had exceeded the speed limit on more than one occasion.

She wiggled in her seat and stretched out her tingly legs. She hoped they would hold her weight, slight though it was, when she finally stood. She also hoped she'd be able to unglue her backside from the seat. The driver had said he planned to stop at the grocery store in Clover Dale. Her *daed* or *mamm* would meet them there. That way the driver could more quickly head back home. Just a few more miles to go.

The *Welcome to St. Mary's County* sign was a welcome sight indeed. They only had to pass a few gas stations and businesses before turning into the store's parking lot. Malinda began counting the seconds as the van waited for the light to turn green. Her head jerked hard when the driver hit the accelerator, and she almost bit her tongue. She strained to see if a buggy was waiting at the far side of the store.

As the van drove around the edge of the parking lot, Malinda spied a dark gray buggy. It could be anyone from the community, since all the Amish in Southern Maryland drove dark gray buggies. If she could catch a glimpse of the horse, she'd know for sure and for certain. *Jah*. It was definitely Mamm or Daed. She'd know their big dark brown horse anywhere. When he flicked his head, Malinda could plainly see the white star above Chestnut's nose. Home. She'd be home very soon.

Malinda fumbled with the catch on the seat belt and finally freed herself as the driver hopped out. How did he jump out so quickly after sitting in the same cramped position for hours? Malinda exited the van more slowly. She even had to hold on to the side of the van to keep her balance as she took baby steps on wobbly legs. She shook each leg a bit, hoping to dispel the pins and needles prickling them from feet to thighs, but her effort was fruitless. She hobbled to the back of the van to claim her suitcase and quilted carryall bag.

Malinda thanked the driver a moment before arms encircled her and nearly squeezed the breath from her body. "*Ach*, Mamm! I didn't even see you get out of the buggy."

"*Wilkom* home, Malinda." Saloma Stauffer released Malinda and fumbled with the purse hooked on her left arm. "Let me pay the driver."

"It's already taken care of, ma'am," the driver replied.

"How? Malinda, did you . . ." Saloma turned to look at Malinda. With one fidgety hand, she tucked a wisp of light brown hair under her white *kapp* and shoved her silver-rimmed glasses back up her nose.

"Miss Mary paid me before we left Ohio," the driver said. "Don't worry about a thing."

"That was *gut* of her."

"I'm going to get back on the road. You ladies have a good day."

"*Danki*. Have a safe trip," Malinda replied.

"*Kumm*, Malinda." Saloma hoisted the heavy suitcase, leaving the lighter bag for Malinda.

Here it kumms. *The invalid treatment.*

Chapter Two

"I can get that, Mamm."

"You don't look like you could carry a gnat. Didn't they feed you in that hospital? I knew I should have gone out there to take care of you." Saloma's voice faded, but she continued talking as she headed toward the buggy.

Malinda stared at her *mamm*'s back and smiled at the continuous mumbling she couldn't decipher. *That's Mamm. Always fussing and worrying over me.* Malinda picked up the carryall bag and followed her muttering *mamm*.

Saloma set the suitcase in the back of the buggy and plucked the bag from Malinda's hands. "Let me look at you." Her brown eyes, not quite as big or as dark as Malinda's, traveled up and down Malinda's body. "Too thin. Way too small."

"Mamm, you're hardly a giant yourself. You're about five feet nothing and probably don't weigh a hundred pounds dripping wet."

"Jah, but I doubt you even weigh ninety."

"You know how it is when I get a flare-up. I was very dehydrated, and I hurt too much to eat."

"Well, you're home now, and I intend to fatten you up a bit."

Malinda rolled her eyes when Saloma's gaze wasn't fixed on her. She knew better than to protest. When her *mamm* got on a roll, she may just as well save her breath.

Saloma paused before climbing into the buggy. "Is there anything you want from the store while we're here?"

"I can't think of anything."

"Okay. Let's go home before the traffic picks up with folks on their way home from work."

"Home. That sure sounds *gut* to me." Malinda grasped the edge of the open buggy door to pull herself up. Ordinarily she could hop right into the buggy like her *mamm* just had, but she still felt a little weak. Her wobbly legs had a mind of their own and offered only minimal support. Malinda plopped onto the seat and gave a weak smile when Saloma peered at her out of the corner of her eye. She settled her skirt and nodded at her *mamm*. "I'm ready."

Saloma clucked to Chestnut, and the buggy rolled forward. The slower pace and rhythmic clip-clop of the horse's hooves calmed Malinda's nerves. Her tight shoulder muscles and stiff back relaxed. She hadn't realized how tense she'd become as the van had raced along the highway. Mamm steered the buggy to the shoulder of the southbound lane of traffic. Malinda relaxed even more when they turned off onto a smaller road leading to their community.

"The honeysuckle has bloomed." Malinda sniffed the sweet fragrance. "I guess I missed the pear trees and apple trees."

"*Jah*. They've already bloomed. I suppose you left before any of the flowers started blooming."

"Spring was just getting under way when I left. Now summer is half gone."

"Ohio must have been pretty, though."

"It was. The fields that hadn't been plowed were dotted with all sorts of wildflowers. Aenti Mary's flowers were pretty. I kept them weeded and watered until I got sick. I felt so guilty, Mamm. I was there to help her, and she ended up helping me."

"I'm sure she was plenty grateful for your company and your help." Saloma stretched out her right arm to pat Malinda's knee. "Besides, she was about well when you took sick, ain't so?"

"She was pretty well recovered."

"Are you pretty well recovered, too?"

"I think so. I still feel a little weak, but being home makes me feel ever so much better."

"*Gut*. We'll get you strong and healthy again."

Malinda sighed and lapsed into silence. She would not give voice to her fears and doubts. She studied the scenery that passed by her. Her neighbors' neat yards looked the same as always. Little brown birds perched in clumps along electric wires strung between the poles along the road. Of course, those wires only led to her *Englisch* neighbors' houses. White, cottony clouds slid across the bright, blue sky. The moving buggy generated a slight breeze to cool the hot afternoon. A young Amish woman and man on the side of the road caught her attention.

"Malinda!" the young woman cried.

"*Ach*! It's Phoebe Yoder." Malinda waved at her *freind*. Phoebe had been a year ahead of her at school, but they had always been *gut freinden*.

"*Wilkom* home, Malinda! I'll visit soon," Phoebe called.

Malinda nodded and turned toward her *mamm*. "Who was that with Phoebe?"

Saloma pushed her glasses up again with her left forefinger. "That's Ben Miller. I guess he arrived here after you left for Ohio."

"Ben Miller. Ben Miller." Malinda tapped her head as if that would jog her memory.

"Ben is Rufus and Lena Kurtz's grandson. He lived here as a boy until his *mamm* died. Then his *daed* moved them to Holmes County. He used to visit, though, in summers."

"I remember now. He's older than me, so I didn't really know him at school."

"He's a bit older than Phoebe, too, I'm thinking."

"Are he and Phoebe, uh, a couple?"

"Now, that I'm not sure about. Phoebe took the kidnapping of her little *schweschder* very hard. She blamed herself and sort of avoided people. It seems Ben has been a great *freind* to her."

"You wrote me about the kidnapping. That must have been so awful. Little Naomi is fine, ain't so?"

"*Jah*. The Lord brought her back unharmed. What a blessing for the Yoders and all of us. Naomi is happy and healthy. Lavina scarcely lets her out of her sight."

"That's understandable. Having your *boppli* snatched away and not knowing if you'll ever see her again must be an awful thing." Malinda sniffed and blinked back the sudden tears that sprang to her eyes at the very thought of the nightmare the Yoders had experienced. She searched for a new topic of conversation. "In one of Phoebe's letters to me, she mentioned something about Micah Graber. She isn't courting him, is she?"

"Now Malinda, you know very well those things are private." A sly smile slid across Saloma's face. She cocked one eyebrow and glanced askance at her *dochder*.

"Right, Mamm. There's nothing private around here. News and even possible news travels faster along the Amish grapevine than it would along that telephone wire going from one *Englisch* house to another."

Saloma chuckled. "And you missed it while you were gone, ain't so?"

Malinda laughed. "It was hard piecing things together from the snippets of information I gleaned from yours, Phoebe's, or Mary Stoltzfus's letters."

"I daresay it gave you something to do when you weren't tending to your *aenti*."

"Aenti Mary healed very quickly from her hip surgery. She's getting around now with barely a limp. I'm just sorry I frightened her and she ended up worrying about me. I-I wish this horrible illness would just go away. I've prayed so much for healing, but it hasn't happened."

"The Lord Gott gives us strength to bear whatever comes our way." Saloma reached over to squeeze Malinda's hand.

"I know, but—"

"The apostle Paul prayed for healing, too. Remember? The Lord had other plans and told Paul His grace was sufficient."

How many times had Mamm reminded her of this Bible passage? The Lord did not remove the apostle Paul's thorn in the flesh, whatever it was. Paul apparently accepted Gott's grace after asking three times for healing. Malinda had asked, *nee*, begged for healing every day since she first got sick three years ago. She hadn't been accepting of her disease, as Paul was of his problem. But Paul didn't feel like no one would ever want to marry him, or like he would be a burden to someone. He didn't have a burning desire to give birth to a *boppli* and nurse that *boppli* at his breast. He didn't even *want* to get married.

Sure, Malinda was only nineteen. It wasn't like time was running out for her to have *kinner*, but joining the church, marrying, and having a houseful of *kinner* were all she had ever wanted. She had no desire to taste the *Englisch* world, where girls her age were working or going to college. She had no desire to wear jeans or makeup or to drive a sporty car. She simply wanted a home and a family.

Most of her *freinden* were courting or were already married. She knew her older *bruders* Sam and Atlee slipped out of the house to visit their girlfriends. No doubt one or both would be marrying this wedding season. Malinda sighed. Mamm would tell her—and had in fact told her on more than one occasion—to wait on the Lord and trust in Him. She would remind Malinda she was only nineteen. But in three years of attending singings when she wasn't sick, no *bu* had ever asked to take her home.

She didn't think her looks were too frightening. Little ones didn't run away in fear, and adults didn't shrink back in disgust. Even Dr. McWilliams must have found her attractive—but she wouldn't let her thoughts go there. It must be her illness that made the fellows keep their distance. What young man would want to be saddled with a sickly *fraa*?

Who would want to take on the expense of her medications and doctor appointments? Of course, there were times she felt well and strong, but when a flare-up hit, she felt like her insides were being ripped out and she had all the strength of a newborn kitten. A man wanted a woman who could keep the household running smoothly every day, who could bear him strapping sons. She sighed again.

"Malinda?"

"Hmm?" Malinda called her mind back from its wandering and focused on her *mamm*.

"Did you hear what I said?"

"*Jah*. I-I need to accept Gott's will."

"Right."

"It's so hard." Malinda flicked away the tear that trickled down her cheek.

Saloma squeezed Malinda's hand again. "I know, dear one." She returned her hand to the reins and guided the horse to make the turn onto the long gravel driveway leading to their house. Chestnut could easily have made the turn without prompting. He acted as eager to return home as Malinda was. "Daed and your *bruders* will be ever so glad to see you."

Chapter Three

Malinda put a hand to her still-tender belly as they bumped along the rutted driveway. She'd told the nurse and Dr. McWilliams she no longer had pain, and that was true for the most part. The sharp, gut-wrenching pain had subsided, leaving behind a dull ache, which had recently turned into a soreness mainly experienced with certain movements.

Never one to miss a thing, Saloma said, "I'll have to get your *daed* to grade the driveway. I told Rufus just the other day it feels like we're driving over a washboard."

"I'm okay." Malinda moved her hand to her lap. She had no desire to return to the hospital or to see a doctor. Mamm's fussing over her would be hard enough to bear. She knew her *mamm* meant well, but sometimes her hovering gave Malinda little peace.

Malinda's gaze soaked in her surroundings. It seemed she'd been gone a lot longer than a few months. The hayfields must have been cut recently, since the grass was fairly short. Daed and her *bruders* must be working in a back field now. Sam and Atlee, at twenty-three and twenty-one, may even be at other jobs. Sam often worked at Swarey's Furniture Shop. Crafting furniture appeared to be his calling.

Atlee put in a lot of time at the fairly new cheese factory. Sixteen-year-old Roman, thirteen-year-old Ray, and even eight-year-old Aden would no doubt be performing whatever tasks Daed had assigned them.

Tears pooled in Malinda's eyes when she drank in the sight of the big two-story white house. She was so very glad to be home. For a while there in the hospital, she had wondered if she'd ever return. That had been her worst flare-up ever. No wonder Aenti Mary had been frightened. Malinda had been frightened herself. She'd heard the murmurings of possible surgery among the hospital staff and thanked the Lord her condition had improved.

Scarlet and salmon geraniums, white and pink begonias, and heavenly-smelling dianthus bloomed near the house in neat flower beds. The lush green grass looked freshly mowed, and the wooden porch swing rocked ever so gently in the slight breeze. *Ach*! It was *gut* to be home. "I'm sorry I haven't been here to help you with the yard and garden. You must have been working so hard. Everything looks nice."

"I had Aden do a lot of the weeding and such. He's still young enough not to mind helping out his *mamm*. Ray, on the other hand, muttered under his breath, but he helped out from time to time."

Malinda smiled. She could imagine Ray mumbling about doing women's work. He wouldn't dare disobey Mamm, though. He may complain, but he'd do as he was told, for sure. "At least we're home in time for me to help you with supper."

"It's mostly done. You just rest up before your *bruders* traipse into the house. A long ride can be most tiring, even for healthy people who haven't just gotten out of the hospital."

Healthy. Would Malinda ever feel healthy again? She knew her *mamm* hadn't meant for her words to sting, but they pierced Malinda's soul nonetheless and reinforced her belief that no man would want a sickly *fraa*. Tears threatened again. Maybe she'd take Mamm up on the suggestion to rest. She must be more tired than she'd thought.

Malinda trudged up the stairs to her room, carrying her belongings. Being the only girl had at least one advantage—she didn't have to share a room. She gratefully dropped the suitcase and bag onto the bed. They had grown heavier with each step and left her gasping for breath by the time she reached the top. She must be weaker than she'd thought, too. It only took a few minutes to hang her dresses on the wall pegs and to put her nightgown and undergarments in the drawers of the big oak dresser. Thank goodness she had washed all her clothes the day before leaving Ohio so she didn't have a pile of dirty laundry staring her in the face.

Her room looked just as she had left it, though she knew Mamm had dusted every week. She breathed a sigh of relief to be back in the familiarity and comfort of her own home. Maybe she'd stretch out on the bed for just a moment before helping Mamm. Despite dozing during much of her trip home, fatigue still gnawed at her. She'd just lie here and look around her room and thank the Lord for bringing her home safely. Her eyes traveled from her solid-colored blue, purple, and green dresses hanging on pegs to the wide dresser with its four deep drawers and two smaller drawers to the brown and beige rag rug on the dark oak floor. Her fingers plucked at the quilt with its blocks of blue, purple, and white. Mamm had stitched it for her years ago. No longer being jostled about in a van or buggy, Malinda finally relaxed her tense muscles. Ahh, just a little rest.

"Malinda, supper is about ready!"

Malinda bolted upright, heart pounding. She must have drifted off to sleep yet again. She slid off the bed and straightened the quilt. She ran her hands down her dress to try to smooth out at least a few of the wrinkles. She tucked loose strands of hair back into her bun where they belonged and pushed her cockeyed *kapp* back into its proper position.

She rushed into the kitchen. "I'm sorry, Mamm. I meant to *kumm* right back down to help. I sat on the bed for a minute and, well . . ."

"That's all right. I told you everything was nearly ready." Saloma pulled a bubbling beef noodle casserole, one of Malinda's favorite dishes, from the oven and set it on the quilted hot pad on the counter next to the stove. "There will be time enough to get back to chores tomorrow or whenever you feel up to it."

Malinda nodded. She needed to get back into her familiar routine, but she knew from past experience she couldn't push herself too hard too fast. "Here. I can at least set the table." She took the stack of dinner plates from Saloma's hands and carried them to the long walnut table Rufus had made for Saloma when they'd gotten married over twenty years ago. Scuffling sounds and voices from the mudroom alerted her to the arrival of her *daed* and *bruders*.

"Malinda's home!" Aden raced into the kitchen to give Malinda a hug. At barely eight years old, he still liked to hug and be hugged, and he was particularly fond of his big *schweschder*.

"Did you miss me?" Malinda hugged the dear little *bu* whose very dark brown hair and big chocolate eyes were so like her own. He even had a smattering of tiny light brown freckles across his nose, just like she had.

"*Jah!*"

"I missed you too, Aden."

"You have to see my frogs." The little boy let go of Malinda's too-slim waist and tugged at her hand.

"Whoa! You can show me after supper. It will still be plenty light enough."

Aden's lower lip poked out, but then he brightened. "Okay. If it starts to get dark, we can catch lightning bugs."

"Young man, did you wash up?" Saloma gave her youngest a stern look.

"Not yet, Mamm, but I'm going right now."

"See that you do."

"Scoot!" Malinda gave him a gentle push in the right direction.

"Wilkom home, Dochder," Rufus's voice boomed. His six-foot stature and broad shoulders belied his gentle nature—gentle, but firm. None of his *kinner* shirked their responsibilities or dared to cross him, but any chiding or correcting was done with love.

Sam, Atlee, and Roman, all clones of their *daed* with light brown hair and green eyes, stomped into the room behind Rufus. They nodded at Malinda and smiled. She knew they were happy to see her but all considered themselves too old to offer any hugs. Ray stomped into the kitchen after his older *bruders*, but not before he told Aden to hurry up before he gnawed his own arm off in his hunger. At thirteen, he was well on his way to his *daed*'s and *bruders*' height, but he was still gangly. He was the only Stauffer sibling who looked a true mixture of his parents. He had his *daed*'s light brown hair and his *mamm*'s dark brown eyes. His temperament combined his parents' personalities as well.

Malinda could tell Ray wanted to give her a hug but didn't want to be teased by his *bruders*. He settled for mumbling a greeting of welcome.

"*Danki*, Ray." Malinda squeezed his arm, the closest thing to a hug she dared offer.

"I'm ready!" Aden burst into the kitchen holding his hands up for inspection. "We can eat."

"Well, *danki* for your permission." Rufus ruffled the boy's bowl-cut hair.

When all had taken their places at the table, Rufus gave the signal for their silent prayer. Silence only reigned in the Stauffer household during prayer time and when everyone was sound asleep. At the conclusion of prayer time, Saloma picked up one bowl after another and passed them first to Rufus, who would then send them around the table. The cacophony of voices began.

How unlike Aenti Mary's house, where the two of them ate mostly in silence. It hadn't been an unpleasant or uncomfortable silence, but Malinda preferred the sharing and teasing that went on at the Stauffer supper table.

"How's the furniture business?" Atlee elbowed Sam, barely choking back a laugh.

"*Gut.*"

"And the Swareys are *gut*, too?"

"As far as I know." Sam studied his plate, as if coaxing noodles onto his fork was the most important thing in the world.

"Even Emma Swarey?"

Sam coughed and swiped his white paper napkin across his mouth. "As far as I know," he mumbled into the napkin.

"Say, was that a big crop of celery I saw growing in their field when I drove by? Could they be thinking of all the celery dishes they'll need at a fall wedding?"

Malinda feared Sam's blood red face would actually burst into flame, and that someone would need to pound his back to stop his coughing fit.

"That's enough, Atlee." Rufus attempted to be stern, but a smile tugged at his lips.

"You know, the Swareys have several girls of marriageable age," Saloma said.

"Emma's the oldest, ain't so?" Atlee feigned innocence.

"How is the fair Lizzie Beachy, Cheese Man?" Sam poked Atlee turning the tables on him.

Now Atlee's face glowed. "I wouldn't know." He elbowed Sam so hard the table shook.

"Let's find another topic of conversation." Saloma's lips twitched in a half smile.

"It sounds like I've missed some things." Malinda pushed fresh string beans from the garden around on her plate. "Mamm, you, Mary, and Phoebe didn't include any of these recent, uh, developments in your letters. Maybe I can meet up with Emma and Lizzie soon."

"Are you going to play with your food, or eat it?" Atlee snapped.

"I'm working on eating it."

"You'd better work on it a little harder. If we get a windstorm or even a strong puff of wind, you're going to blow away.

"Ha! Ha! You're so funny, Atlee."

"It's so *gut* to have all our loving *kinner* sitting around our table, ain't so, Saloma?" Rufus looked across the table at his *fraa*.

"I'm glad to be home," Malinda declared. "It was hard getting used to the quiet at Aenti Mary's house." She speared a single green bean and raised it to her mouth, determined to eat something even though her stomach still felt queasy. She wrinkled up her nose at Atlee as if to say, *So there!*

"It's never quiet here, that's for sure and for certain." Roman looked from one older *bruder* to the other.

"I'm interested in the cheese factory, Atlee." She resisted teasing him by calling him "the Cheese Man." "I think it's great they're up and running. How is business?"

"Great." Atlee sat up straighter. Excitement lit his eyes. "It's actually getting better all the time. We have a lot of Plain and *Englisch* customers."

"Do you like working there?"

"I'm learning how to do a lot—"

"I like cheese," Aden interrupted. "Maybe I can work there when I get older."

"We don't eat the cheese," Atlee stressed.

"But maybe you could if they had extra or if you bought it," Aden insisted.

"Sure." Atlee turned his attention back to his second helping of casserole.

"How did they treat you at that big hospital?" Rufus brushed bread crumbs from his long, brown beard.

"F-Fine. Just fine." Malinda didn't dare mention any of the disturbing things Dr. McWilliams had said to her or his almost-too-familiar demeanor. Daed would hire the first driver he could find to transport him nonstop to the doctor's doorstep in Ohio. She didn't know what her *daed* would do once he arrived there, though. Since the Amish believed in nonviolence, he definitely could not punch the doctor in the nose, but he would undoubtedly give the man a piece of his mind.

At least Malinda wouldn't ever have to see Todd McWilliams again or hear his declaration of some special feeling between them or feel his hand grasp hers. She wouldn't ever have to see Nurse Trudy's piercing stare as if accusing Malinda of some inappropriate behavior. Malinda barely suppressed a little shiver.

"Are you feeling better, then?"

Daed's voice broke into her thoughts, calling her back to the Stauffer supper table. "*Jah*, not quite back to normal, but definitely better." Malinda had practically forgotten what normal was, but maybe she'd know again one day. That didn't seem too likely, but she could always hope.

"We need to fatten her up, ain't so, Saloma?" Rufus passed Malinda the bowl of green beans cooked in bacon drippings.

"I still have some, Daed." Malinda set the bowl down in front of Ray. The thirteen-year-old was an eating machine.

Malinda believed he could gobble up her share of food as well as his own. She wished her family understood her insides didn't feel like being bombarded with food. She knew they meant well, and she truly didn't want to be so scrawny, but she often didn't feel like eating during or soon after a flare-up of the evil Crohn's disease.

Malinda cleared the supper table when everyone had had their fill of casserole, green beans, pickled beets, crusty homemade bread, and peach pie. Saloma tried to shoo her out of the kitchen to rest, but Malinda was determined to prove she felt stronger than she really did. She insisted on carrying out her usual duties. Aden hopped up and down from one foot to the other, waiting for Malinda to check out the frogs with him.

"Aden, I am going to put you to work if you keep pestering us," Saloma told him. "Your jumping about is not going to make Malinda and me work any faster."

"I'll help. What do you want me to do?" Aden stopped fidgeting and turned big hopeful eyes from Mamm to Malinda.

"Gee, he really wants me to see those frogs," Malinda whispered.

"*Jah*. Then he'd better turn them loose."

"Maaamm!" Aden dragged the word out in a whine. "Do I have to?"

"You do. Gott did not intend for frogs to live in captivity. Here, now you can put these pans away for us in the bottom cabinet."

Eager to help, or more likely to get outside, Aden snatched up the pans, shoved them into the cabinet, and slammed the door. "There."

"We'll have to remember to stand back next time we open that door or we'll get clobbered," Malinda muttered.

Saloma turned a stern look on her youngest. "Young man, you put those away properly or no one will see the frogs. I'll have Ray turn them loose now."

Aden's shoulders slumped and his lower lip protruded, but he didn't utter a word. He dropped to his knees and yanked open the cabinet door. "Aaahh!" He threw his hands up as metal pans crashed around him.

"See, Aden." Saloma shook a finger at him. "You made more work for yourself. Now put them away neatly. No one wants to be attacked by pans."

When the kitchen had finally been restored to its normal pristine condition and Malinda had hung up the red-and-white-checked dish towel, she grabbed Aden's hand. "Okay. Let's go see those frogs. Where in the world are they that they can't hop away?"

"I'll show you." Aden tugged her toward the door.

"You make sure he lets those critters go!" Saloma called after them.

"You heard Mamm, right?" Malinda nudged Aden.

"I heard." The little voice sounded totally dejected.

"Cheer up, Aden. I'm sure the frogs will be glad to be free again. You'll be doing them a favor." Malinda gently squeezed his hand and trotted along beside him.

"Here. Look in here." Aden stopped beside an old metal washtub behind the shed. A discarded window screen served as a lid. Aden let go of Malinda's hand and whisked the screen aside.

"*Nee*! Wait!" Malinda's cry came too late. A huge, ugly toad, seeing its chance at freedom, leaped high enough to clear the side of the tub and slammed into Malinda's neck. She grabbed at the slimy creature, but it slipped through her hands. Brown globs of mud dotted her blue dress.

"You let him go!" Aden wailed. He shoved the screen back over the tub.

"You let him go. You lifted the screen. The poor thing probably got tired of being confined to the tub. There's one free one." Malinda peeked through the screen. "Four more to go."

"What do you think of them?"

"I think they are toads, not frogs, and I think you are a very clever *bu* to have caught five of them."

Instantly Aden retracted his pout and puffed out his chest. "*Jah*, I guess I am."

"And you've kept them alive for how long?"

"Three days. I wanted to show them to you."

"Well, I'm quite impressed. You've done a fine job of taking care of them. Now don't you think the others would like to be free like the first one?"

"I suppose so."

"Just let me stand back this time." Malinda shuffled backward, keeping her eyes fastened on the screen Aden was preparing to shove aside until she slammed into a brick wall. "*Ach*!" She stumbled until strong arms steadied her. She whipped her head around, *kapp* strings swinging across her face. Her eyes connected with the big, sky blue eyes of the tall young man whose strong arms held her upright. She jumped back with a little shriek as if the man had a hissing snake wrapped around his neck. "I-I'm sorry. I-I didn't know you were there."

Chapter Four

Not sure what to do with his hands after Malinda pulled free of them, Timothy Brenneman slapped one against his thigh and used the other to fiddle with the straw hat on his head. "I-I came by to talk to Sam." Now, why was he nervous? "*W-Wilkom* home."

"*Danki*, Tim."

Malinda swiped at the spatters of mud on her dress, smearing them even worse than they were. A crimson color swept up her pretty face, probably matching the color Tim knew was flooding his own face. What was wrong with him? He was a grown man of twenty-two, and he'd known Malinda all her life.

"See ya." Malinda dashed over to Aden's side. "You'd better rinse out this tub and scrub the mud off yourself before Mamm sees you. I'll help you with the tub." Malinda grabbed one side as Aden grabbed the other. Tim started to offer to carry the tub for them but instead stood rooted to the spot.

"What about lightning bugs?" Tim heard Aden ask.

"We'll have plenty of evenings to catch them," Malinda told him.

Tim yanked off his hat and ran a hand through his hair. Now, why had Malinda rushed off like she couldn't wait to get away from him? A firm hand clamped down on his shoulder, halting his rambling thoughts.

"*Was ist letz*?"

"Huh?" Timothy turned to look at the young man who, though older by one year, stood an inch shorter. "Hello, Samuel. Nothing is the matter."

"Did you *kumm* to see me?"

"Uh, *jah*." Timothy's made-up reason to visit Sam had fled without a trace. He couldn't tell Sam he'd heard Malinda had arrived home and he wanted to see her with his own eyes. For the life of him, though, he couldn't remember the excuse he'd concocted.

"Was it something about work?"

"Uh, *jah*. Work." Timothy and Sam both worked at Swarey's Furniture Shop. His flimsy excuse did have something to do with work. His mind raced, searching for something halfway logical to latch onto. "I have to deliver that new bedroom suite over to the Kurtz place tomorrow. Would you be able to help me?" Dumb excuse. He could easily have waited until the next morning to discuss this with Sam. He shifted from one foot to the other like a scholar called before the teacher. His eyes darted to Malinda, who was trying to help Aden wash off mud at the outside pump, and then slid back to Sam's face. He willed his cheeks not to turn as red as a sun-ripened tomato.

"Sure, I'll help you. By the way, she just got home a little while ago."

"Huh? Who?"

"Malinda, of course. That's what you really came to see about, ain't so?"

Now Tim was absolutely convinced his cheeks looked like two bright tomatoes ready for picking. He shrugged as nonchalantly as he could manage. "I'm glad she made it home okay. She looks a little peaked."

"She's scrawnier than ever, for sure, but she'll perk up now that she's home."

"Scrawny" was not a word Timothy would use to describe Malinda Stauffer. Beautiful, kind, caring—those were better words to describe her. Sure, she looked mighty thin and frail at the moment, but she would get better. "I'm sure she will," he managed to mumble.

Sam punched Timothy's upper arm. "Do you want to *kumm* inside and visit?"

"Another time, maybe. I'm sure everyone is tired tonight." Malinda certainly looked about done in. Maybe she'd feel up to attending the next young folks' singing.

"Any time."

"I'll see you at work tomorrow." Timothy gave a final glance in Malinda's direction just in time to see her usher Aden inside. She turned his way for the briefest of moments and offered a hint of a smile. He couldn't be sure if that smile was meant for him or for Aden, but it gave him a flicker of hope. He'd been waiting for years for her to grow up.

"Let's finish cleaning up and get you ready for bed," Malinda told Aden. She supposed Timothy had dropped by to see Sam about something. Even though Sam was a bit older, the two had been *freinden* for a long time. Why had Tim been watching her? Was it pity she saw etched on his face? She did not want to be pitied by anyone, especially Timothy Brenneman. Would all of her *freinden*—and all the young men—look at her the same way? *Poor, sickly Malinda Stauffer. Be nice to her but keep your distance. She's too fragile and weak to make anyone a* gut fraa. Would those be the words whispered behind her back?

"Here, I'll take this one off your hands." Saloma grasped Aden's arm to lead him in the right direction. "You've had a long day and probably need some rest. He is going to require some serious scrubbing."

Malinda nodded and trudged off to perform her own bedtime preparations. Even Mamm thought her incapable of completing a task as simple as getting Aden ready for bed. Well, with Aden, maybe that task wasn't always so simple. That *bu* could find more diversions to prolong bedtime than she could ever have imagined at his age. The very thought brought a smile to her lips.

Malinda blew out a long, deep sigh. She hated to admit it, but Mamm had been right. Exhaustion threatened to claim her. Hopefully, after a full night's sleep in her own bed she'd rise bright and chipper in the morning. Wearily she shrugged out of her clothes and pulled on her long, white nightgown. She removed her *kapp* and loosened her hair to fall to her waist. She quickly brushed it and wove it into one long braid. *Ach*, she was tired of being tired!

Why did she have to have this horrible Crohn's disease? She had felt perfectly fine up until a couple of years ago. She'd become so sick that Dr. Nelson sent her for all sorts of nasty tests to confirm the diagnosis. Various medicines, costing a lot of money, helped, but flare-ups could occur at any time. She knew there was no cure for the disease, but she prayed for a remission. Instead, each flare-up seemed worse than the previous one and probably caused more and more damage to her intestines.

Malinda feared surgery would be required at some point, and she feared that even more than the flare-ups. Dr. Nelson had told her she might experience much pain relief and might be able to stop some of her medications if she had surgery, but that was a step she was not yet ready to take. She'd overheard Dr. McWilliams discuss the same thing with medical students at the Ohio hospital. They had all stared at her as if she was some exotic fish in a bowl of guppies. Besides, she did not want to create more of a financial burden. Since the Amish carried no health insurance, her family and community would have to foot the hefty surgery bill.

She fell onto her knees, propped her elbows on her bed, and dropped her head into her hands. "Please, Gott, please take this horrible disease away. I don't want to be a burden. I just want a normal, healthy life." One tear and then another slid down her cheeks.

My grace is sufficient.

Malinda jerked her head up and looked around the lamp-lit room. Had Mamm slipped in and overheard her prayer? No one lurked in the shadows. Malinda was alone—or was she?

Chapter Five

Malinda tried to get back into the swing of life at home. She dragged herself out of bed in pre-dawn darkness to help her *mamm* get breakfast on the table for her *daed* and *bruders*, she cooked and cleaned, and she fought to hang heavy, wet bedsheets on the clothesline. She was well aware that Saloma watched her like a hawk and often urged her to rest, but Malinda did not want to be treated like an invalid. She would prove she was not a weakling even if that meant collapsing into bed each night feeling like she'd been plowed over by a team of horses. She had even let Mamm talk her into attending the singing with Sam and Atlee on Sunday evening. That had proven to be a mistake she did not intend to repeat.

"I'm glad you came to the singing," Phoebe Yoder said on Tuesday.

"*Jah*. Did you have a *gut* time?" Mary Stoltzfus asked around the bite of oatmeal cookie she was chewing.

Phoebe and Mary, though a year older, had been Malinda's *freinden* for years. As promised, they were paying her a visit after morning chores had been completed, the noon meal eaten, and the kitchen cleared. The three girls sat in green metal lawn chairs in the shade of a big oak tree, sipping lemonade and munching cookies.

"I-it was, uh, okay," Malinda hedged.

"Did you get a ride home?" Phoebe playfully poked Malinda's arm. "I kind of left ahead of you."

"I know. I saw you slip out with Ben Miller. I rode home with Atlee. I drove to the singing with Sam but figured he'd want to slip away with Emma Swarey, so I persuaded Atlee to drive me home. He wasn't exactly thrilled about it."

"Oh, I thought . . ." Phoebe began.

"I'm sickly. What *bu* wants a sickly girl?"

"You're too hard on yourself." Phoebe reached over to pat Malinda's arm. "You aren't 'sickly.' You have times when you feel poorly, but most times you're just fine."

"I may seem just fine, but the disease is always there ready to rear its ugly head. And I have to be careful what I eat. And . . ."

"A lot of people have to watch what they eat." Phoebe swiped at a fine strand of strawberry blonde hair that sailed across her face in a sudden wisp of breeze. "Some people have diabetes and have to stick to a certain diet."

"Some just need to diet." Mary giggled and patted her belly.

"Not you," Malinda said. "I don't know where you put all those cookies."

"There is always room for cookies." Mary helped herself to another cookie loaded with plump raisins. "And pie and cake and—"

Phoebe wadded up her paper napkin and threw it at Mary. "You're impossible!"

"I am different, though," Malinda insisted. "I never know when I'll have a flare-up. I have to take medications that aren't cheap. After a flare-up I feel weak, and during one, I'm worthless."

"As I said before, you are way too hard on yourself. The

disease is not your fault, and it's not in your control. You can't blame yourself. I know all about blaming one's self, and it's not *gut*."

Malinda knew Phoebe had had great difficulty overcoming self-recrimination after her little *schweschder* was kidnapped. Thankfully, little Naomi had been found safe and sound, but Phoebe had suffered guilt and self-doubt for a long time. Malinda's *mamm* had told her all about that. "I know, Phoebe. I'm trying not to blame myself. Maybe you didn't notice how everyone at the singing looked at me in pity."

"I think they were all concerned. You probably saw caring, not pitying." Mary popped the last of her cookie into her mouth.

"No *bu* approached me—as usual."

"Did you give one a chance? You sort of hid in the shadows." Mary licked cookie crumbs off her lips before reaching for her lemonade.

"I noticed Timothy Brenneman's eyes following you." Phoebe winked at Malinda.

"Pshaw! Tim is Sam's *freind*. Sam was too preoccupied so probably asked Tim to keep an eye out that I didn't collapse somewhere."

"It didn't seem like he minded watching you."

"You're *narrisch*, Phoebe!"

"Not so crazy as you think, Malinda Stauffer." Phoebe picked up the plate of cookies. "Here. You'd better grab another one before Mary eats them all. I see her eyeing the plate again."

The girls talked and laughed for another hour, then Phoebe and Mary had to head home to help with chores. "Can we expect a wedding this wedding season?" Malinda looked directly at Phoebe.

Phoebe pressed her hands to her crimson cheeks. "I'm sure there will be several weddings."

"Will yours be one of them?" Malinda turned to look at Mary. "Or yours?"

"Not me." Mary shook her head. "I'm still looking. After things didn't work out with Aden Zimmerman, I'm taking it slow. You'd better pin your hopes for a wedding on Phoebe."

Malinda smiled as she gathered up cups and the empty cookie plate. Her *freinden* had cheered her up, and the little respite from work revved up her energy. She set the tray on the step and decided to remove laundry from the line while she was already outside. Stepping into the sunlight after her time in the shade felt like stepping into the woodstove. The heat of the summer afternoon nearly stole her breath. The laundry would definitely be dry. Ohio had been a tad cooler, but she was ever so glad to be back home in Maryland.

Malinda unpinned the big bedsheet, folded it, and tossed it into the laundry basket she'd left outside earlier. She continued unpinning, folding, and tossing as her thoughts rambled. She really was happy for Phoebe. After her devastating experience, Phoebe appeared to have found love with Ben Miller—not that anyone in the community out-and-out discussed such a thing. It was a blessing Ben came back to Maryland when he did. Apparently those two were meant for each other.

Was there a young man meant for her? The faces of the fellows at the singing flitted across Malinda's mind. She couldn't imagine a single one of them wanting to take her on with all of her medical issues. She dropped the last clothespin into the bag. Had Timothy really been watching her, as Phoebe had said? If so, why? Malinda tossed her head. No doubt Sam had asked Tim to keep an eye on her so he wouldn't feel guilty about sneaking away with Emma. Sam knew Atlee would get too caught up with the other fellows to pay any attention to her. That had to be it.

* * *

"You need to try to eat more, Malinda. You've been working hard and need to keep up your strength."

Malinda followed her *mamm*'s gaze down to her still-full plate. "I know, Mamm. I'm trying."

"I don't mean to nag, dear, but you have lost a good deal of weight."

Malinda nodded. She was well aware that her dresses hung like feed sacks on her despite pinning them tighter. She'd always been thin, but now her ribs and hip bones had become even more prominent.

"If you get any skinnier, you'll be able to slip through the door cracks. You need to eat like me." Atlee speared a hunk of meat loaf and stuffed it into his mouth. Aden, Roman, and Ray burst out laughing.

Malinda wrinkled her nose at her *bruder*. "Funny, Atlee." She picked up her fork and stabbed a slice of pickled beets.

"She'll be like the wind just blowing through. Whoosh!" Roman picked up where Atlee left off.

Adam and Ray laughed harder. Sam, who had seemed lost in his own world somewhere all throughout the meal, chuckled. Even Rufus hid a smile behind his napkin.

"Now, *buwe*, don't tease." Saloma shook her finger at her sons. "Our Malinda looks fine, just a bit too thin."

"*Ach*! Before I forget," Rufus interrupted. "A letter came for you today, Malinda. It's with the stack of mail on the counter."

"For me?" Who would be writing to her?

"The return address said it was from that hospital in Ohio. If it's a bill, just leave it for me."

Malinda nodded. That's probably exactly what it was. Or maybe it was one of those customer satisfaction surveys someone had mentioned when she'd been discharged. She picked at the food on her plate and managed to eat a few bites of meat loaf and boiled potatoes. Her stomach should be able to handle that. Of course, Mamm set a huge piece of peach pie in front of her when she passed out dessert to everyone else.

"Mamm, this looks great, but I don't think I can eat it all. I don't want to waste your pie."

"You're absolutely right, Malinda. We don't want to waste Mamm's pie." Atlee reached to snatch Malinda's plate.

"Eat your own!" Saloma smacked Atlee's hand.

"I'm only trying to help her out, Mamm."

"You're only trying to get a second piece of pie. I don't know where you put the mountain of food you eat." Saloma turned toward Malinda. "Just eat what you can. You always liked peach pie, and the early peaches are coming in now."

"I do like peach pie. Here, let me cut this piece in half. I'll try to eat half, and someone else can have the rest."

"Such a generous *schweschder*." Atlee's voice came out muffled by the pie he was chewing. He reached again for Malinda's plate.

"I said *someone*, not necessarily Atlee." Malinda scooted her plate out of reach. She had missed her *bruders'* banter while she had been in Ohio with Aenti Mary.

When the kitchen had been restored to order, Malinda picked up her letter from the pile of ads and assorted junk mail on the counter and stuffed it in her pocket. It didn't look like the usual bill envelopes she'd seen before, so she assumed it was that survey. She'd complete it in her room after her evening prayers.

Malinda trudged up the stairs, weariness seeping into her bones. She hoped she hadn't overdone it today, but she had wanted to prove—mainly to herself—that she was a fully functioning, capable member of the family and community. Her right hand, on its way to her head to remove her *kapp*, changed directions and plunged into her pocket to extract the envelope she'd stuffed in there earlier. She really didn't feel up to answering any sort of survey questions with another busy day only a few hours away. She merely wanted to climb into her bed and sink into sleep. She'd better glance at the contents of the envelope, though, just to be sure a bill did not lurk inside.

Malinda slid her finger beneath the flap of the envelope and tugged out a single sheet of paper. It must be a very short survey. At least it wasn't a bill. She unfolded the paper and gasped as she read the handwritten words. Todd McWilliams. Dr. McWilliams. Why on earth would he write her such a letter—any letter? Malinda felt almost positive busy doctors did not take the time to handwrite letters to their patients, and even if they did, by some peculiar chance, they certainly didn't write the kind of message this letter contained.

She stumbled across the small bedroom and dropped onto the quilt-covered bed to reread the letter. It started out fine. The doctor inquired about her health and expressed his hope for a remission. Then it got weird. He said he missed seeing her every day. Malinda's face flamed when she reread the words where he described her beauty.

No one had ever called her beautiful. Sure, like anyone else, she hoped she was pleasing to look at, but the Amish did not dwell on looks. The women all dressed in the same style dresses, though color may vary slightly; they all parted their hair down the middle and twisted it into a bun; they all pinned a white *kapp* on top of their heads. Sameness. Conformity. It was their way.

Malinda's hands trembled as she continued reading. The doctor continued on by saying how much he wanted to see her again. He mentioned a conference he might attend in Baltimore in the fall and said he might be able to visit her then. Could he find his way all the way down here to St. Mary's County?

Of course he could! *Englischers* had all kinds of fancy contraptions in their cars, and even on their phones. She'd heard they could find out all sorts of information on their computers. She could only hope the doctor would be too busy to track her down, or better yet, he wouldn't attend the conference at all. She planned to join the next baptismal class in late summer. By fall, she'd be getting ready to join the church.

Ach! What should she do with this letter? Should she answer to say she felt better and, by the way, please don't try to find her? Had she done something or said something when she'd been in a groggy state that had given the doctor the wrong impression? She thought she'd tried to discourage him.

What should she do? For one thing, she couldn't let Daed see this letter. She hastily stuffed the sheet of paper back inside the envelope, scooted across the room to pull open a bureau drawer, and thrust the offending note beneath her undergarments. She finished preparing for bed but knew sleep would now be out of the question. Who would have thought a Plain girl could get into such a predicament?

Chapter Six

Malinda's strength returned a little more each day. Her stomach calmed so she could eat a bit better, much to Saloma's delight. She kept up with her chores but often caught Saloma's watchful eyes on her. No matter how busy she stayed, she couldn't keep the words of that letter from running across her brain over and over again.

"I think you need to get out of the house for a bit, Dochder," Saloma announced on a Friday afternoon.

"Huh? What do you mean, Mamm? I've been outside plenty. I've hung out laundry and weeded the garden and picked vegetables and—"

"Let me rephrase that. You need to get away from the house, and I have the perfect solution."

"I really am fine, Mamm. I don't need to go anywhere."

"Well, I need some cheese for supper, so you can take a little outing to the cheese factory for me."

"Can't Atlee bring home whatever you need if you tell him tonight?"

Saloma shook her head. "*Nee*, your *daed* has his heart set on my macaroni and cheese, and I don't have enough cheese."

"Daed won't mind waiting another day."

Saloma continued as though she hadn't heard Malinda. "I also need you to pick up a couple of spools of thread from the quilt shop." She paused to fish around in her pocket, and then held up little snips of fabric. "I need two spools of this medium blue color here and two of the light lavender color here." She pointed out the colors on the fabric she held out to Malinda.

Malinda sighed and tucked the clippings into her own pocket. "I'll go hitch up."

"You can manage that okay?"

"Sure."

"Wait a minute. Let me get you some money."

Malinda struggled to curb her tongue and not complain. If Mamm had told Atlee at breakfast yesterday, he could have brought the cheese home last night. As for the thread, she could probably rummage through her *mamm*'s thread box and find exactly the right shades already there. Mamm just wanted to get her out of the house, but Malinda felt more comfortable at home, away from pitying glances. And then, too, Isaac Hostetler worked at the cheese factory. She wanted to see Isaac. Her heart even leaped at the thought, but she didn't want his look of pity.

She talked to the big, sleek, brown horse as she hitched him to the buggy. "Are you ready for an outing on this hot summer day, Chestnut?" The horse snorted and stomped. Malinda's fingers fumbled briefly when her mind wandered to that letter again. "Maybe we do both need an outing." Malinda patted the horse. Maybe Isaac wouldn't be working today.

Malinda kept Chestnut trotting at a moderate pace. She was in no great hurry, and she didn't want to overtax the horse in the afternoon heat. She stopped at the quilt shop first to pick up the thread she was almost one hundred percent sure her *mamm* did not need. She would make the cheese factory the last stop. Even though she'd brought a small cooler along, she didn't want to arrive home with gooey, melted cheese.

The ladies working on a quilt in the back of the shop had plied her with so many questions about her health and her trip to Ohio, the simple stop for thread stretched into a visit much longer than Malinda had intended. She knew the women really cared and weren't simply being nosy. It's just she didn't relish all the attention to her health, or lack thereof. She clucked to Chestnut and set out for the cheese factory so Mamm could prepare Daed's favorite macaroni and cheese dish. She couldn't believe Daed would have minded waiting a day or two, but when Mamm took a notion to do something—or in this case, for someone else to do something—there was no talking her out of it. Malinda sighed. She'd zip in, buy the cheese, and zip back out, all relatively unnoticed, she hoped.

She slid from the buggy and patted Chestnut's neck. "Be right back." A few cars in the lot told her *Englisch* customers were milling about inside. That could work to her advantage. Maybe everyone would be busy with them so she could quickly pick up what she needed and scoot back out.

Maybe not. Standing across from the entrance with hazel eyes fastened on the door was none other than Isaac Hostetler. Malinda's heart tripped over itself. Her throat suddenly felt as dry as the dirt in the parking lot, and her tongue attached itself to the roof of her mouth. *Relax. You've known Isaac forever.* Not only did she know him, she truly believed he would have asked to take her home from a singing if she hadn't been sent to Ohio and stayed there longer than expected. For some unknown reason, Isaac hadn't attended the singing she recently went to, and he hadn't visited or inquired about her as far as she knew.

Malinda coaxed her lips into a tremulous smile. She looked into the eyes that captured the hues of his green shirt and today looked green instead of hazel. She pried her tongue from the roof of her mouth and dragged in a deep breath. Her feet, as if they had a mind of their own, carried her closer to where Isaac stood. "Hello, Isaac." She hated that her voice wobbled, making her nervousness obvious.

"Hello, Malinda."

Isaac's mouth snapped shut after just those two words. No *How are you feeling?* or *It's great to see you.* No polite pleasantries at all. Just two little words. It looked like any conversation would be up to her. "I—we missed you at the last singing."

"I, uh, was busy."

"I thought we could have talked then—you know, caught up a bit, since I've been away." Malinda studied the unsmiling face in front of her. She watched the hazel eyes shift from side to side. She waited a few endless seconds, but no reply came from Isaac's lips. "Will you be at the next singing?" Malinda pinned him with her eyes and saw him squirm.

"Uh, I don't know."

"Oh." Malinda searched her mind for something else to say. Conversation between them hadn't been so difficult before. She heard the screen door swish open behind her but kept her gaze on Isaac's face, which suddenly paled.

"*Ach*, Isaac! I thought maybe you'd be ready to leave early like you said."

Malinda watched Isaac's brow wrinkle and caught the slight shake of his head. Before she could turn around to utter a greeting, the newcomer flounced in front of her, touched Isaac's arm almost possessively, and spoke in a syrupy voice. "Why, hello, Malinda."

"Hello, Becky." Malinda looked from Isaac to Becky and stumbled backward a step as realization dawned. No wonder Isaac hadn't asked about her or visited since she returned home. He'd even kept his distance after last church day's common meal, staying with the other young men. Now she understood why. He wasn't giving her time to adjust to being home like she'd thought. He'd taken up with Rebecca Zook! Had he started seeing Becky as soon as Malinda left town, or did he wait until she'd been gone at least a few days? Was she gone too long, or had her illness played a part in Isaac's obvious change of heart?

Malinda felt as if Isaac had plunged a knife into her chest, and Becky's self-satisfied smile twisted the blade. Becky batted her long, pale lashes at Isaac and then fixed Malinda with a wide-eyed, innocent stare. With the hand that wasn't still grasping Isaac's arm, Becky tucked an imaginary stray wisp of honey blonde hair beneath her *kapp*.

Fake! Malinda wanted to cry, but held her tongue. Not for one minute did she fall for Becky's innocent act. That girl, with her slightly tighter and slightly shorter dresses, knew exactly what she was doing. And she knew Isaac and Malinda had often talked after singings. She probably also knew Isaac was about ready to ask to court Malinda. When Malinda had to leave suddenly to help her *aenti*, Becky must have considered that the perfect opportunity to sink her claws into Isaac. *Ach*! The nerve of the girl, to play all pure and innocent now!

"I heard you were home," Becky said.

"Didn't you see me at church?" Malinda could hardly get words out through her clenched teeth. Of course Becky had seen her. They both carried food to the tables after church, for goodness' sake. Becky must have sat behind her during church, too. That was probably a *gut* thing. Malinda would have gotten sick if she had seen Becky making goo-goo eyes at Isaac across the way.

"I guess I didn't pay much attention." Becky gave a little giggle and cut her eyes up to Isaac's.

"I don't remember you being at the last singing, either, so you wouldn't have seen me there."

"We, uh, I had other plans that evening."

"I see." Malinda began backing away from the obviously

smitten pair. "Well, I'd better get Mamm's cheese." She continued backing up. She would not give Isaac and Becky the satisfaction of seeing her shed a single tear, even though the pain of betrayal seared her heart. She stumbled as she abruptly spun around.

"Whoa!" a deep voice called as strong hands steadied her. "We meet again." A note of merriment colored the voice.

"*Ach*, Timothy!" Malinda looked up and up into the clear, blue eyes with laugh crinkles at the corners. "You saved me from falling again. It's getting to be a habit."

"I'm glad I've been at the right place at the right time." Timothy chuckled. He dropped his hands from Malinda's arms and gave an exaggerated bow. "At your service, miss." He swept his straw hat across his broad chest.

Malinda couldn't help but laugh at Tim's antics, despite her heavy heart. "What are you doing here?"

"I'm glad you're feeling better." Becky laid a hand on Malinda's arm. She tugged Isaac along behind her. "Excuse us. Isaac and I need to talk."

Malinda nearly gagged at Becky's sickening, sweet smile. When Becky batted her lashes at Isaac and squeezed his arm, Malinda feared she would lose the snack she'd eaten earlier. She stared after the departing couple and caught her lower lip between her teeth to stop its trembling. She would not cry. Not here.

"Malinda? Malinda?"

Malinda dragged her gaze away from Isaac and Becky. "Hmm?"

"Are you all right?"

Malinda started to nod, but an affirmative answer would be a lie, and lying was a sin. Instead she shrugged her shoulders.

"You asked what I was doing here."

"I did? Right, I did."

"My *mamm* asked me to pick up some cheese on my way home. Are you here to see Atlee?"

"*Nee*. I'm fetching cheese for my *mamm*, too." Malinda raised her eyes to meet Timothy's. If eyes could speak, his would express his concern. At least she hoped it was concern she saw, and not pity. He had to have heard the entire exchange with Becky. "I guess we'd better get that cheese, ain't so? My *mamm* wants to make macaroni and cheese tonight."

"Mmmm! That sounds *gut*." Timothy rubbed his belly. "I think my *mamm* is planning to use the cheese for sauce on broccoli. I'd rather eat at your house."

Malinda laughed a real laugh. "I'm sure there will be plenty for one more. You're always *wilkom*, you know."

"I may just take you up on that offer." Timothy smiled down at Malinda before strolling over to the cheese case.

Chapter Seven

What was wrong with Isaac Hostetler? Couldn't he see through Becky Zook's facade? Didn't he remember or even notice Becky's penchant for worming her way into relationships, tearing couples apart, and then dropping the fellow to move on to her next conquest? Timothy cast a brief, sidelong glance down at the petite young woman beside him. Didn't Isaac know what a true gem Malinda Stauffer was? Any fellow should be thrilled and honored to have Malinda's devotion. He knew he would be. Isaac's loss could be his gain. He hoped.

How would Timothy go about getting Malinda to see him as something other than her *bruder*'s *freind*? How would he get Malinda to care for him the way he cared for her, the way he'd cared for her for the past several years? Timothy couldn't even remember when his emotions had shifted. It seemed one day he had thought of Malinda simply as Sam's little *schweschder* who sometimes tagged along on their fishing adventures to the Wicomico River. Then, practically overnight, she had become a beautiful girl who made his heart do crazy little somersaults at the mere sight of her. So what if he was three years older? He'd never found any girls closer to his own age who intrigued him nearly as much as Malinda did. He'd been biding his time, waiting for Malinda to finish school, grow up, and start attending singings.

To Timothy's dismay and because he hadn't had the nerve to approach her, he'd had to stand by and watch her talk and laugh with other young folks after singings. He'd about abandoned all hope of winning her heart when Isaac Hostetler began paying extra attention to Malinda. When she seemed to reciprocate the interest, Timothy felt actual physical pain, like a worm was gnawing away at his gut. Now he might have another chance. He didn't want to blow it by doing or saying something stupid.

Timothy took a quick, deep breath. It wouldn't do for him to say what a dolt he thought Isaac was or how he'd like to throttle Isaac for causing Malinda any heartache. Should he mention Isaac at all? He certainly couldn't blurt out his feelings. He'd need to take it slow, but not so slow that he missed this unexpected opportunity altogether.

"Which kind of cheese did your *mamm* need?"

Timothy didn't realize they'd reached the counter already. How long had they been standing here? What a *dummchen* he must seem to Malinda. Heat flooded his cheeks. Had she asked him that question more than once? "Um, cheddar, I think. I've, uh, had a busy day, and it sort of slipped my mind. Does that sound like the right kind for sauce?"

"I believe your *mamm* would probably use cheddar for a sauce."

"If I'm wrong, we can eat the cheese on sandwiches, ain't so?"

"For sure. You can do about anything with cheddar. I have to get several kinds. Mamm likes to use a mixture in her macaroni and cheese."

"That sounds *appeditlich*. Save me some, if you can."

"I'll put some aside before my *bruders* and Daed have a chance to inhale it. If you want to join us, just *kumm* on over." Malinda turned her attention to the clerk to place her order.

Timothy couldn't believe he'd spent all this time talking about cheese. What else could he say? He needed his brain to think faster before they both completed their purchases and went their separate ways. He stuffed his change into his pocket and took giant steps to catch up with Malinda. "Are you going to see Atlee while you're here?"

"*Nee*. Mamm wants to make her macaroni, I'm sure, so I'd better get Chestnut moving toward home."

Timothy matched his pace to Malinda's and accompanied her to her buggy. He untied the horse for her and reached out a hand to help her climb into the buggy.

"I can manage."

Malinda's mutter sounded like it had *kumm* through clenched teeth. Timothy thought he detected a trace of annoyance in her voice. Did she think he believed she was incapable of caring for herself or of even climbing into a buggy on her own? He knew very well she was not an invalid. In fact, she looked healthier than she had last week. Of course, she always looked beautiful to him. He'd better make amends fast. "I know you can manage just fine, Malinda. You are a very strong, capable person. I-I'm only trying to be, uh, gentlemanly."

"*Ach*! I'm sorry, Tim. I didn't mean to snap at you. I feel like everyone considers me a helpless invalid. Even my own *mamm* keeps one eye on me nearly every waking second."

"She cares about you, Malinda. I'm sure that's all it is. Everyone cares." He almost said *he* cared, but modified his response. Before he could bridle his wayward tongue, though, he added, "I don't think you're an invalid at all. I think you are just perfect." Timothy watched the crimson color stain Malinda's pale cheeks.

"You're very sweet." Malinda ducked her head as if suddenly embarrassed by her comment.

Before his nerve completely abandoned him, Timothy reached out a hand to lightly grasp Malinda's chin. He gently tilted her head up so her chocolate-drop eyes had to look into his own eyes. He wanted her to know he meant every word he uttered, that he was sincere and could be trusted. "I'm only saying what is true, what I feel inside." Malinda's cheeks flushed an even deeper crimson. Timothy smiled. He could gaze at Malinda Stauffer forever.

"*Danki*, Tim." She once again stared at her feet.

Timothy didn't mean to embarrass her. Somehow his tongue had acquired a mind of its own and was flapping out whatever thought popped into his head.

"I'd better get Mamm's cheese home before it melts in this heat."

"I know what you mean. Did you bring a cooler? I have my lunch box you can use. My *mamm* is making sauce with the cheese, so a little melting won't be a major catastrophe."

Malinda smiled up at Timothy, causing his heart to tumble over itself. "Your *mamm* probably doesn't want to use a straw to suck up her cheese, either. I brought a little cooler. I even have an extra cold pack if you need it."

"I think I'll be okay. May I offer you some assistance?" Tim nodded toward the buggy and bent in a playful bow.

Malinda picked up on his playfulness. "Why, yes, sir. I'd be most obliged."

Timothy took one of Malinda's arms and assisted her into the buggy. He wished he didn't have to let go of her—ever. As she wiggled to get situated, Timothy's hand slid down her arm, and his fingers intertwined with her small, soft ones. *This is nice.* If he couldn't hold her in his arms, holding her hand was the next best thing. And she didn't rush to pull her hand away. Dare he get his hopes up?

"Will you attend the next singing?" Timothy gave Malinda's hand a gentle squeeze.

"I-I don't know."

Timothy's eyes followed Malinda's gaze toward the entrance of the building, where Isaac emerged with Becky close by his side. Becky's exaggerated giggle could be heard over top of any of his air tools, Timothy thought. "He's not worthy of you." He spoke only half under his breath. If she followed her usual pattern, which Isaac evidently was too besotted to recognize, Becky would soon tire of Isaac and move on. Timothy hoped by that time Malinda would be completely over Isaac and would be courting him.

"What did you say?" Malinda slid her hand from Timothy's grasp.

Timothy felt a sudden emptiness without Malinda's tiny hand in his. "Uh, I, uh . . ." He searched for words. "I hope you'll *kumm* to the singing. I'll attend if you will."

"Why?"

"Why not?"

"Timothy Brenneman, it is not polite to answer a question with another question."

"It isn't? All right then. I-I'd like to talk to you at the singing. That's all."

"You can talk to me any time you *kumm* over to see Sam."

Suddenly emboldened, Timothy said, "Maybe I'd like to talk to you without Sam around."

Malinda's eyes flew up to stare into Timothy's. Her mouth dropped open. "I . . . you . . . why?" She shook her head as if confused.

Timothy wished he could retract his last comment. Obviously he had upset Malinda. That was the last thing he wanted to do. He wanted a closer relationship with her. He didn't want to frighten her or drive her away. "I-I like talking to you. Is that all right?"

"Well, sure, I guess so. Why not?"

"It isn't polite to answer a question with a question, Malinda Stauffer."

Malinda burst out laughing, the musical sound dispelling the tension growing up around them like weeds in a strawberry patch.

Timothy laughed, too. "I'm not just Sam's *freind*," he began when their laughter died away. "Do you think you could think of me as a person?"

Malinda giggled. "You are a person, silly."

Timothy smacked his forehead. "That didn't *kumm* out right. What I meant—" He paused, took a deep breath, and wondered how best to continue. Finally the words burst from his mouth. "What I meant was, could you ever think of me as someone other than Sam's *freind*, as someone interested in you?" Interested? He'd been fighting feelings much stronger than "interested" for ever so long.

Timothy's eyes traveled down to his toe, which was stirring up dirt and assorted pebbles, then to Isaac, who was leaning into Becky's buggy, and then back to Malinda's lovely face. He was apparently going about this all wrong. Now he'd put Malinda on the spot just after Isaac had trounced on her heart.

"I-I'll attend the next singing," Malinda whispered. She cleared her throat and stared into Timothy's eyes. "It might be fun talking to you and getting to know you as 'a person.'"

"Really?" Timothy feared he had imagined her response. He searched her face to make sure she wasn't teasing or mocking. *Nee*, Malinda would never be cruel or anything other than completely honest. Of that he felt certain.

"Really." Malinda glanced at the cooler beside her. "I'd better get Mamm's cheese home."

"Me too. See you soon, Malinda."

Malinda nodded. "I'll save you some macaroni and cheese." She clucked to the horse and urged him forward at a trot.

Timothy barely kept from jumping and shouting. Did Malinda mean she'd give him a chance? Could he imagine that one day she would care for him the way he cared for her? He hoped she didn't have second thoughts before the next singing.

Chapter Eight

It was a *gut* thing Chestnut could find his way home blindfolded in a snowstorm, since Malinda's mind had wandered a million miles away. Actually, just a few miles. It had stayed behind at the cheese factory. What had just happened? Had she misunderstood completely, or had Timothy Brenneman, Sam's *freind*, the older *bu* who had often been a fixture at their house, just indicated his interest in her? Not a casual interest, as in inquiring about a *freind*'s little *schweschder*. He specifically asked if she'd attend the next singing so they could talk.

Normally the couples who spent time talking after the last song had been sung ended up leaving together. Many ended up courting. Is that what Timothy wanted—to court her? And exactly how did she feel about that? She had always thought of Timothy as Sam's pal. Of course, he had always been nice to her, even when she was a pesky little girl. Could she think of him in a different way?

Malinda's brain conjured up Timothy's image. He was nice to look at. Very nice. In fact, Timothy was very handsome. He must be well over six feet, since he stood several inches taller than Sam. He was strong. Malinda had seen him lift heavy pieces of furniture by himself when she'd visited

Swarey's Furniture Shop. But those strong arms were also gentle. She felt heat, and not heat from the afternoon sun, rise to her cheeks when she remembered how those arms had steadied her several times recently. His pale blond hair reminded her of the corn silk she liked to rub between her fingers when she shucked corn. Would Timothy's hair feel the same between her fingers? His eyes were the bluest she'd ever seen. His furniture-making skills surpassed even Sam's. Malinda had seen some of the fancier pieces Timothy had designed for *Englisch* customers. But those eyes . . .

Ach, *Malinda! Get hold of yourself!* She could not allow herself to think of a fellow in any way other than as a *freind*. Look how Isaac had treated her. He'd forgotten all about her the instant she left town. To be perfectly honest, she couldn't imagine Isaac understanding her illness or helping her through a bad time. In fact, she couldn't ever remember him coming around or even asking about her when she felt sick like Timothy always did. That should have been a warning sign, but she'd totally ignored it.

Well, she wouldn't let herself get hurt again. And she wouldn't impose her weakness, her illness on anyone. That would not be fair—even if there ever was a fellow who would give her a second look once he knew the seriousness of her disease.

Malinda sighed and sniffed back tears. Like the apostle Paul, she would have to live with her thorn and not subject others to it. Somehow she'd learn to be content with remaining single all her days. Her *bruders* would most likely all get married and give her plenty of little ones to dote on.

"Hello, Malinda. Please pass me the macaroni and cheese." Atlee drummed his fingers on the table.

"Huh?"

"*Kumm* back to earth, Malinda," Sam chimed in. "Atlee

has asked you three times to pass the macaroni and cheese. Please give it to him before he eats mine from my plate."

Malinda wrinkled her nose at her older *bruders* and lifted the big casserole dish. "Here you go." She thrust the bowl into Atlee's outstretched hands.

"Ow! It's still hot."

"Grasp the handles. See, I didn't get burned." She turned her palms out to face Atlee.

"That's because you're out in la-la land somewhere."

"I am not."

"You have seemed rather distracted, Dochder." Rufus glanced up briefly before slathering butter on a third homemade biscuit.

"I'm sorry, Daed."

"Are you feeling all right?" A worry frown creased Saloma's forehead. Her gaze latched onto Malinda's mostly untouched plate.

"I'm fine, Mamm." Immediately Malinda picked up her fork and scooped up a bite of cheesy noodles. She'd just managed to poke them into her mouth when Atlee pointed his fork at her.

"I saw you with Timothy."

Although Atlee's words were garbled by the noodles stuffed in his mouth, Malinda understood them quite well. She hoped no one else did. Maybe she could divert the conversation to some other topic. "Atlee, you act like you haven't eaten in a month."

"I'm a growing *bu*." He gulped down the wad of food.

"Growing out, not up. You'll be as big as the barn, eating like you do."

"*Nee*. I work it off just fine." He loaded his fork again. "So what kept you and Timothy so engrossed?" Atlee elbowed Sam and chuckled before shoveling the next bite into his mouth.

"I was picking up cheese so you could stuff yourself

tonight. Timothy was fetching cheese for his *mamm*, too. He wondered which kind she would need for her cheese sauce."

"It seemed like a pretty lengthy conversation to be only about cheese."

Malinda nearly crumpled her napkin to hurl at Atlee's head but didn't give in to the temptation. She willed her cheeks not to flush but felt the heat rise in spite of her best effort. "Timothy was just being nice and asking how I was. You must have been shirking your duties to take such notice of the customers' conversations."

Sam guffawed and nearly choked on his butter-oozing biscuit. He licked his fingers before elbowing Atlee. "She got you there, Bruder."

Out of the corner of her eye, Malinda caught her parents exchanging smiles. They seemed to be enjoying the banter, so Malinda doubted they would help her out of this uncomfortable predicament.

"For your information, Miss Know-It-All, if you hadn't been staring so intently at Timothy Brenneman, you would have noticed the cheese factory wasn't overrun with customers at that time." A smug smile tugged at Atlee's mouth.

"I was not staring at Timothy. I was taught to be polite and give my attention to the person talking to me."

"I thought you liked Isaac Hostetler," Roman chimed in.

"It looked to me like Isaac only had eyes for Rebecca Zook today. He seemed to hang on her every word and every flutter of her lashes." Atlee batted his eyes.

Malinda gasped. Her nose burned and her eyes filled. She blinked hard.

"Such things are not your concern, Roman, or yours, either, Atlee." Saloma gave each of her sons a stern look.

Roman shrugged. "Just wondering."

"Tim didn't have a message for me or anything, did he?" Sam juggled fresh garden peas on his fork.

"*Nee*. Why? Didn't you see him at work today?"

"I did, but he left early to pick up a few supplies, and apparently to pick up cheese, too." Sam wiggled his eyebrows at Malinda.

"Apparently." Malinda refused to say more on the subject. She studied the food she'd been shuffling around on her plate.

"I think we need to eat more and talk less," Rufus announced.

Malinda held back her sigh of relief. She couldn't decide which subject was touchier—her relationship or nonrelationship with Isaac, or her meeting with Timothy. She sent up a silent prayer of thanks for her *daed*'s intervention.

As usual, her *bruders* had scarfed down their food while Malinda toyed with hers and only pretended to take an occasional bite.

"Can we have cobbler now?" Aden pushed his empty plate away from him.

"Cobbler? Peach cobbler?" Ray's excitement nearly matched Aden's. "Peach cobbler is my favorite. Can we have ice cream with it?"

"I think we can have one dollop of vanilla ice cream." Saloma smiled at her sons.

"I'll get it, Mamm." Malinda pushed back her chair, jumped to her feet, and stacked her *bruders*' empty plates on top of her own to hide the food still covering it.

"*Danki*, Malinda. I'll be along in a minute." Saloma glanced at the stacked plates in Malinda's hands and then at her daughter's face. Malinda pretended not to notice and whisked the plates from the room.

After taking the ice cream to the table, Malinda busily scrubbed plates and scarcely heard Saloma enter the kitchen. Her brain whirred with her *bruders*' comments, interwoven with Timothy's words and Isaac's betrayal. It wasn't like she and Isaac had been officially courting, but she thought they'd had an unspoken understanding. Evidently the feelings had been one-sided—her side. She exhaled a deep sigh.

"That sounded almost painful. Is there anything you'd like to talk about?" Saloma set leftovers in the refrigerator.

Malinda's jaw tensed hard enough to cause a pain to shoot straight up to her forehead. She shook her head. She pulled a soapy hand from the dishwater to rub her cheek.

Saloma ripped a paper towel from the roll on the counter and dabbed at the bubbles on Malinda's cheek. "Are you sure?"

"Are all fellows so fickle?" Malinda blurted.

"Are we talking about a particular fellow?"

"*Ach*! I don't know. I guess it's just me. Maybe if I hadn't gotten sick and stayed in Ohio so long, things would be different." Malinda drew in a shaky breath. Before Saloma could respond, she added, half to herself, "Maybe he just wants a healthy girl. I wish . . ." She let that thought evaporate into the stuffy kitchen air, knowing full well how her *mamm* would reply to that.

"Gott's grace is sufficient, Malinda."

"I know." Mamm didn't understand how hard it was to have a chronic disease that could wreak havoc on her body at the drop of a hat. She held her tongue, though. No use hearing the apostle Paul spiel again.

"Maybe Isaac isn't the right *bu* for you, and Gott has a different plan."

"What if His plan is for me to stay single? I really want a family of my own, Mamm."

"Sometimes our ways aren't His ways."

Malinda sniffed but could do nothing to stop the tear trickling down her cheek. She stared into the murky dishwater and clamped her teeth together to bite back a sob.

Saloma gently raised Malinda's chin. "Maybe He has

someone else in mind for you. Be open to His will, *jah?*" She pulled Malinda away from the sink and into her arms.

Malinda wrapped her arms around her *mamm*, wet hands soaking Saloma's back. "*Ach*, Mamm! I've gotten you all wet!" She started to pull away.

Saloma tightened her hug. "A little water never hurt anyone. I don't think I'm sweet enough to melt." She chuckled, and even drew a little giggle from Malinda.

Chapter Nine

What was Gott's plan for her life? Malinda pondered that as she crawled into bed. Even though the night was still warm, she pulled the sheet up to her chin. Something about having the cool sheet covering her body comforted her. She had prayed long and hard, until her knees throbbed against the wood floor despite the throw rug beneath them. She heard no voice in reply and felt no real direction. Maybe she hadn't prayed hard enough or listened as closely as she should have. It would be so *wunderbaar* if the Lord would speak to her directly as He had to Abraham and Moses or if He sent an angel to her as He had to Mary and Joseph. Her decisions then would be so simple—either obey or disobey. She wouldn't have to figure out which path to take. She would be told, and then she would simply obey. It appeared, though, that the Lord would not answer her in such a manner. It looked like He was leaving her to forge a path of her own.

Malinda sighed and shifted to her right side. Mamm said to be open to Gott's will. If only she knew for sure and for certain what that was. She had thought Isaac was the man for her. Wrong! If she'd been mistaken about Isaac, how would she ever trust her own judgment again? How would she know what was Gott's will and what was her own notion?

She punched her pillow to plump it up. Maybe the Lord had someone else for her, like Mamm said. Or maybe there would be no one willing to be saddled with a sickly girl. Could she be content to be an *aenti*? Or maybe she could be a schoolteacher? Either way, she'd be loving other people's *kinner*. She wouldn't be holding her own *boppli* in her arms.

Malinda flopped back over onto her back. Surely Gott didn't want her to be alone. She doubted she could be content with remaining single all her life like the apostle Paul. He accepted Gott's answer and Gott's grace and found contentment. Could she do the same? She didn't want to!

"Forgive me, Lord Gott. I don't mean to be contrary or demanding. I want to do Your will. Really I do. Is it too much to ask that Your will include a home and family of my own?" She snaked one hand out from under the sheet to swipe at the tears trailing down her cheeks. "And, Gott, I-I forgive Isaac and Rebecca."

When the last tear had trickled off her chin, Malinda sniffed and made up her mind to think rationally now that her emotions were spent. Mamm had probably been right when she said Isaac might not be the right one for her. After all, if he truly cared about her, he would have inquired about her and would have been eager to see her the moment she arrived home. He certainly wouldn't have fallen prey to Rebecca's charms the instant Malinda left town. But what was the *Englisch* saying? "Out of sight, out of mind" or something like that. Well, she had certainly been out of Isaac's mind as soon as she was out of his sight. Most people, at least the girls, anyway, had figured out Rebecca's game a long time ago. It seemed pretty obvious that Rebecca must be keeping a tally of all the *buwe* who succumbed to her fluttering eyes and sweet voice. Evidently Isaac wasn't so astute or sincere. If he could turn off his feelings at the drop of a hat, he definitely wasn't right for her. They hadn't officially been courting. And to be honest with herself, she wasn't in love with him, but she had thought she was moving in that direction. No more. Isaac was now part of the past.

But what did her future hold? Who was right for her, and how would she know? Surely she would appeal to someone. The image of a tall, dark-haired, dark-eyed man with a black stethoscope circling his neck flashed through her mind. Dr. Todd McWilliams seemed interested, for sure. If a sophisticated, intelligent, important man like him could be attracted to her, she must not be too homely. Ach, *Malinda! Looks aren't important. And for goodness' sake, the man is* Englisch*!* He definitely was not the right man for her. Besides, he frightened her with his gaze that seemed to penetrate her mind and soul. He seemed too sure of himself, too sure he could convince her to leave her faith, her whole way of life. As if that would be possible! She had no desire to jump the fence. It was rather flattering, though, that she sparked his interest. She most likely was an enigma, a challenge for him.

She shivered despite the warm night and the cotton sheet pulled up to her chin. She feared the doctor was not used to accepting *nee* for an answer. She prayed he wouldn't try to locate her if he came to Baltimore. She turned to the other side, twisting herself in the sheet. It would definitely be best not to think about him at all. His attention may have given her ego a little boost, but he scared her more than anything.

Why in the world did he behave the way he did? Was that how he treated all of his female patients, or just her? Sure, she was young and naïve and Amish, but she wasn't unintelligent. She knew when something wasn't right. And Dr. McWilliams definitely had not acted as a doctor should. None of the other doctors or male nurses or technicians who entered her hospital room in Ohio acted inappropriately in any way. They did their jobs and maintained a pleasant but professional manner. At first she thought Dr. McWilliams was merely trying to put her at ease in a strange place. But he overstepped the boundaries of a doctor-patient relationship and made her nervous, even fearful. Another little shiver snaked its way up her spine. *I'm glad I'm in Maryland and he's in Ohio. I just hope he stays there!*

Malinda grunted as she fought the sheet again. She squeezed her eyes tightly shut. Her whirling brain refused to allow sleep to claim her. Thoughts of the fellows her age flashed through her mind. She'd known them forever, had sat through eight years of school with them, had played tag and softball on the playground with them. They were nice enough, for sure, but not a single one made her heart skip even half a beat. Only Isaac, who had been a grade ahead of her in school, created a little stir, and that had only begun shortly before she left town.

Her mind examined and rejected other older fellows before settling on Timothy Brenneman. What had possessed Tim to speak to her as he had today at the cheese factory? Had he had such thoughts for a while and only gotten up his nerve to voice them today? She couldn't remember him giving any indication he was interested in her in all the years he had been hanging around their house with Sam. When had he begun to think of her as anything other than Sam's pesky little *schweschder*? Had she been too caught up in her dreams of Isaac to notice any subtle changes in Tim's behavior? She searched her memory.

Of course Malinda had stopped trailing along behind her older *bruders* and their *freinden* years ago, but she had almost always been around when the other fellows came to the house. Most of Atlee's and Sam's buddies greeted her politely and then promptly ignored her. But, now that she thought about it, Tim had been different. He always asked about her plans, her latest quilting project, and even her health, once the Crohn's disease began making its ugly appearance. The look in his big blue eyes always made her feel he was genuinely interested in her replies rather than merely attempting to exchange pleasantries. He always looked down into her eyes as he spoke, not all around as if in a hurry to escape. His smiles always reached his eyes, making little crinkly lines at the corners. Had he always done this, or had his attitude changed recently?

What did Malinda really know about Tim? He and Sam had been *gut freinden* forever, so he'd always been a part of her life. He had tolerated her presence and had never been mean to her. In fact, if she remembered correctly, he often jumped in to stop Sam or Atlee from teasing her. When she got older and no longer tramped after her *bruders*, her contact with Tim became a bit more limited. But she did notice when he was around.

Timothy Brenneman was hard not to notice. He stood taller than Sam, and Malinda used to think Sam was a giant compared to her own slight, five-foot-one-inch frame. Tim's muscles rippled beneath the sleeves of his shirt from all his hard labor on his *daed*'s farm and all his lifting of heavy furniture. Yet, despite his obvious strength, Malinda sensed gentleness about him. His deep voice had a soothing quality, and his expressive sky blue eyes beneath pale blond hair could trip any girl's heart. But her own heart still smarted from Isaac's betrayal.

Why did she tell Timothy she would go to the next singing? Why did she say she'd like to talk to him, too? Unsure if she could think of Tim as more than a *freind*, Malinda didn't want to give him false hope. Maybe she could find a reason not to attend the singing. She had promised, though. "*Ach*, Malinda! How do you get yourself in such messes?" She spoke aloud as if expecting the darkness to answer her.

How should she act next time she saw Timothy? She would always look at him differently now. Was that a *gut* thing or a bad thing? He had been very sweet at the cheese factory today, and playful, too. She liked both qualities. Despite the sight of Isaac and Rebecca in her periphery, she had enjoyed the moments with Timothy. Malinda sighed and flung the sheet off of her. Maybe she could settle down and sleep if she was cooler.

Maybe not.

Chapter Ten

Despite her restless night, Malinda stumbled into the kitchen before Mamm the next morning. She peeled off slices of bacon from the plastic-wrapped slab she pulled from the gas-powered refrigerator and stretched them out in the cast-iron frying pan. They popped and sizzled while she whisked enough eggs to feed all her hungry family. She was laying crisp bacon strips on a paper towel–lined plate to drain by the time Saloma appeared.

"Goodness, am I that late?" Saloma stole a glance at the apple-shaped, battery-operated clock on the far wall.

"You're not late, Mamm. I woke up early."

"Here, I'll do the eggs." Saloma took the large ceramic mixing bowl from Malinda's hands.

"I'll pack the lunches, then." Since the younger *buwe* were out of school for the summer, she only had Sam's and Atlee's lunches to pack. Stealthily she slid the small plastic container of macaroni and cheese into Sam's lunch box and attached a note on which she had written "give to Tim" in bold, black letters. When she looked up, she caught her *mamm* looking askance at her with raised brows, but she didn't say a word. Malinda hastily added fruit and cookies to the lunch boxes and fastened them while asking her *mamm* about the day's plans. That was the only subject she could think of on the spur of the moment to divert attention from her secretive action. Knowing her *mamm*, though, Saloma's curiosity would get the best of her before too long.

"Did Sam ask you to squirrel away some macaroni and cheese for his lunch today?"

The question came as Saloma and Malinda systematically canned tomatoes in the hot kitchen. They had gotten an early start right after breakfast with the intention of finishing the job before the oppressive afternoon heat and humidity set in. They had scalded and peeled the baskets of tomatoes and now had them bubbling on the stove. Saloma ladled tomatoes and their liquid into quart-sized canning jars. She then passed the jars to Malinda, who ran the long handle of a wooden spoon inside the jars to dispel air bubbles before she screwed on lids and set the jars in the canner.

Malinda nearly dropped the jar she was holding in midair on its way to the canner. She shouldn't have been surprised at the question, but she started nonetheless. Actually, what was surprising was that her *mamm* had waited this long to ask her question. She must have been burning with curiosity all morning. Malinda steadied the jar and gently lowered it into the canner. "*Nee*, Sam didn't ask for the mac and cheese—and he'd better not eat it, either!"

"Then why on earth did you put it in his lunch box? You know he and Atlee eat like there's no tomorrow."

Malinda suppressed a sigh. There would be no way to sidestep Mamm's questions. She couldn't be untruthful. She hadn't planned to divulge the details of her encounter with Timothy. She was still trying to sort things out in her mind. "You know I ran into Timothy yesterday."

"So you said last night."

"Well, I happened to mention you needed cheese for

your macaroni dish. Timothy said his *mamm* needed cheese for a sauce for broccoli. Tim said he'd rather have mac and cheese. I told him I'd save him some."

Saloma chuckled. "That *bu* always did like my macaroni and cheese. He could almost out-eat Sam."

"That would be pretty hard to do."

"Did you put a note on that container so Sam would know it was for Tim?"

"I did. I wrote in big, bold letters. Sam had better not ignore that note!"

"Did you and Tim discuss anything else?" A sly little smile played at the corners of Saloma's lips.

"Uh, we talked a little more. We both needed to get the cheese home before it turned into sauce all by itself." Malinda couldn't bring herself to tell Saloma that Timothy thought she was perfect, that he wanted her to think of him as more than Sam's *freind*, that he wanted her to attend the next singing so they could talk. She and her *mamm* had always been close, but some things needed to be savored for a while before they could be shared. Warmth crept up from her neck to her cheeks, and she raised an arm to swipe at her face. "It's sure hot in here!" Judging from Saloma's expression, Malinda was fairly certain she hadn't fooled her *mamm* one bit. She prayed Mamm wouldn't question her further.

"Timothy is a *gut bu*. I guess I should say he's a *gut* young man. He's much more thoughtful than Isaac Hostetler. Isaac is fine, I suppose, but not nearly as mature, though I'm sure I know Tim much better than Isaac. It's hard to believe Tim and Sam are grown up and ready to head their own families. Tim has always been the nicest of Sam's *freinden*." Saloma's eyes slid over to rest on Malinda's face. All the while, she continued to ladle tomatoes into the hot, sterile jars without sloshing any liquid over the sides.

Malinda thought her *mamm* could can tomatoes or perform practically any household chore in a dead sleep.

Certain her face was blushing as red as the tomatoes in the jar she was lowering into the canner, Malinda pretended the task at hand required her utmost attention and avoided looking up. If Mamm looked into her eyes, she'd be bound to see Malinda was withholding some tidbit of information and would probably dig until she dragged it out. Malinda's brain scrambled to find a way to steer the conversation away from the topic of Timothy Brenneman. "We sure got a lot of tomatoes this year, ain't so?"

"*Jah*, and we'll probably have two or three more pickings. I've got enough left in this pot to make some stew. Do you think it's too hot for stew?"

"I think Daed and the *buwe* will eat anything you put on the table, hot or cold."

Saloma laughed. "I'm sure you're right about that."

Malinda held in her sigh of relief. Maybe she had escaped further scrutiny for now.

The day passed in a flurry of activity with canning, cleaning up, cooking, and more cleaning up. Malinda managed to sidestep any references to Timothy until her *mamm* reined in her curiosity and stopped asking questions. Until after supper, that is.

Out of the blue, a horse and buggy kicked up dust as they advanced up the dirt driveway. Malinda had perched on the wooden front porch swing, which she had set gently swaying to create a small breeze. Her bag of knitting supplies lay beside her. She watched her *bruders* trying to play volleyball in the front yard. Aden, Ray, and Sam faced Roman and Atlee. Malinda smiled as Aden missed the ball time and time again. He tried so hard. Thank goodness Sam and Ray didn't scold him.

"Hey, it's Timothy!" Sam shouted as the buggy rolled to a stop. "Hurry up, Tim. We need some help here."

"Tim's on our side," Roman called. "It's already three against two."

"But . . ." Sam's eyes darted to Aden. "Okay."

Obviously Sam wanted to spare Aden's feelings. Malinda's heart swelled at her oldest *bruder*'s kindness to her youngest *bruder*. Sam would be a great *daed* one day. She wondered if he and Emma Swarey were headed for marriage. At twenty-three, Sam was definitely old enough to start his own family.

Malinda's eyes followed Timothy as he jogged over to join the game. She saw his gaze sweep the house before his blue eyes connected with hers. Malinda couldn't be sure, but she thought Tim gave her a quick wink. Her heart flopped like a rockfish on the bottom of the old fishing boat. Her cheeks warmed, so she hastily shifted her eyes to the game. To make her embarrassment complete, Atlee had caught Timothy's action and smirked in her direction.

Malinda snatched up the as-yet-untouched ball of dark blue yarn and yanked out the knitting needles poked inside of it. Drat! Why did Atlee have to witness that unspoken communication between her and Timothy? She knew she should have stayed inside tonight, but she had wanted a breath of fresh air after being cooped up in the stifling kitchen all day. She'd never be able to count on Atlee to keep his mouth shut, so she should expect teasing or, at the very least, questions later.

"Hey, Malinda, are you sure you don't want to play?" Atlee yelled. "You can even pick whichever side you want to be on. Hmm, I wonder which side that might be?"

"I'm fine right here, Atlee. Don't mind me. You go right ahead and enjoy your game."

"I'm sure some of us would enjoy it much more if you played."

Malinda just knew her face would glow in the dark if the sun had already set.

"Let's play!" Sam served the ball before Atlee had a chance to focus and return the ball that dropped at his feet.

"Yeah!" Aden jumped up and down.

"Aw, Atlee, you missed it!" Roman wailed.

"Well, you could have run over here to spike it," Atlee retorted.

"It came right in front of you. I would have had to knock you down."

"That's okay," Tim said soothingly. "We'll score next time."

Fingers of dusk squeezed the sky by the time the volleyball players collapsed on the ground, breathing hard. Malinda glanced at the scarf she'd been knitting by rote. It was a *gut* thing she knew her pattern well and was an accomplished knitter, since her attention had been focused on the game instead of on her stitching.

"Hey, who wants to help me catch lightning bugs?" Aden was the first to hop to his feet.

Five groans rose in unison from the ground.

"Maybe next time, Aden," Sam said.

"Tomorrow?"

"We'll see."

"How about you, Malinda? Will you help me?" Aden hollered toward the porch.

"I think I'm going to head inside, Aden. Remember, I helped you the other night. Maybe it's Atlee's turn next."

Atlee groaned. He answered before Aden even asked. "Maybe tomorrow." He raised his voice a bit louder. "*Danki*, Malinda. I owe you."

Aden stomped across the yard and up the front steps, mumbling under his breath.

"Aren't you tired?" Malinda asked. "You played a *gut*, hard game."

"I'm not very *gut* at volleyball." Aden's shoulders slumped.

"You're getting better all the time. You know you're playing with guys who are a lot bigger than you. They can reach higher and hit the ball harder. If you played with people your size, you'd probably be one of the best players."

Aden instantly brightened. "Do you think so?"

"For sure and for certain." Malinda didn't want her little *bruder* to become prideful, but she did want him to have confidence in himself. Surely it wouldn't hurt to give him a little boost. She didn't think her compliment would go to his head.

Aden smiled. "*Gut nacht*, Malinda."

Malinda squeezed his hand as he walked past. "Sleep well." She stole a glance toward the yard before gathering up her knitting. Timothy now stood talking to Sam, his body angled so he halfway faced the house. It would be pretty difficult for Malinda to sneak inside unnoticed. She'd never shied away from Timothy before, but now she felt so mixed-up. How should she behave around him?

Malinda gave her head a little shake. This was ridiculous. He was the same Timothy as always. She was the same Malinda as always. She snatched up her yarn and needles and pushed herself to her feet. She should follow Aden and get inside before the mosquitoes decided to feast on her.

"Hey, Malinda, wait!"

Malinda shifted around to see Tim loping across the yard toward her. Sam stared after him, mouth agape. That familiar flush swept up Malinda's neck and face.

"Close your mouth, Sam." Atlee's voice was overly loud. "You'll suck in all those lightning bugs Aden wanted to catch." Atlee punched his older *bruder*'s upper arm.

Malinda blocked out her *bruders*' antics and focused on the young man climbing the porch steps to tower over her. She looked up and up into his mesmerizing eyes. Funny, all these years she'd never paid much attention to Tim's eyes that were the exact color of a cloudless summer sky. Her heart did that crazy little flip-flop that almost made her catch her breath.

"Hi." Tim practically whispered.

"Hi." Malinda wondered if he had charged across the yard and risked teasing simply to say hi to her. For some strange reason, though, her own tongue seemed incapable of forming any more words. She could only stare expectantly at Tim and wait for him to speak.

Timothy cleared his throat. "I, uh, didn't want to leave without saying hello to you."

"Th-that's nice."

"*Ach*! I don't know why I'm so nervous. I've known you forever."

"I know."

"Do you feel the same way?"

"*Jah*. It's kind of silly, ain't so?"

"*Jah*." Tim blew out a breath and visibly relaxed. "I'm glad you were outside. You could have joined us. I think Sam could have used some help."

"I probably would have hindered more than helped."

"I doubt that. I've watched you play volleyball at gatherings."

"You have?"

"I-I've watched you a lot, actually."

"You have?"

"I don't mean that in a bad way. I-I've just been, uh, interested in you, uh, for a long time."

"You have?" Malinda wanted to smack herself. She certainly wasn't presenting herself as a person with any intelligence when all she could utter were the same two words.

"Well, Tim, I'm glad you came over to see *me*." Sam stomped up the steps, followed by Atlee, Roman, and Ray. He chuckled and slapped Tim on the back. The others guffawed as if Sam had told the funniest joke in the world.

"*Gut nacht*." Malinda scowled at her *bruders* as they trooped past her. She rolled her eyes, drawing a laugh from Timothy.

When the screen door had slammed shut, Tim spoke again. "I guess I'd better get home. It was great to see you again, Malinda."

"You too." It wasn't like they hadn't just seen each other a few days ago, but it was sweet of him to say.

"You are still planning to attend the singing, ain't so?"

"I'm planning on it." The next singing was more than a week away. Timothy sure seemed to be anxious that she show up.

"*Gut*. Well, I guess I'll see you soon. *Danki* for sending me the macaroni and cheese. I'm glad you remembered."

"Of course I remembered. I'm glad Sam didn't eat it."

"*Danki* again." Tim backed away without taking his eyes off Malinda, until he nearly stumbled down the steps.

Malinda gasped and reached out a hand. "Careful."

Tim grabbed the rail to keep from falling. "*Gut nacht*, Malinda."

"*Gut nacht*." Malinda heard the shuffling sound of running feet as soon as she entered the house. Sometimes *bruders* could be such a nuisance!

Chapter Eleven

Late summer in Southern Maryland brought oppressive heat and humidity. Even after the sun slid from the sky, the heat persisted. Darkness gave little relief, and any cooling breezes were few and far between. Trips to the grocery store became events to look forward to. If Malinda took her time rolling the cart up and down each aisle, she could enjoy the *wunderbaar* cool air for as long as possible. Sometimes, though, prolonged exposure to air-conditioning made the heat nearly unbearable when she did emerge from the store.

Now was the time for frantic canning of the last pickings of green beans, tomatoes, and other vegetables. Peaches had ripened as well and would need to be canned to be enjoyed as a sweet treat on winter days. Jellies and jams needed to be put up, too. For Malinda and most Amish females, many hours would be spent working in hot kitchens. Malinda reminded herself that the work would slow down soon. Apples wouldn't be ready for a few weeks yet, and fall vegetables were not as abundant.

The canning didn't change the host of other chores. Laundry, cleaning, cooking, and weeding all still had to be sandwiched in with the canning and preserving. Malinda worked beside Saloma from sunup until sundown. Grateful her stamina had returned, she never complained about the hard work and never took the breaks her worried *mamm* often encouraged her to take.

Sundays provided a respite from all their labor. The previous Sunday had been an off Sunday, and the Stauffers had stayed home to rest from the busy week. That meant church services would be held this Sunday. Since everyone had been so busy, this would be the first chance most people had to visit lately. The young people's singing would also take place in the evening.

Thankfully, the heat wave had abated a bit, so the early-morning drive to church was more pleasant than it had been lately. Malinda didn't feel like her dress had adhered to the seat, and sweat didn't trickle down her back for the first time in quite a while. A parade of dark gray buggies that stirred up little clouds of dust rolled up the long driveway to the Swareys', where church services would be held in one of the big barns. Since they were a little early, they might even have a few minutes to mingle before filing into the barn that had been transformed into a meeting place.

Malinda smoothed her good blue dress after hopping out of the buggy. At least it wasn't stuck to her legs today. She walked with her *mamm* to join clumps of women and girls waiting to enter the barn. Saloma hurried over to talk with some of the women, leaving Malinda alone for a moment. Before she could propel herself over to where Phoebe Yoder stood talking to Mary Stoltzfus, someone approached from out of her field of vision and lightly tapped her arm.

"I'm glad to see you felt up to coming out today," a syrupy voice said.

Malinda involuntarily cringed. Without even turning to look, she could identify the owner of that voice. If words had a color, those words hanging in the air would be the same honey gold color as Rebecca Zook's hair.

"I've been to every service since I've been home." Malinda

forced a pleasant note into her voice. She pasted on a little smile before shifting to look up into the taller girl's green eyes. She raised a hand to check her *kapp*, which was already properly positioned, just to shake Becky's hand off her arm.

"But I know how sickly you are—never sure from day to day if you'll feel like doing anything."

"I'm not sickly, Becky. I have a medical condition that flares up sometimes, but I've been fine lately." Malinda gnawed her tongue to keep from saying if Becky hadn't been staring at the men's side of the gathering during church services, she would have known Malinda had been in attendance.

"I guess Isaac had it wrong. You know how fellows can mess things up." Becky forced a little laugh.

"Isaac?"

"*Jah*. He said you were just so sickly it was hard to count on you."

"Really?" Tears burned the backs of Malinda's eyes. She would not let Rebecca Zook make her cry. She would not!

Becky grasped Malinda's arm again. "Isaac is such a nice fellow and so much fun to be with. He likes to do so many active things—you know, taking long walks, playing games, taking his *daed*'s little boat out on the river. I guess these things would be kind of hard for someone in delicate health, but we are certainly having a great time." She batted seemingly innocent eyes and smiled her sugary smile.

Malinda tried to figure how she could politely shake Becky's hand off her arm. Now she wished they had arrived too late to mingle. She wished they had rolled up just in time to file inside. "I-I'm glad you're enjoying life," Malinda managed to say. She opened her mouth to speak again, but before any coherent words tumbled out, someone looped an arm through her free arm, pulling her away from Becky's grasp.

"There you are, Malinda. We've been waiting for you."

Phoebe tugged on Malinda's arm again. Mary stood on Phoebe's other side. "I know you and your *mamm* have been as busy canning and working as we have. It's nice to have a day off, ain't so?" Phoebe paused for a breath. "*Ach*! Hi, Becky. We're going to steal Malinda away from you. We have ever so much to talk about."

"For sure." Mary wormed her way in between Malinda and Becky. "You know the singing tonight will be back here at the Swareys'," Mary began as she and Phoebe propelled Malinda away from Becky.

Malinda blew out an exaggerated sigh. "*Danki* for rescuing me." She let Phoebe and Mary lead her into the barn, where they assumed more solemn countenances fitting for church.

Malinda couldn't miss the flirty glances Becky continued to shoot at Isaac or the periodic winks he aimed back at her. But her reaction surprised her. Her heart no longer hurt. She didn't feel sad or jealous. All her recent prayers and petitions must have been answered, and she'd only just realized it. Now relief flooded through her. The Lord Gott had spared her future pain. If she had become more involved with Isaac, his betrayal would have been ever so much harder to bear.

She wiggled slightly to find a more comfortable position on the backless, wooden bench. She straightened her shoulders and willed her attention back to the minister delivering the second sermon. Before long the tingly sense of being watched raced up her spine. Malinda cautiously slid her eyes to the men's side of the barn to locate the source. Right away she found Tim's blue eyes fastened on her. His ever-so-slight smile raised a crop of goose bumps all along her arms. Malinda returned a wisp of a smile before refocusing on the sermon. She admonished herself to pay closer attention. After all, she'd be starting baptismal classes next week to join the church in early fall.

* * *

Malinda sat with Phoebe and Mary at the singing that evening. She sang the old songs with enthusiasm, her voice blending in with those around her. She knew Phoebe would be slipping away with Ben Miller later. They seemed to be a perfect match. They shared a fondness for the prissy-looking alpacas and would probably raise a passel of them if they got married. She didn't know if Mary had her eye on any special fellow since her interest in Aden Zimmerman had waned.

As the singing neared an end, Malinda's nerves caused quivery waves to roll through her stomach. Would Timothy make *gut* his intention of talking to her? Would he ask to take her home? Should she go with him if he did ask? She didn't remember feeling a flock of butterflies fluttering around inside of her at thoughts of Isaac when they had first started talking. What did that mean?

"Let's go get some snacks." Mary nudged Malinda with her elbow when the notes of the last song faded away.

"I-I'm not really hungry."

"You're going to dry up and blow away. *Kumm* grab something."

Malinda trudged along with Mary and Phoebe to the tables where bottled water, sodas, chips, and cookies awaited. Malinda never liked to call attention to her illness and sometimes, out of a desire to fit in, ate foods she knew could give her problems. After her recent severe flare-up, she hesitated to eat just about everything. Besides, her appetite still had not quite returned to normal.

She was well aware that her dresses hung on her sticklike body—as Atlee so kindly described it—no matter how tightly she pinned them. She could encircle her upper arm with her thumb and index finger and could visibly count her ribs. No wonder Isaac had dropped her like a hot potato. A man wanted a woman with a little more substance. Timothy would probably lose interest in a sick-looking person, too. She had been making progress, though. She had added at least a couple pounds onto her frame in the weeks since she returned home.

Malinda eyed the refreshments. Phoebe grabbed a soda and a handful of cookies. She searched the room, most likely looking for Ben. Mary grabbed a napkin, opened it, and filled it with greasy potato chips and two of each kind of cookie. Malinda's stomach churned just looking at Mary's fare. She snatched a bottle of water, the least offensive treat for her. Chips were definitely out of the question, but a plain oatmeal cookie should be all right, especially if she just nibbled at it.

"Is that all you're having?" Mary stuffed several salty, oily chips into her mouth.

"This is fine for now." She twisted the cap off her water bottle and took a sip. She replaced the cap as she scanned the group of young people. Several couples had paired up to eat and chat. Phoebe had made her way over to Ben and looked totally absorbed in whatever he said to her. Malinda caught Mary stealthily glancing in first one direction and then another. "Are you looking for anyone in particular?"

"Uh, I'm just looking to see who is still here."

"I don't think anyone has disappeared yet, have they?"

"Probably not." Mary craned her neck to look over and around clumps of people.

"Maybe I can help if you tell me who you're searching for. I know it isn't Aden."

"*Nee*, not Aden. Let's just say a certain fellow with the initials J.K. has caught my eye."

"Joshua King from the next district?"

"Shhh!"

"Oops. Sorry." Malinda bit her lower lip. "I guess it didn't hit me that people from the other districts would be here." Malinda didn't mention that her own thoughts centered on a certain tall, muscular, blue-eyed fellow.

"I may mosey around a bit." Mary's words came out garbled.

"You might want to swallow that wad of chips first."

Mary nodded, gulped, and took a big swig of soda. "I love potato chips, but you can't stop eating them once you start."

Malinda wrinkled up her nose. She hadn't been all that fond of potato chips even before her Crohn's diagnosis. With Mary moseying, she'd be left standing alone. Her other *freinden* all seemed to be paired off or involved in conversations. She supposed she could join one of the little groups, but for some reason, she felt a little self-conscious.

Maybe she'd slip over to the fringes of the barn, out of sight in the shadows. That would make it easier to sneak out. She'd never persuade Sam or Atlee to leave early, but maybe she could escape unnoticed and walk home. The evening was pleasant enough, and the walk would probably be *gut* for her.

"Finally you're free," a deep voice said close to Malinda's ear, causing her to nearly jump out of her shoes.

"*Ach*, Timothy!" She patted her chest, where her heart was galloping like a horse racing home in a thunderstorm. "I didn't see you walk over here."

"I'm sorry I scared you. You were staring at the door like you were planning to bolt, so I figured I'd better hurry over to see you."

"I-I thought you were busy talking to some of the other fellows."

"I was biding my time until you were free." Timothy paused as if weighing his next words. He lowered his voice a bit more. "I'm glad you came tonight."

"I enjoyed the singing. I always like how our voices all blend together."

"*Jah*, that is nice. Did you get something to eat?"

Malinda looked down at her empty hands. She didn't remember setting her water and cookie down anywhere. "I had some water and a cookie somewhere."

Timothy smiled that smile that lent a sparkle to his blue eyes. "Would you like something else?"

"*Nee*, I'm fine, but you go ahead and get something if you like."

"I'm not really hungry, either."

"What?" Malinda gave an exaggerated gasp. "I don't believe my ears. Timothy Brenneman is not hungry?"

Tim laughed. "That is rather surprising, isn't it?" He glanced toward the dwindling refreshments.

"Go grab a cookie, Tim. I can see you might need a little something to tide you over until you can get home and raid your *mamm*'s kitchen."

"*Ach*, Malinda, you know me too well."

Did she? How well did she really know this *bu* who had been a regular fixture at her house all her growing-up years? Sure, she knew him as a nice fellow and Sam's best *freind*, but what about the person deep down inside? To her surprise, Malinda realized she wanted to know that person.

Tim scooted over to the refreshment table, wrapped two cookies in a paper napkin, and snatched a bottle of water. "Would you like more water, since yours took a hike?"

Malinda smiled. She started to refuse, but then figured holding the bottle of water would give her something to do with her hands. At least Tim didn't try to foist food on her. "Sure, I'll take another bottle of water."

Tim grabbed a second bottle and held it out to Malinda. "We'll keep a close eye on this one so it doesn't wander off."

Malinda giggled. "*Danki*." She almost giggled again when, out of the corner of her eye, she caught Mary sashaying around the area where Joshua King stood talking to a couple of other fellows from his district. She'd like to keep watching that scene unfold, but turned her attention back to more important matters, namely Timothy.

"It's a nice evening, not too hot and sticky. Would you like to step outside?"

"Sure." Malinda felt a little awkward with Tim in this new relationship. She was beginning to consider him in a totally different way, which, while pleasant, was still a bit confusing. She walked toward the doorway beside Tim, telling herself to relax and breathe normally. This was Timothy, after all, not some stranger.

Several couples strolled around outside the barn, and two open courting buggies rolled down the driveway toward the paved road. In the waning light, Malinda recognized Phoebe's beautiful strawberry blonde hair beneath her white prayer *kapp* in the last buggy. She wouldn't be at all surprised to hear a wedding was in Phoebe's near future. Phoebe and Ben made such a perfect couple. Of course, any such news would be kept a secret until the couple was published during a church service shortly before the wedding.

Malinda couldn't determine the identity of the couple in the first buggy. She did a quick sweep of all the parked buggies and found that Sam had already slipped away. Maybe a wedding was forthcoming this season for him and Emma, too. It might turn out to be a very busy fall indeed.

Another couple wandering around outside so close together their arms appeared joined caught Malinda's eye. Without having to squint to enhance her vision, she knew it was Isaac and Becky. Funny, that jolt of pain didn't shoot through her heart. Involuntarily, her shoulders gave a little shrug, as if saying, *So what?*

"I'm sorry about, uh, about, well, how things turned out with Isaac."

Malinda turned to look into Tim's caring blue eyes. "You

are? It was for the best. We were definitely not right for each other. I'm fine with it now." She had to look away lest she drown in those crystal clear eyes.

"You are? That's *gut* to hear." Timothy shuffled along beside Malinda, close but not touching. "I have a little confession to make."

Malinda's heart skipped a beat. *Here it comes,* she thought. Timothy was going to say he'd changed his mind and didn't want to get any further involved with a sickly girl. "Wh-what kind of confession?" Malinda held her breath, anticipating his polite but definite let-down. She ventured a peek at his face.

"I'm not really sorry."

Malinda quirked her eyebrows and tried to decipher Tim's words. "About what?"

"I'm not really sorry that you and Isaac aren't a couple. I'm also sorry if that makes me sound mean."

"I don't believe you could ever be mean, Tim."

"I always want to be truthful. That's why I had to tell you I'm actually glad you and Isaac aren't a couple. I was afraid I'd lost my chance when you started talking to Isaac."

"Your chance?"

"*Jah*. I've been waiting for years for you to grow up and, uh, maybe notice me as someone other than Sam's buddy and, uh, maybe let me take you home." Tim's gaze dropped from Malinda's face to his feet.

"You have?"

"*Jah*. You couldn't tell?"

"I guess I thought you were being polite when you asked about me or talked to me."

"I really cared . . . care."

"Oh."

"I suppose I didn't want to be too obvious in case you rebuffed me. I'd never live down Sam's or Atlee's teasing in that case."

Malinda smiled. “My *bruders*, especially Atlee, can be rather relentless. Sam may have teased a little, but Atlee would go overboard. I don’t think he intends to be mean, but he can get carried away with his teasing.”

“That he does.” Timothy chuckled. “Would you let me drive you home?”

“That would be nice, Tim. I’ll tell Roman I have a ride home. He can let Atlee know.”

Chapter Twelve

As summer wound down, a hint of crispness tinged the early morning air. Malinda breathed deeply as she battled the wet sheets to pin them onto the clothesline. The cumbersome things always had a mind of their own and resisted Malinda's efforts to neatly stretch them out to dry. Malinda's breath came in pants and hiccups by the time she'd finished wrestling sheet after sheet, but finally they were all gently flapping in the breeze. Thank goodness the morning had not started out hot and sticky. An early fall would be a welcome relief from summer's heat and humidity.

Malinda sighed and took her time heading back to the house to continue with the laundry. Robins were already singing, and blue jays squawked. Squirrels skittered about gathering acorns. Did they know a hard winter was approaching? Malinda had already seen fat, fuzzy caterpillars. The old folks said the caterpillars were a sure sign of a cold winter. Malinda hoped it wouldn't be unbearably cold this year.

Right now, though, she planned to enjoy this day the Lord Gott made. She'd been feeling well—no sign of a flare-up. She'd been attending baptismal classes and would soon join the church. She'd been picturing in her mind a quilt she wanted to start sewing as soon as apple season was over, with its busy days of putting up sweet, dark apple butter and chunky and smooth applesauce. The apples weren't quite ready yet, so today, if she hurried through chores, she could pull out fabrics she and Mamm had on hand and plan her quilt.

Malinda would make a list of other things she needed and maybe head out to the quilt shop if she had time. She loved the smell of the bolts of crisp cotton fabrics lining the walls of the shop. Something about the scent of new material called to her. She could spend hours browsing through the fabrics neatly displayed in color-coordinated groups of blues, greens, purples, and whatever other hues might be in stock. Then she would sort through the spools of thread to find perfect matches. Starting a new project always sparked her excitement.

To be entirely truthful, though, another reason for her happy, lighthearted mood probably had something to do with a certain blue-eyed young man who had appeared outside her window several evenings now. She smiled as she remembered his first visit a few weeks ago.

It was the Saturday following the singing. The next day would not be a church Sunday, so Malinda had stayed up a little later playing a board game with her *bruders*, followed by knitting in her room. She had been standing at the dresser reaching for the pins holding her *kapp* in place when she heard a pinging noise outside her window, followed by a flash of light. She tiptoed along the wall to the window, careful to stay out of sight until she could determine what was going on. She stayed close to the wall and leaned forward slightly to peek out the window. Her heart tripped over itself and her breath caught when she recognized Timothy's pale blond hair in the faint glow of his flashlight. His other hand was clenched as if it held more pebbles to toss at her window. Isaac had never appeared at her window. He'd just knocked at her door early in the evening before her parents had even gone to bed. He'd chatted with the whole family as much as with her.

"Timothy!" Malinda called as loud as she dared. "Just a minute." She prayed he had heard her and wouldn't throw more pebbles, lest he wake up Mamm and Daed, or worse, Atlee. Sam was most likely still out with Emma, so she didn't have to worry about him. Malinda sailed across the room and yanked open the door. She paused for only a moment, listening for the sound of anyone stirring. The silence assured her no one else had awakened.

She crept down the stairs and through the dark house to the back door. She slowly pulled the door open to avoid the creaking noise it sometimes made. She closed it gently behind her. "Psst, Tim!" She sighed in relief when he joined her at the back steps. "Whew! I was afraid you hadn't heard me."

"And I was afraid you'd gone to fetch a pitcher of water to dump out the window on my head."

Malinda giggled. "Why on earth would I do that?"

"I-I was afraid you wouldn't want to see me."

"*Ach*, Tim! Did I give you that idea when we rode home from the singing?"

"*Nee*, but I figured you had a chance to think and might have changed your mind."

"I did not change my mind."

"Me, neither."

"I assumed you hadn't, since you're here."

"Right."

"Would you like to *kumm* inside?"

"Would you mind sitting here on the steps awhile? It's a nice evening, as long as the mosquitoes leave us alone."

"Sure. We can sit." Malinda plopped down on the top step and slid her dress out of the way to give Timothy room. Their arms and legs touched as he settled his large body on the step beside her. Malinda's pulse sped up to double time.

She really couldn't wiggle over any farther. She heard his sharp intake of breath. Was he experiencing a reaction similar to hers? Malinda willed herself to calm down. She gazed at the star-sprinkled sky while she searched for something to say. "Look! Did you see it?" A star had shot across the sky with a long tail of light trailing behind it.

"*Jah*. Isn't it amazing? I love looking at the stars." Timothy pointed out constellations.

"How do you know all those? I only know the Big Dipper and the Little Dipper."

"I've always been interested in the stars and nature and, well, all the beauties the Lord Gott has made. I've borrowed books from the library and read a fair amount."

"That's *wunderbaar*." Usually Malinda checked out inspirational novels whenever she visited the library, not educational materials. It pleased her, though, that Timothy was so smart and so eager to learn things on his own. "What else do you read?"

"Well, let's see. I've read all sorts of woodworking books. I like to see the different styles and techniques. We have a lot of *Englisch* customers, so I want to be able to build all kinds of things."

"You do very nice work. I think you may have a natural gift."

"Maybe. I know I enjoy creating things and making people happy."

"I think you do both quite well." Malinda's voice had dropped to a whisper.

"Huh?"

Malinda gave a little cough. "Do you read other books?"

"I've read some farming books and magazines—you know, about plants, soil, and things like that. The modern way of doing things wouldn't work for us, of course, but I have been reading some about organic farming. I've convinced Daed to at least think about that."

"You are quite a scholar, even though our school days are long gone."

"We're never too old to learn new things."

"I suppose that's true."

"Do you like to read, other than the Bible, of course?"

"Sure. I usually stick to fiction, but I do like to look through quilting books and cookbooks."

"There you go. You're still a scholar, too. We have that in common."

"I suppose we do."

Suddenly Timothy grasped Malinda's hand. "Look! Another shooting star." He pointed at the sky with his other hand.

"Amazing!" Malinda couldn't be sure if she meant Gott's display of lights in the night sky or the tingling feeling that traveled from her fingertips up her arm and throughout her body. Her heart danced when Timothy threaded his fingers through hers. Surely he felt this electric shock wave, too.

Timothy lightly squeezed Malinda's hand. "It's like the Lord has put on a little show just for us, ain't so?"

"*Jah*. I'm glad we stayed outside, or we would have missed this."

"I've missed seeing you this week. I guess we've both been busy. I had several big orders I just finished today." His voice softened a bit. "You've been well, *jah?*"

"I'm not sick all the time!" Malinda attempted to pull her hand from his.

"I didn't mean to imply you were, Malinda." Timothy didn't loosen his grip on her hand. "I've been around here enough to know you are usually fine, but you were pretty sick when you were away. I only wanted to make sure you're okay."

"I was sick weeks ago. I've been fine since I returned home."

"*Gut*." Tim fell silent.

"I-I'm sorry, Tim. I didn't mean to bite your head off. I guess I'm a little sensitive about my illness."

"A little?"

Malinda laughed, dispelling the tension that had grown between them. "Okay. Maybe more than a little. I-I don't want you to think I'm, uh, sickly and incapable of doing things."

"I would never think that, Malinda. Time after time I've seen your strength and determination. If I ask how you are, it's because I care."

"*Danki.*" Malinda squeezed Tim's hand this time.

By the time Malinda said goodbye to Timothy and slipped back upstairs to her room, several hours had passed. She never would have believed they had talked so long if she hadn't checked the little battery-operated clock on her nightstand. As it was, she shook it and put it to her ear to listen for its faint ticking. She quickly undressed, brushed out her hair and wove it into a single braid, and slid between the crisp cotton sheets on her bed.

No amount of willing would make sleep claim her, despite the late hour. Her mind spun like the carousel she'd seen at the Fireman's Carnival as she passed by it a few years ago. She had peered out the buggy window at the painted horses bobbing up and down and going around and around. Her present thoughts were just as sporadic and dizzying.

Malinda had really enjoyed sitting on the step and talking with Timothy. To her surprise and delight, she and Tim had a lot in common. They had talked easily, and any lapses in conversation had felt comfortable, not awkward. Holding Timothy's hand felt natural and somehow right. What would it be like to kiss him?

Malinda's cheeks burned even though she was alone in the dark. She'd never been kissed. She'd thought Isaac had been close to kissing her once, but something—she couldn't remember what—had interrupted that moment. That had never happened again, to Malinda's relief. Since Isaac had turned out to be so fickle and insincere, she was glad her first kiss had not been with him.

Tim, on the other hand, was altogether different. He was definitely more mature. Tim had a *gut* head on his shoulders. He was serious about his work, yet he had a lighter side as well. He teased, but not in a mean way, and he laughed easily. Malinda had always known Tim to be polite and considerate, but he was proving to be fun, too.

Her mind, true to its usual rational nature, sifted through the facts that all painted Timothy in a favorable light. Her heart, however, ventured into uncharted territory. She didn't remember it flip-flopping in her chest one moment and skipping beats the next when she was near Isaac. She didn't remember any electric current racing through her body when Isaac held her hand, like it did when Timothy merely brushed against her.

How did this change occur so suddenly? She had known Tim all her life and hadn't experienced any of these strange emotions before. Had her feelings changed this drastically in the blink of an eye, or had she always had a soft spot for Timothy? Of all her *bruders' freinden*, Timothy stood out as the nicest. Maybe deep down she had cared for him more than she'd even realized. Maybe she suppressed those feelings because Timothy was older and she figured he would be more interested in an older girl, a healthier girl.

Ach! She couldn't subject Timothy to a life of putting up with her illness. Granted, she sometimes went for long stretches feeling fine, but when a flare-up hit, she could be useless. She could even end up in the hospital again, or need surgery like Dr. McWilliams had hinted at. That would be a severe hardship on a family and on a family's finances. And the cost of her medications! Malinda experienced more than a little guilt every time she had to pick up a prescription at the pharmacy. She hated that Daed had to spend so much of his hard-earned money on her. Of course, he never complained.

She'd better nix any budding romance right away and forget all about Timothy Brenneman—or any other fellow, for that matter. What she really needed to do was find some way to earn money to pay for her own doctor visits and medications. A salty tear slid down her cheeks, followed closely by a silent deluge. She smashed her face into her pillow to muffle any sound of her sobs. In a few weeks she would be joining the church with her baptismal class, but an upcoming marriage for her would never be published at the conclusion of a Sunday morning service.

Chapter Thirteen

As summer's long days shortened and the oppressive heat lessened, instructional classes drew to a close. Baptismal candidates would soon be ready to make a commitment to their faith. Malinda had been attending classes on church Sundays for the past several weeks. There would be nine classes total. The candidates had completed eight of them. Only one more to go and Malinda would be ready to become a full-fledged member of the church.

Her parents had provided an ample background on the Amish church and beliefs and had always set a fine example of Christian living for her and her *bruders*, but the classes had been quite intensive. Malinda had studied the Eighteen Articles from the Dordrecht Confession of Faith and corresponding scriptures. She'd delved into a more thorough study of the Ordnung. She understood what was expected of her as an Amish woman and a member of the church. And now she felt ready for baptism.

The decision to join the church had been an easy one for Malinda. She had no desire for the *Englisch* life and didn't really partake of any worldly ways even during her *rumspringa*. Surrounded by all kinds of beeping machines and flashing lights while she was in that Ohio hospital had provided more exposure to technology than Malinda cared to have. Sure, cars and buses were great when a person needed to get to some far-off place or needed to arrive somewhere quickly, but she much preferred her dependable horse and buggy.

Malinda knew many Amish young people, even in quiet, largely rural Southern Maryland, purchased cell phones, iPads, radios, and computer gadgets she didn't even know the names of. A few even purchased cars. She'd had no desire for any of these modern inventions. The old ways suited her just fine. She had no idea how difficult sacrificing any of those gizmos might be for some of her fellow candidates.

Isaac never gave Malinda any indication he had tried out many *Englisch* ways, and most of the others in her class seemed to have no commitment issues. The only person she had qualms about was Becky Zook. Several times Malinda had heard Becky humming songs that were definitely not in the Ausbund. Many of her flirty, flouncy ways seemed more *Englisch* than Amish. Occasionally her lips had seemed brighter and shinier and her pale eyelashes darker. Malinda had heard through the grapevine that Becky had a cell phone, one of those fancier ones that could even take pictures and connect to the Internet, but she had no firsthand knowledge of that.

Whatever the case may be, Malinda sincerely hoped Becky would be able to make her commitment and that she would not lead Isaac astray. Not that she cared about Isaac in any sort of romantic way, but she would hate for Isaac—or any of her *freinden*—to jump the fence. It would be especially devastating if Isaac left the community to please Becky and then she dropped him like a hot potato, as she'd done with so many other fellows. The two of them had been reprimanded by the bishop several times for being late to class or for not showing the proper attitude. Malinda couldn't help but wonder what would happen when the candidates met with the bishop and ministers one final time the night before their baptism.

Would any of the young folks in her group change their minds or say they weren't yet ready to make a commitment? Malinda couldn't imagine going through all the classes and then backing out at the last minute. She shuddered just thinking of such a thing, but she knew it was not unheard-of. She supposed it would be much better to postpone the decision rather than have a change of heart after joining the church and risk shunning. How horrified parents and families would be!

Malinda prayed she'd never give her parents cause for concern, except for her illness, which, of course, she couldn't control. How she wished and prayed she could be rid of that thorn in her flesh. Would she ever learn to accept it?

"How are classes going?" Tim sat on the top front porch step beside Malinda on Saturday evening.

"Fine."

"You don't have any qualms about joining the church?"

"None whatsoever. Did you?" Timothy had been baptized several years ago, along with Sam and Emma Swarey and others their age.

"*Nee*. It's what I always wanted. I never really had any desire to run around and try out a different lifestyle or *Englisch* ways."

"Me, neither. I'm perfectly content to live the way our people have always lived."

"That's *gut*."

Timothy patted Malinda's hand before lacing his fingers with hers. Chills still shot through her at his touch. She had wanted to discourage his attention, not only to be fair to him but also to avoid any heartache she'd likely experience when he bolted. And surely he'd run for the hills when he realized how awful her illness could be. It was only a matter of time. For all his goodness and kindness, Malinda did not expect Tim to be a saint who could blindly accept her with all her medical issues and associated expenses.

She toyed with the idea of asking the bishop to recommend her for any teaching position in any of the local districts after she joined the church. Teaching would be a fitting occupation for a *maedel* throughout her whole, long unmarried life. Malinda loved *kinner*. Teaching would be the next best thing to having a houseful of her own. She had yet to voice this idea with anyone. It was something she'd been mulling over.

Timothy left earlier than usual, since tomorrow would be a church day. Malinda had grown more and more comfortable with him and, to her chagrin, more and more fond of him. If he felt the same way, as she suspected he did, they could both be in for heartache. Malinda sighed deeply as she climbed the stairs in the sleeping house.

He sure did enjoy spending time with Malinda. The more he got to know her, the more he liked her. He wondered if she realized how pretty she was with that raven-colored hair and eyes as dark as midnight. Physical beauty wasn't that important, but it sure didn't hurt any. Timothy smiled to himself at the thought of the beautiful, tiny young woman who'd just sat beside him on the porch step.

He had wanted to put his arms around her and never let her go, but that would definitely not have been appropriate. Maybe her slight build and small stature made him want to protect her. Yet, she had a determination and strength that belied her size. And she seemed so sensitive about her illness, as if it made her inferior in some way. Timothy could never tell her about his desire to shield her and take care of her for fear she'd misinterpret his meaning. That desire came not from any thought that she was sickly and unable to fend for herself, but from his genuine feelings of . . . what? Concern? Love?

Timothy stopped in his tracks. Love? Did he love Malinda? Signs seemed to point in that direction. Timothy yanked off his hat and ran a hand through his hair. Why should he be surprised that the word popped into his mind? He'd had the feelings for years.

During every visit with Sam, he'd been aware of Malinda's presence. He'd sought her out whenever he could do so inconspicuously. He'd tried to keep her in his line of vision whenever possible, whether she hung laundry on the line, weeded the flower beds, or played with Aden in the front yard. *Jah*, he'd had it bad for a long time.

What were Malinda's feelings? She allowed his visits and always seemed happy to see him. She didn't shrink back when he sat so close to her their arms touched. She didn't pull her hand away when he took it into his own—her little soft hand, delicate but strong. They talked easily about all sorts of things . . . the starry sky, their homes and families, his furniture making, her quilting. They laughed and teased each other. Her smile lit up his whole world, and her laugh rang in his ears like a pleasing melody. They certainly seemed well suited.

Yet sometimes Timothy sensed a hesitation on Malinda's part. Did she have misgivings about allowing his visits? Did she have doubts about her feelings for him? She definitely had no doubts about her faith or her upcoming baptism. Maybe she was simply shy or cautious, though he'd never considered her to be shy. He remembered she had been rather quiet at school, but she had participated in activities and always had an answer when the teacher called on her. He'd paid attention to her even then.

Maybe he only imagined any reticence on Malinda's part. Maybe he was afraid to believe she could be interested in him instead of Isaac Hostetler, even though she'd stated on several occasions she was glad she had made no commitments to Isaac.

Timothy shook his head and shrugged his tense shoulders. He plopped his hat on his head and shuffled a little farther down the driveway. He was glad he had walked this evening, since it gave him more thinking time. He'd always known Malinda to be an honest person. Surely she would say so if she didn't want him to visit. She would have snatched her hand away when he reached out to hold it. Did she feel the same jolt of electricity he did whenever they touched?

In another week, Malinda would be joining the church. Next fall they could be published. Maybe before then. Not everyone waited until the official wedding season. Some couples married at different times. Marriage? He was really jumping ahead! But he was ready, and he wanted to marry Malinda. She had been his choice for ever so long. He wanted to share his life with her and raise *kinner* with her, but he couldn't move too fast. Somehow he had to slow down and give Malinda whatever time she needed. "Please, Gott, let her feel the same way I do. I've waited so long."

As the whispered prayer died on his lips, Timothy turned to throw one final glance at the Stauffer house. There! He saw it! In a flicker of lamplight he saw Malinda at her bedroom window. He raised a hand to wave. She pumped her hand up and down in response. Timothy chuckled aloud. She did care! He would have turned a cartwheel if he could do so without pulling every single muscle in his body.

Chapter Fourteen

A flock of butterflies, if that's what you called a huge group of them, flapped wildly inside Malinda's stomach. She feared her nerves would cause a flare-up of her Crohn's disease. She'd toyed with her supper, half afraid to introduce any food to her already misbehaving intestines. Mamm had watched with a concerned expression but had held her tongue. Malinda gulped in several deep, calming breaths. She really had no cause to be so nervous. She would be meeting with the same ministers and bishop she'd met with for all nine baptismal classes. But this was the final meeting. Tomorrow was Baptismal Sunday. Malinda's nerves were taut. She had no doubts about her own decision, but some little concern wagged a finger in her mind. Were the other candidates as sure as she was? She prayed nothing would go wrong.

Malinda dressed carefully and made sure every unruly wisp of hair behaved. She'd do the exact same thing before heading to church tomorrow morning. They were meeting at Bishop Menno Lapp's house this evening. She decided to take the buggy rather than walk so her dress wouldn't become saturated with perspiration and cling to her body.

Daed had hitched Chestnut for her. He squeezed her arm as she prepared to climb inside. "I'll be home soon," she assured him.

Rufus simply nodded and offered an encouraging smile.

Other baptismal candidates arrived at the bishop's house at the same time as Malinda. She took some small comfort in the obvious jitteriness of the other young people. Apparently they were all in the same boat. She hoped no one would cause the boat to tip. She wanted all of them to join their community of faith tomorrow.

Bishop Menno, a tall, wiry, usually stern-faced man, invited them all into his home. A thin smile above his salt-and-pepper beard softened his expression a bit. Martha, the bishop's *fraa*, couldn't be more opposite from her husband. She was short and round and always had a ready smile. Her light brown hair showed no hint of gray, though she and the bishop were probably in their late fifties.

"*Kumm* in. *Kumm* in. I have lemonade and cookies." Martha bustled about trying to put the young folks at ease.

The candidates solemnly filed into the living room to perch on the straight-backed wooden chairs set up there. The girls sat on one side, and the *buwe* on the other. An empty chair on each side caused them all to exchange nervous glances. Malinda mentally ticked off the attendees to determine who would dare to arrive late to this highly important meeting. The missing candidates happened to be the same two people who'd been reprimanded previously for their tardiness. Surely Isaac and Rebecca hadn't changed their minds about joining the church. Even if they had, wouldn't they at least show up to tell the bishop their decision?

"We will wait just a few more minutes," Bishop Menno mumbled to the other ministers, who nodded in agreement.

Malinda's heart pounded so hard she feared it would burst through her chest. Those butterflies churned her meager stomach contents and threatened to send everything straight up her esophagus. She forced herself to take slow breaths. One of the other girls fidgeted in her chair until Bishop Menno shot her a stern look. Although there was no clock in the room, Malinda imagined a ticking sound that grew louder and faster in her head.

Just as Bishop Menno roughly cleared his throat, the door flew open. All heads turned to watch Isaac and Becky rush into the Lapps' living room. Malinda hazarded a glance in the bishop's direction in time to note his deeply furrowed brow. Personally, she would not want to cross the man. The Isaac she knew—or thought she knew—would not have been so blatantly disrespectful. She hoped he and Becky had a plausible excuse this evening.

"Well?" Bishop Menno scowled at first one and then the other of the latecomers, who slid into the two vacant chairs.

"I—We're sorry," Rebecca sang out sweetly without a trace of remorse in her voice or demeanor.

Isaac coughed. "Uh, *jah*. We're sorry." He at least had the decency to look ashamed as he hung his head, probably to avoid the bishop's glare, which could easily melt a foot of snow on the Lapps' pond in the middle of a February blizzard.

"And?" After a brief pause with only silence as an answer, the bishop continued. "What was more important than this meeting?"

"I, uh . . ." Isaac looked toward Becky. Malinda shifted slightly so she could observe Becky. Apparently Becky was going to let Isaac handle the whole excuse business. Becky daintily arranged her dark purple dress and pushed a tendril of pale blonde hair beneath her *kapp*. Her pale lashes fluttered, but she did not lift her green eyes in Isaac's direction. Her focus remained on some spot on the wall high above the bishop's head.

"We were, uh, visiting." Isaac's voice barely crossed the

threshold of whispering. "We lost track of time. Then I had to race home to help with chores."

"I see. We'll begin now." Bishop Menno fixed each candidate with a solemn expression one by one, though his gaze lingered a little longer on Isaac and Rebecca. "As you all are well aware, baptism is a very serious commitment. Once you are baptized and join the church, there is no going back without serious repercussions for you and for your families."

Malinda's ears picked up a slight rustling sound. She stole a quick glance sideways, allowing her to bring Becky into her peripheral vision. The girl squirmed on the wooden chair and picked at her apron. Whatever could be in her pocket to create that sound? Generally, cotton dresses did not rustle. Malinda's eyes snapped back to the ministers, who took turns reviewing the lessons from the previous classes.

Malinda held herself erect. Her shoulders and neck began to ache from the strain of sitting perfectly still. At least during three-hour church services she could shift positions periodically without drawing attention to herself. Here, under the scrutiny of Bishop Menno and the ministers, she felt her every breath was counted.

"What questions do you have for us?" Bishop Menno asked when the last minister finished speaking.

Malinda had no questions. Evidently no one else did, either. No one coughed, or even exhaled audibly.

"All right," the bishop continued. "Now is the time to change your mind if you have any doubts. It is better to wait and be sure of your commitment than to forge ahead only to change your mind later. This is a lifelong commitment."

Heads nodded, but no one spoke.

Bishop Menno looked at each of the fellows and asked if they were ready. All answered affirmatively, though Isaac cleared his throat twice before choking out his answer. Then the bishop turned to each girl and repeated his question. Each answered without hesitation. All except one. Becky squirmed again, fidgeted with the edge of her apron, looked at the rag rug on the wooden floor, and then raised her eyes to stare at that fascinating spot over the bishop's head.

"Rebecca?" Bishop Menno asked again.

"Um, *jah*." She stopped fidgeting and tucked her hands beneath her legs.

Bishop Menno kept his eyes on Becky a moment longer before surveying all the candidates. "I encourage you to spend the rest of this evening at home praying and reading the Scriptures."

In unison, the candidates nodded and filed from the room. Martha gave each a smile and a package of cookies to take with them. "A little nourishment for the body as you nourish your souls." She smiled as she held the door for the young people to depart.

Malinda suddenly felt she could breathe again as she made her way to her buggy. She dragged in a huge gulp of fresh air. The young people remained silent as they prepared to depart, all except for one voice, which called out, "Wait, Isaac. I want to show you . . ."

Chestnut nuzzled the hand Malinda placed on his head before climbing into the buggy. She let him set the pace for home. She nibbled at a chocolate chip cookie as the buggy rolled along. She prayed all went well tomorrow.

Chapter Fifteen

Darkness still swirled around the room when Malinda slipped out of bed Sunday morning. She pressed one hand to her belly and prayed it would not betray her today of all days. She carefully pulled on her crisp blue dress and smoothed every little tendril of hair beneath her precisely pinned *kapp*. This was the day she'd been waiting for, preparing for practically her whole life. Nervousness mingled with excitement. She whispered another prayer that the day would be a joyous, memorable one for everyone.

The family got an early start to the Yoders' house, where church services would be held. No doubt there would be many extra people, with families of the baptismal candidates in attendance.

"Are you feeling all right?" Saloma turned from the front of the gray buggy to look at Malinda. "You didn't eat enough breakfast to last you through the long morning."

"I'm fine, Mamm, just a little nervous. I'll probably be starving after church." Malinda couldn't imagine that at the moment, though.

Buggy after buggy rolled up the Yoders' long, gravel driveway. Some of them Malinda didn't recognize. Folks from neighboring districts must have already arrived. Those butterflies from last night had again taken up residence in Malinda's stomach. Maybe she should have forced herself to eat more than three small bites of the thick, sticky oatmeal that had congealed in her intestines.

Phoebe Yoder and Mary Stoltzfus, already church members, met Malinda and offered words of encouragement before Malinda crossed the yard to stand with the other girls in her baptismal class. Becky had arrived on time today. She looked nervous instead of prissy. A quick glance at the fellows told her Isaac had almost the same sickly pallor as Becky.

Malinda murmured a greeting to the other girls and then stood silently wringing her clammy hands. She gulped in a last breath of fresh air before filing into the service with the other girls. They would most likely be bunched closer together because of the extra guests in attendance today, so fresh air might be in short supply.

The ministers expounded on various Biblical stories pertaining to baptism, and Malinda kept her attention focused on them. Only once did her gaze stray briefly to the men's side. Timothy offered her a tiny smile and nod of encouragement. Malinda was amazed at the calmness that washed over her at Tim's simple gesture. Last to speak, Bishop Menno reviewed the story from the book of Acts about Philip baptizing the Ethiopian eunuch. Then he called the candidates forward. All seven of them knelt beside one another.

Malinda breathed a quick sigh of relief as she knelt between two other girls. She feared her knocking knees would be heard by the whole congregation, or even worse, would refuse to hold her upright. Becky, at the end of the line of girls, still wobbled slightly, although she no longer stood. Her nervousness seemed totally out of character, but Malinda assumed they were all experiencing overwhelming emotions.

* * *

Timothy released his lower lip from beneath his teeth only when the metallic taste of blood invaded his preoccupied senses. He hadn't even been aware he'd been gnawing a hole through his lip, since he'd been focused on the young people rising from the wooden benches and filing forward to where the bishop waited. Timothy's heart pounded hard, threatening to shatter his ribs. His breath came out rapid and shallow. And he wasn't even one of the baptismal candidates!

Tim's own baptism had been several years ago, but he remembered every detail. It had been the most momentous day of his life so far. It was the day that sealed his membership in the Amish community. He'd never had any desire to be otherwise. Sure, he ran around a little as a teenager, but he never smoked or drank or even drove a car. His most daring venture had been the purchase of a prepaid cell phone that had a camera in it and that he'd had no problem relinquishing when he began baptismal classes. *Jah*, he felt perfectly content as an Amish furniture maker and farmer. He'd, of course, feel even more content once he had a *fraa* by his side to share his life. He hoped that time wouldn't be too much longer getting here.

No amount of persuasion by his brain could calm his nerves. Timothy's gaze flicked briefly across the three *buwe* standing in front of the congregation and then the four girls before coming to rest on the second girl in line, the beautiful, dark-haired one. He knew his sweaty palms and ragged breathing were because he understood her nervousness. He felt it. He shared it.

Somehow he had taken her jitteriness upon himself. Is this what it meant to care for someone, to love someone? He forced a slow, deep breath, which instantly calmed him. As inconspicuously as possible, he wiped his hands on his *gut* black trousers. He willed calmness into Malinda. He prayed for her and released her to the Lord Gott's care. He prayed nothing would mar her special day. He'd never experienced such intense feelings for another person before. This must be love.

After a lengthy prayer, Bishop Menno asked the candidates to kneel. Malinda had felt her body sway during the prayer and was glad she wasn't standing. The bishop would ask each candidate the baptismal questions, one person at a time. Malinda had no qualms about her answers. She would respond with wholehearted affirmation. She believed Jesus was Gott's Son. She recognized this as a Christian church. She renounced the world and the devil with all his subtle ways. She desired to serve only Jesus, who died on the cross for her. She would promise before Gott and His church that she would support the teachings and regulations, would attend church services, would work in the church, and would not forsake it. *Jah*, she was ready.

Bishop Menno began with the *buwe* and asked them each question. The first *bu* answered flawlessly. Isaac answered the first question without hesitation. After the bishop asked the second question, a pregnant pause filled the room. Malinda held her breath. What was wrong with Isaac? She wanted to look in his direction but didn't dare. Isaac coughed, cleared his throat, and finally offered the expected answers to the bishop's remaining questions.

A little gasp from Becky almost made Malinda lean around the girl between them to look at her. Becky sniffed softly and fidgeted slightly. The girl between them slid a tissue from her pocket and handed it to Becky.

The bishop moved to Malinda. She responded to his questions with no trace of doubt in her heart or her voice. The girl beside her answered with equal assurance. Then the bishop faced Becky, the last candidate. Like Isaac, she replied quickly to the first question but stared at the floor after Bishop Menno asked her the second question. He lowered his voice. “Rebecca, did you hear the question?”

Becky sniffed. “I heard . . . I feel sick.” Becky pushed to her feet and turned away from the other candidates. A ripple of shocked gasps washed over the congregation.

In an instant, Becky’s *mamm* approached the bishop. “I’ll take her out.” She wrapped an arm around Becky’s waist and led the girl to the door. Her own sniffling mingled with Becky’s.

“We will continue.” Silence reigned for a moment. Either the bishop needed to reorder his thoughts or he was praying for Becky. At his signal, the congregation rose, while the candidates remained kneeling for the prayer. His final words reminded them that those who believe and are baptized shall be saved.

After everyone had resettled on the wooden benches, Bishop Menno began the baptism. He held cupped hands over each candidate’s head. One of the ministers poured water into the bishop’s hands three times as the bishop pronounced them baptized in the name of the Father, the Son, and the Holy Ghost.

Malinda’s hands trembled as Bishop Menno approached her, even though she had them clutched together so tightly her knuckles turned white. She trembled, not in fear but in anticipation. Her emotions threatened to overwhelm her. Tears flooded her eyes and mingled with the rivulets of water trailing down her face. A sudden joy burst into bloom in her heart and sent warmth throughout her body. She somehow felt pure and clean and determined to live up to the promises she had just made.

Bishop Menno shook hands with all the candidates and gave the *buwe* the holy kiss of peace. His *fraa*, Martha, did the same for the three remaining girls. The bishop offered a benediction and stated the six young people before him were no longer guests and strangers but were members of the household of Gott.

Malinda walked on marshmallow clouds as the new members filed back to their seats. She couldn't keep the smile from her lips or contain the joy that radiated from her soul. She wondered if the others were experiencing anything similar. Now she would really be considered an adult member of the community. She would willingly accept the responsibilities that accompanied that status. She felt as bright as a brand-new shiny copper penny. She prayed Gott's light would always shine in and through her, no matter what may happen.

The church service concluded in normal fashion. The women hurried to bring out food, while the men arranged the wooden benches into tables for the common meal. The women whispered to one another as they headed for the kitchen, probably discussing the same thing as Malinda and her two fellow new members. What was going on with Becky?

Chapter Sixteen

Timothy thought Malinda looked lovelier than he'd ever seen in her crisp blue dress and her raven hair tucked neatly under her white *kapp*. Of course, she always looked beautiful to him, even when she was sick. Today, though, she fairly glowed. Her big brown eyes sparkled, and she walked with a spring in her step. This had been an important day in her life. Only one little blip had threatened to spoil the day, but Bishop Menno had handled the interruption well. He didn't allow Becky's outburst to break the mood of the service or to disrupt the baptism. What on earth had possessed Becky to run out of the service like that? She should have told the ministers of any doubts long before today.

He gulped the iced tea one of the women set in front of him. His throat felt as dry as the creek bed at the end of a rainless August. Tim looked around the table at the other men gathered for the meal. Most looked as hot as he felt, but at least a slight breeze brought a small measure of relief. Two of the new members talked animatedly with the fellows around them. Tim smiled to himself. He remembered feeling so different after his baptism—so clean, so new, so adult. His gaze traveled around the table and stalled on Isaac Hostetler.

Isaac looked anything but happy. In fact, he looked downright sullen. His pasty appearance reminded Timothy of the ashes he shoveled out of the woodstove, all white and gray. Was Isaac sorry he'd made his vow to the church? Did he wish he had bolted, as Becky had done? Maybe Tim should try to talk to him.

Timothy hoped to catch Malinda's eye as she bustled about refilling cups. He hoped he'd get the chance to talk to her later—maybe even take a walk with her. When she finally glanced in his direction, he smiled and winked at her. He nearly laughed aloud at the crimson flush that crept up her neck and across her cheeks. She averted her eyes and moved on to refill another cup.

While he waited for the women to finish eating, Timothy decided he would seek out Isaac. Maybe he could help the younger man. Even though he'd been furious with Isaac for hurting Malinda, things had worked out for the best. Poor Isaac looked like he could use a *freind* right now.

Timothy sidled up to Isaac, who stood alone in the shade of a huge, old oak tree. "Big day."

"*Jah*."

"You don't seem particularly happy."

Isaac shrugged and turned to walk away.

Timothy clamped a large hand on Isaac's shoulder. "What's troubling you, Isaac? I'm a *gut* listener."

"Why should you care?"

Isaac sounded like a petulant little *bu*, but Timothy kept that thought to himself. "I remember my baptism day as one of the happiest days of my life, but you seem troubled. I'd like to help if I can. That's all."

"*Ach*! You can't help. What's done is done."

"Are you afraid you made a mistake by joining the church?"

"*Nee*. *Jah*. I don't even know." Isaac rubbed a hand over his clean-shaven jaw.

"Does your confusion have anything to do with Becky Zook?"

"Why would you think that?"

You're too defensive. Dead giveaway. "Well, you two seemed kind of, um, close. She didn't get baptized, and you did. I figured that might make a problem for you."

Isaac shrugged again and then jerked his head toward the far reaches of the yard, indicating for Timothy to follow him farther away from any listening ears. Isaac didn't stop until he'd practically reached the woods bordering the Yoders' property. Timothy thought their trek seemed a little extreme, since everyone else looked preoccupied with eating or visiting, but he'd placate Isaac.

"*Was ist letz*?"

"Everything is wrong!"

"Do you want to explain?"

"I-I don't even understand myself. Why do we do the things we do?" Isaac let out a long, exasperated sigh.

"That's hard to say, but we all do things we wonder about later."

"I'm so befuddled."

"Do you know why Becky changed her mind?"

Isaac nodded. A tortured expression crossed his face. "I-I guess."

Timothy waited, trying very hard not to tap his foot or show any other sign of impatience. He wanted to talk with Malinda, but he had initiated this interaction with Isaac, so must see it through. Besides, he really did want to help Isaac, or at least persuade him to talk to the bishop about whatever was troubling him. He didn't know if he would be successful with either option, but he needed to at least try.

"Becky showed me something after our meeting at Bishop Menno's last night." Isaac's voice dropped so low Timothy needed to strain to hear him.

When Isaac didn't continue right away, Timothy prodded. "What was it?"

"Papers."

"What kind of papers?"

"Train schedules and prices."

"Was she planning to go on a trip?"

"She was planning on *us* going on a trip."

"You and Becky? Just the two of you?"

"*Jah*."

"A trip where? For how long?"

"To New York. She said she wanted to see the big city and all it had to offer before she settled into a humdrum, boring life. Those are her words, not mine. She said there had to be more to life than cornfields and cows."

"Did you want to go along?"

"We had talked about how much fun it would be to travel someplace and see new things, but . . ."

"Did you change your mind?"

"Traveling a bit would be fine, but . . ."

"How long were you planning to be gone?"

"That's just it, Tim. I wanted to go on a trip. Becky didn't want to *kumm* back."

"She wants to jump the fence?"

"I'm not sure if she even knows what she wants. I thought maybe she wanted me, but I guess not."

Timothy could have told him Becky didn't seem to be the "settling down" kind. She liked flirting with all the fellows too much. "What happened?"

"Becky was all excited and wanted to leave as soon as we got an *Englisch* driver lined up to take us to the train station. I asked her about baptism, and she said we could always do that later if we came back. That's when I knew for sure and for certain she didn't want to *kumm* back. Tim, I never wanted to leave the community forever. I just wanted to see other things."

Timothy nodded. Each person had to make his own decision. Many young folks grew restless and wanted to try new things, but, thankfully, most got baptized and stayed in the community. "Did you tell Becky your feelings?"

"*Jah*. She wasn't too happy, and she kept trying to change my mind. She didn't want us to show up for the service today at all. She kept trying to convince me, but I didn't want to disappoint my *mamm* and *daed*. Maybe I should have waited. Now Becky will go off without me and-and I-I've lost her."

"Do you think you ever really had her?"

"I thought we had something special." Isaac held up a hand as Timothy opened his mouth to speak. "Before you say anything, I know Becky was a bit of a flirt, but things were different with us."

Timothy held his tongue before the words "That's what all the fellows believed" slipped out. "Were you courting?"

"Sort of."

"Sort of?"

Isaac's face flushed bright red. "We were going to settle down and court properly after we took a few little trips. That's what I thought, anyway."

"Who was going to chaperone those little trips?"

"We hadn't gotten that far with the plans."

"It sounds like Becky got a lot farther with them than you did, if she had train schedules and such."

"I guess so. She'll probably leave now, and I'm stuck here. I thought since she showed up at church and walked forward with the rest of us she had decided to join the church after all."

"Are you having second thoughts about your commitment?"

"I-I don't know."

"Maybe you should talk to Bishop Menno. He's pretty understanding and wise."

"I can't. It's done now."

Isaac's shoulders slumped, and he had the most hangdog expression Timothy had ever seen. Isaac reminded him of a balloon that had sprung a leak, allowing all the air to seep out. "Where is Becky now?"

"Who knows? She's probably trying to get a ride to the train station."

"You don't think she'd go ahead with her plans all alone, do you?"

Isaac shrugged. "It's hard to tell. She can be pretty impulsive."

That was an understatement if Tim had ever heard one. "She's probably at home right now. Maybe if you go there, you can talk some sense into her."

"I doubt that, but I'll think about it. *Danki* for listening, Tim." Isaac turned and raced away like a dog fleeing from a rabid fox.

Timothy shook his head. He prayed Isaac would sort out his feelings. Maybe Tim could put a bug in one of the ministers' ears to have a chat with Isaac. One of them or the bishop would most likely head over to the Zook place soon, if they weren't already there.

Timothy strode off in the direction of the tables. The conversation with Isaac had eaten up more time than he had planned. Surely Malinda would be finished her meal by now. He hoped her family hadn't already started home.

Chapter Seventeen

Malinda continued to float on air as she tackled the mountain of laundry Monday morning, still buoyed by the warm, *wunderbaar* memories of her baptism. She hoisted the laundry basket full of wet clothes and headed for the clothesline. She'd felt a few twinges of disappointment that she'd been unable to speak with Timothy after the service, but maybe that was for the best. She really needed to force herself to end any serious relationship with him before either of them could get their hearts broken. She hoped she wasn't too late. It would not be easy to pretend she desired nothing more than a casual relationship with Tim. He'd already become so much more than a *freind*.

Putting distance between them would be best for both of them, Malinda reminded herself. She needed to end things before she had another flare-up that sent Timothy fleeing in the opposite direction. He had some inkling about her disease from hanging around with Sam, but he'd never personally experienced the extent of her illness. It was not a pretty sight. What if she had a severe flare-up like she'd had in Ohio and ended up in the hospital? Tim would be horrified to see that or to learn how expensive her treatment could be.

Malinda could be content to live with her *mamm* and *daed* and to help care for her *bruders*. Maybe she wouldn't be completely happy, but she would be content. She loved her family. Aden was still young enough that she'd have a few more years to play games with him and help him with schoolwork. What would happen to her, though, when her *bruders* married, her parents moved into the *dawdi* house, and Sam and his wife took over the farm? What would become of her then?

She sighed. No use in thinking of those things yet. She should just enjoy this beautiful, sunny, late summer day with the laundry flapping gently on the line. Malinda snatched up the empty basket. One more load of laundry to wash and hang out this morning. Wheels crunching on the gravel captured her attention. She raised one hand to shield her eyes from the bright morning sun. Who was visiting so early in the morning?

Malinda watched as the horse and buggy raced up the driveway, kicking up a cloud of dust. Whoever it was either was in a terrible hurry or had some sort of news to share. Malinda reached the front yard just as a female voice hollered, "Whoa!" A moment later, Becky Zook hopped from the buggy. Loose tendrils of pale blonde hair flew about her head. She must have been driving furiously to stir up enough of a breeze to loosen her hair from its pins. She swatted at the hair to get it out of her eyes, but she didn't even attempt to poke the strands back under her *kapp*.

"Becky, *was ist letz*?" Malinda's heart thumped a wild rhythm. Had something happened to one of Becky's parents? The Stauffers weren't the Zooks' nearest neighbors. Why would Becky drive all the way here if they needed help?

"As if you don't know what's wrong!"

"What are you talking about? How would I know why you zoomed up my driveway?"

"Don't you look all innocent!"

"*Kumm* sit on the porch, Becky, and explain what you're talking about."

"I'm not going to sit on the porch so all your eavesdropping family can hear me through the open windows. Walk a ways with me."

Malinda dropped the laundry basket at her feet and approached Becky's horse. "Do you want me to tie him for you?"

"Just leave him alone! I don't plan to be here that long."

Malinda and Becky had, of course, known each other forever, but they had never been much more than acquaintances. Lately, they had practically avoided each other, except at the baptismal classes.

"How could you turn him against me?"

"Turn who against you?"

"Isaac. Who else?"

"Becky, I've barely spoken to Isaac in weeks. You should know that. I thought he spent every spare moment with you."

"Who else could persuade him to abandon our plans?"

"What plans? I assumed you both planned to join the church, since you attended the classes."

"That was Isaac's idea. I figured he'd change his mind after the first two or three classes and stick with our plan to get out of here."

"You were going to jump the fence?"

"We were going to travel."

"Then why did you bother going to the classes at all?"

"Isaac felt pressured to go. I wonder who could have pressured him." The sarcasm dripped from Becky's voice.

"It certainly wasn't me. I don't have any influence over Isaac. Besides, a person shouldn't be coerced into joining the church. He should want to join."

"Exactly."

"I'm sure Isaac's parents hoped he'd join, but I doubt they pressured him."

"Well, now he's gone and joined. He'll be under the ban if he goes off to travel with me."

"Were you going to get married?"

"Pshaw! We just wanted to see the world a bit before settling down. Or maybe we'd find someplace we liked better than Maryland. Now he can't go with me." Becky stomped a foot like a pouty, spoiled *boppli*.

Malinda gasped. "You were going to go off together, just the two of you?"

Becky burst out laughing. "If only you could see your face, Malinda. You look positively horrified." With one hand, Becky wiped the moisture from her green eyes.

Malinda snapped her mouth shut when she became aware it was still hanging agape. "It doesn't seem a laughing matter to me. What would your *mamm* and *daed* say? What would the bishop say?"

"We had planned to recruit someone to be a chaperone, silly. I haven't strayed that far away."

"Have you strayed, Becky? You could always talk to Bishop Menno. You can always repent and be baptized. You did attend classes."

"I don't have anything to repent for . . . yet."

Except being devious, Malinda almost blurted out. "You made it sound like you had when you said you hadn't strayed *that* much."

"Well, you know, just the normal petty sins."

"A sin is a sin."

"Aren't you the pious one?"

"I just mean we all sin and all need to repent."

"Surely not you!" Becky clapped a hand over her mouth

and gasped in mock horror. "Not perfect little Malinda Stauffer!"

"I am not perfect. I'm just trying to do the best I can." Malinda took a deep breath to calm down. She would not let Becky get under her skin. "What will you do now, Becky?"

"Don't you worry yourself about it."

"You could always join the next baptismal class if Bishop Menno won't consent to your baptism now."

"I'm not ready yet. I couldn't go through with it during the service with everyone's eyes boring holes into my back, so it's not likely I'll do it now."

Malinda reached out tentatively to touch the bigger girl's arm. "Think about it, Becky. I'll pr—"

"Don't you dare say you'll pray for me. I don't need your prayers. I'm still going to see New York and any place in between here and there I feel like seeing."

"Alone? That's not very safe. Aren't you afraid to go alone? You could get lost, or worse."

Becky laughed, a harsh sound rather than a pleasant one. "I'm sure I'll find someone to go with me." With that, Becky flounced off toward her buggy without so much as a backward glance at Malinda, who stared after her.

When the gray buggy had disappeared from sight, Malinda shook her head in an effort to clear her troubled mind. What in the world was that all about? Why would Becky think she had any influence over Isaac? Surely Becky knew Malinda and Isaac only spoke to each other to exchange pleasantries these days. Becky would have had much more influence over Isaac, for sure and for certain. If Becky couldn't convince Isaac to forsake his baptismal plans, then surely it must be Gott's will for him to join the church.

Malinda sighed and reached down to retrieve the straw laundry basket. She absently plucked at the edges as she pondered what she should do. Would Becky really go off on her own? Of course, she'd have to get an *Englisch* driver to transport her all the way to the train station, but then she'd be on her own. Should Malinda tell someone about Becky's plans? Who? Becky's parents or one of the ministers or Bishop Menno?

"Are you going to bring that basket inside?" Saloma called out the open kitchen window.

"Be right there, Mamm." Malinda clomped up the back steps. The screen door slipped from her fingers and slammed shut behind her. "Oops!" she called. "It got away from me." She started for the laundry room, but Saloma's words stopped her in her tracks.

"Was that Becky Zook out there talking to you?"

"*Jah*." Malinda scooted closer to the laundry room. "I'll get that last load done."

"What did she want?" Saloma dried her hands on a blue-and-white-checked dish towel. "That girl sure put her parents in a bad way. They must be so disappointed, not to mention embarrassed."

"I-I think Becky is confused. Maybe she needs a little time to sort out her feelings."

"Hmpf! She should have done that before she knelt in front of the whole church on Sunday."

Malinda agreed, but merely nodded. Should she confide in her *mamm*? Becky didn't say not to tell anyone. She didn't make her promise to keep any secrets. Besides, if Becky took a notion to set out right away, everyone would know.

"*Was ist letz*, Dochder?"

Malinda shrugged. "I'm all right, Mamm. I'll get to the laundry." She took two steps, her black sneakers squeaking on the linoleum floor.

"Malinda Stauffer, you wait one minute! I know when something is wrong with you."

Slowly Malinda turned around to face her *mamm*. Why

did she have to have one of those faces that mirrored her every thought? Why did her *mamm* have the capability of reading her like a book? Maybe that was a skill that came with motherhood. She supposed if she had five sons like Mamm did, she'd learn a thing or two about the working of her *kinners'* minds, too. And she and Mamm had always been close, so Mamm would naturally pick up on her moods.

Malinda sighed for about the millionth time this morning. "Nothing is wrong with *me*, Mamm."

"But?"

"Mamm, I don't know what to do about Becky." The words flew from her mouth.

"Why do you have to do anything at all about Becky? I think she needs her parents or the ministers or Bishop Menno to straighten her out."

"I don't think any of them know her plans."

"And you do?"

"I know what she just told me."

"What was that?"

Malinda hesitated for a moment. "Well, she didn't make me promise not to tell, and somebody has to do something!" Malinda dragged in a deep breath and repeated the gist of Becky's tale. "What should I do, Mamm? Something bad could happen to her, running around all alone."

"It's a wonder you're concerned about her after the way she treated you—stealing your beau the minute you left town."

"That was just as much Isaac's fault, ain't so? I don't think Isaac and I were right for each other, anyway. It's best the way things worked out."

Saloma raised an eyebrow in question but didn't pursue that subject. "Do you think Isaac will go with Becky?"

"He's a church member now."

"He wouldn't be the first to change his mind and jump the fence."

"Surely he wouldn't do that, Mamm."

"After you finish hanging out that last load of laundry and I finish my dinner preparations, maybe we'll take a little drive over to the Zooks' house. We might have to make a little visit to the Hostetlers, too. We can leave it up to their parents then."

"Okay, Mamm. *Danki*."

During the entire ride to the Zooks' farm, Malinda sat on her hands to keep from picking at her fingernails. Mamm must have sensed her trepidation. Every now and again she would cast a sideways glance at Malinda.

"It's all right, dear." Saloma reached over to pat Malinda's knee. "You didn't betray any confidences. I would certainly want to know if one of my *kinner* planned to go off on some wild goose chase."

Malinda nodded. She knew her parents would do everything in their power to dissuade one of them from traipsing off into the unknown. "Maybe Becky will be there working alongside her *mamm*, and we could just go home."

"That would be nice, but that Becky Zook is a pretty headstrong girl. She may have her parents wrapped around her little finger like she has most of the fellows at one time or another. I'm thankful Sam and Atlee never fell prey to her charms."

Or Timothy, Malinda almost added. "Do you think Sam and Emma will get married this fall?" Malinda desperately needed to divert her attention.

"Of course, I wouldn't know for sure, but I wouldn't be one bit surprised if they did."

"I like Emma."

"She's a nice girl. I think she'll make a fine *fraa* for Sam. It's about time for Atlee to think of settling down, too."

"That's hard to imagine." Malinda smiled. Atlee always

liked to laugh and joke. The thought of all her *bruders* moving out and leaving her alone with their parents was a hard pill to swallow. She didn't want to be a burden to anyone. She would have to figure out a way to earn money to pay for her medication and doctor appointments.

Malinda pushed the image of Timothy's bluer than blue eyes and his caring expression out of her mind. She was glad he'd never gotten together with Becky Zook, but she couldn't lead him on, either. The Lord Gott hadn't seen fit to remove her thorn despite her desperate pleas, so she needed to resign herself to spending her life alone. She'd worry about that later. Right now, she had to figure out what to say to Becky if she was at home, or worse yet, to Becky's parents if she was gone.

She heard muffled sniffling sounds the instant she and Saloma stepped inside the back door of the Zooks' house. She elbowed her *mamm*. "Someone's crying."

Saloma grabbed Malinda's hand and pulled her along as she hurried into the house. "Sylvia! It's Saloma and Malinda." Louder sniffles came in reply. Saloma sped through the kitchen to the living room, still tugging Malinda along with her. She dropped Malinda's hand and rushed to where Sylvia Zook was rocking in a big oak chair with an embroidered pillow clutched to her chest. Tears streamed down her cheeks and dripped off her chin. Malinda tiptoed closer, but remained in the background, happy to let Saloma handle this situation.

"What is it, Sylvia?"

"My *b-boppli*." Sylvia sniffed again.

Mamms referred to all their *kinner* as *bopplin*, but Malinda was pretty sure which of her seven Sylvia meant.

"What happened?" Saloma asked.

"Sh-she's gone. Sh-she said she wanted to see other things, visit new places. Sh-she just up and left."

"All alone?"

"She called an *Englisch* driver, not one of our usual ones. She didn't give up her cell phone when she started baptismal classes."

"Do you know where she wanted to go? Maybe we can see if relatives or acquaintances can look out for her."

"She mentioned Philadelphia, New York, and I don't remember where else. I-I tried to talk her out of leaving. I told her we could arrange for her to visit family in Ohio or Indiana or even Florida. She said she didn't want to visit any Amish communities." At this, Sylvia broke down and sobbed.

Saloma knelt beside the rocking chair and gathered the grieving woman in her arms. In between sobs, Sylvia sputtered, "Why couldn't she join the church like the others?"

"Some take a little longer to make the decision." Saloma patted the heaving back of the woman she was holding. "We'll pray for her."

"Amos headed over to the bishop's place as soon as Becky left. He doted on our *dochder*, you know."

"I'm sorry Becky left." Malinda spoke softly.

"Did you know about this?" Sylvia raised her tear-streaked face to look into Malinda's eyes.

"Becky showed up at our house a little while ago." Malinda relayed to Sylvia what had transpired between the two young women. "I tried to get her to change her mind."

"We hoped we'd get here before Becky took off," Saloma added.

Sylvia drew in a shaky breath. "She stormed in, blurted out her announcement, and grabbed a few belongings. By that time, a car was blowing its horn in the driveway." Fresh tears filled her eyes. "D-Do you think Isaac went with her?"

"She told me she would go alone now that Isaac joined the church," Malinda answered.

"At least she won't be under the ban, Sylvia," Saloma said soothingly. "She'll be free to return at any time. Lots of young folks do crazy things during their *rumspringa*."

"Not many run off. At least not many here," Sylvia replied. "We'll pray she *kumms* to her senses soon."

By the time they left Sylvia, Malinda felt like she'd been dragged by a horse. Exhaustion, jangled nerves, and an aching stomach plagued her. She prayed she wasn't heading for another flare-up. She slumped onto the buggy seat beside Saloma.

"Are you all right, Malinda?" Saloma raised the back of her hand to Malinda's forehead.

"Just tired." Malinda smiled at her *mamm*'s automatic reaction. Any time any of her offspring looked the tiniest bit peaked, Saloma pressed a hand to their foreheads.

"It has been a stressful day." Saloma clucked to the horse to get the buggy rolling. "You can close your eyes and rest a bit."

"I'll be fine." Malinda forced a confidence she didn't feel into her words. "Do you think Sylvia will be okay?"

"*Ach*! How does a parent deal with such a thing? I'm thankful mine have joined the church. Of course, I've got three more to worry about." Malinda couldn't imagine her *bruders* running off, but one never knew what the future held.

A gray buggy approached from the opposite direction. The horse plodded along as if in no hurry. Malinda strained to see the lone occupant. "It's Isaac. I thought that looked like his horse."

"It's a relief to know he didn't go traipsing off into the unknown with Becky. One set of grieving parents is more than enough."

"*Jah*," Malinda mumbled.

Saloma nodded to Isaac as the buggies passed each other and then cut her eyes over to Malinda.

"Don't worry, Mamm. I'm not pining away over Isaac. I hope he finds the right girl when he gets over Becky. I know that girl isn't me."

"What about you, dear? Aren't you looking for the right person, too?"

Malinda shrugged. "I'm too much trouble for anyone." She closed her eyes. She didn't want to hash this out with her *mamm* again. "Maybe I will rest for a minute. That way I'll be ready to get the laundry in when we get home."

Chapter Eighteen

It might not be Saturday, but Timothy couldn't wait any longer. He wanted to see Malinda. He needed to see Malinda. Sam had mentioned in passing that Malinda didn't feel well the other day. He prayed she wouldn't end up in the hospital again. Sam didn't seem worried, so maybe she'd just had a headache or something.

Since news of Becky Zook's escapades had spread throughout the community like fire in a haystack, Tim harbored an icy fear that Malinda would get back with Isaac. No matter what she had told him before, Tim couldn't seem to stop the crop of insecurities that had rooted and spread in his mind. A quick visit with Malinda would ease his worries.

Timothy glanced down to give himself a once-over. He had rushed home from Swarey's Furniture Shop to clean up and change clothes. His blue shirt, which had been crisp when he left home, had wilted a bit in the waning heat of the day, but he looked decent enough. Early September days had been plenty warm, but at least they cooled off more quickly as sunset approached, unlike July and August, where one day melted into the next.

Tim found himself talking to the horse as they trotted along. It could be he was actually talking to himself, but it didn't seem as pathetic if he believed he was talking to the horse. His respirations became quick and shallow as he turned the buggy onto the Stauffers' gravel driveway. Why should he be nervous?

Maybe he should have waited until Saturday evening, but he'd never gotten the chance to talk with Malinda after church, and he hadn't seen her out and about anywhere. Maybe she didn't want to see him but was too kind to say so. "Stop it!" He spoke louder than he'd intended. The horse paused and threw his head back to look at Timothy. "Not you, boy. Keep going." Great! Even his horse thought he was crazy. He needed to relax. If Malinda decided not to see him, he could pretend he had come to visit Sam.

Timothy had decided not to wait for the cover of darkness to visit Malinda, in case she was sick and needed to sleep. Now the whole family would witness his approach. Since the supper hour had passed, some of them may even be milling about outside. He hoped he would spot Sam first, unless by some stroke of grace Malinda was rocking on the porch swing.

"Hey, Malinda!" a male voice shouted. "I think you have company."

Atlee. Why did it have to be Atlee? Tim liked Atlee. It was just that Atlee could be such a huge tease. He raised a hand in greeting as Atlee burst from the house and trotted down the steps. In a few long strides, he reached Tim's horse.

"Hey, Tim. What brings you by this fine evening? Let me think." Atlee's forehead wrinkled and he tapped his chin as if in deep thought. "Maybe you came to chase lightning bugs with Aden, or maybe some urgent furniture-making issue can't wait until you see Sam at work tomorrow. Or maybe . . ."

Timothy jumped from the buggy and punched Atlee's upper arm. "Maybe I just happened to be in the neighborhood and stopped by."

"*Gut* one, Tim." Atlee glanced at the front porch. "Maybe the real reason just stepped out onto the porch."

Timothy's eyes flew to the porch. Heat crawled up his neck. "Maybe you're right."

"Well, don't mind me, then. I'll water your horse and just mosey around."

Anything else Atlee may have said was lost on Timothy. Once his eyes locked on Malinda, all other thoughts vanished. She still looked fresh and lovely at the end of the day in her dark purple dress. She had probably been cooking or cleaning or working outside all day, but she was just as pleasing to his eyes as ever. An almost-shy smile tugged at her lips as she captured a tendril of dark hair and poked it beneath her *kapp*.

"Hi, Tim."

"Hi, Malinda. How are you?"

"I'm fine."

"Sam mentioned the other day you hadn't been feeling well." *Bad choice of topic, Tim. Now she'll believe you think she's sickly.*

To Tim's surprise, Malinda didn't take offense. "It was nothing serious. I'm fine."

"I'm glad to hear that." Tim twisted the straw hat he'd swiped off his head and was holding in his hands. "Would you like to go for a ride?" At her hesitation, he amended the offer. "We don't have to be gone long." Why did she hesitate? Had he done or said something to offend her? Maybe it was the stupid comment about how she was, after all. Why did he never know the right thing to say?

Malinda walked toward Timothy and his buggy, but her steps did not seem light, and her face was devoid of enthusiasm. "Would you rather go for a walk instead?" he asked.

"A ride will be fine."

Tim offered a hand to help Malinda into the buggy, though she'd made it perfectly clear on a previous occasion that she was entirely capable of climbing in all on her own. He was glad she chose a ride over a walk so they could be away from her family's watchful eyes and listening ears. Even though the Stauffers had been like a second family to him while growing up, he preferred they didn't witness his bumbling efforts to court Malinda, if she allowed that.

Timothy suppressed a sigh. He thought he and Malinda had gotten far enough in their relationship that he wouldn't still feel this awkwardness and confusion. Confusion about Malinda's feelings, not his own. His feelings had remained constant for more years than he could remember. He settled himself and picked up the reins. "Ready?" When Malinda nodded, he shook the reins to get them moving. "It's *gut* to see you."

"You too." Malinda plucked imaginary lint from her dress.

"Is anything wrong?"

"*Nee*. Why do you ask?"

"I don't know. You don't seem too happy. Did I do something wrong?"

"*Ach*, Timothy! It's me. I'm feeling a little, um, jittery, I guess."

"To be with me? We've known each other forever."

"I know. I'm sorry. You haven't done anything wrong."

"You aren't having doubts about . . ." Timothy wanted to say "us" but opted instead for, ". . . joining the church, are you?"

"Never."

He gnawed the inside of his cheek to keep from asking if she had doubts about him. Maybe he should be brave and ask. "That's *gut*."

"I've never wanted anything else except to join our church."

"That's *gut*." Timothy ran his tongue over the now-sore spot in his mouth. The metallic taste of blood surprised him.

He'd better control his teeth before they chewed a hole clear through his cheek. He forced his muscles to relax. He'd never been so tongue-tied in his life. This was Malinda, for Pete's sake. *His* Malinda. Or was she? That he had to find out. He cleared his throat, causing Malinda to jump. "Um, Malinda?"

"*Jah?*"

"Are—do—have you seen Isaac?"

"*Nee*. Why do you ask?"

"I, um, I guess I'm feeling insecure."

"Insecure about what?"

"About us."

"Us?"

"There is an 'us,' isn't there, Malinda?" Timothy felt sure his heart would crumble if Malinda answered negatively. He held his breath and gripped the reins so tightly he expected them to saw into the flesh of his palms. He turned his head so he could look into Malinda's chocolate eyes. He had to see what her face told him in case her words said something different. The pause stretched into eternity. Tim had to jump in and say something, or else the wait for her response would kill him. "You do want there to be an 'us,' ain't so?"

"Tim, um, you are a very nice person . . ."

He gripped the reins even tighter, if that was humanly possible. There was a "but" on the tip of her tongue. He just knew it. It had only to fall off and drag words he didn't want to hear behind it. He forced himself to wait. He leaned a little closer so he wouldn't miss a single syllable she uttered. He glanced at the road to make sure the horse wasn't veering off into a ditch and then looked back at Malinda. Maybe they should have walked instead so he could concentrate solely on Malinda.

At last she spoke again. "It wouldn't be fair to saddle you with my problems."

"What problems do you refer to?"

"My health problems. You know I have Crohn's disease and take medications. Expensive medications."

"I'm not worried about money. And if you have days you don't feel well, I'll help you."

"You'd soon get tired of that."

"That's not the way it works, Malinda. If two people, um, take vows, it's for all time—in sickness and in health."

"Vows?" Her voice squeaked. She gave a little cough. "You don't know how bad it can get."

"I know it was bad enough to land you in the hospital. I don't want you to be sick, Malinda, but your condition doesn't scare me off. I want to help you, to take care of you."

"No man wants to take on extra household duties with his own chores and work. It would definitely be a burden."

"Why don't you let me decide that?"

Silence.

"I decided." Timothy sliced into the silence. "I can handle that." He didn't know if Malinda would slap his hand away or not, but he reached over to squeeze one of hers. Despite the warm evening, her hand was cool. He urged the horse off the road and into a neighboring field so he could focus on Malinda. Her furrowed brow had smoothed and a tiny smile curved her lips upward ever so slightly, but tears shimmered in her dark eyes. He gently squeezed her hand again.

"Y-You don't know . . ."

"I know what I feel."

"I feel guilty enough that my *daed* has to spend so much money on my medicine. I wouldn't want someone else to take on that burden. Besides, I should find a way to help with those expenses."

"Malinda, I am not worried about the money. Gott will provide. Just think, maybe you will be so happy it will cure your disease."

"That would be a miracle." Malinda smiled a smile that lit her face and made Timothy smile in return.

"Could we . . . could you give us a chance? We can take it slow, if you like." That wasn't especially to Timothy's liking. If he had his way, they'd be published at the next church service and be married as soon as she could sew her dress and food could be prepared. In fact, he wouldn't mind being like the *Englischer*s who got married at the courthouse without all the fuss, but that wasn't their way. "Can I court you, Malinda, or can you honestly say you don't care at all for me and want me to leave you alone?" He crooked an index finger under her chin to raise her face. His own pleading image reflected in her eyes.

"I, um, I . . ." Her voice dropped so low it was barely audible. "I would be lying if I said I didn't care."

Timothy's heart soared higher than the crimson setting sun. He tried to reel it back in, but it flew ever higher.

"I'd like to keep seeing you," Malinda continued, "but if I get sicker, I may change my mind."

"If you get sicker, I will be there for you." Before he could stop himself, he leaned down to brush her soft cheek with his lips. For just a moment, Malinda leaned her head against his shoulder. *That's right where she belongs,* he thought. He'd like to wrap his arm around her in a tight embrace and never let her go, but that would have to wait. Now he had to make sure she always wanted to stay by his side. He couldn't let anything or anyone change her mind.

Chapter Nineteen

Fall crept into Southern Maryland early that year. The heat and humidity slithered away practically overnight, leaving the air crisp and fresh. Soon Malinda would be spending her days helping Saloma put up apple butter, applesauce, apple pie filling, apple jelly, and any other apple treats they could concoct. The trees had been loaded with McIntosh, Stayman, Winesap, and Rome apples that would be ready for picking at different intervals. The house would carry the sweet, spicy scents of apples and cinnamon for days.

Malinda loved clear autumn evenings. She could wrap a shawl around her shoulders and sit on the step to gaze at the bright stars twinkling in an inky sky. The round, orange harvest moon would be so big she could almost reach up and pluck it from the sky. When the chill seeped through the shawl and into her bones, she could retreat to the cozy blue armchair near the woodstove and knit until her eyes grew too heavy to hold open. She loved knitting or crocheting hats, gloves, scarves, afghans, or whatever else she could think of for gifts for *freinden* and family. This year she needed to think of a special gift for Timothy.

The thought of Timothy brought a smile to her lips and

heart. She truly did care for him but knew she was still holding him somewhat at arm's length, afraid to let him get too close lest he bolt when her disease flared up. She feared, though, her heart had already dragged her deeper into the relationship than she had intended to go.

Timothy had abided by his promise to take things slowly, but he'd been coming by more frequently. Sometimes it was a quick stop on his way home. Other times they sat together or took rides on Saturday evenings after her family had gone to bed. All except Atlee, who occasionally visited with *freinden*. Malinda sometimes wondered if Atlee would ever become serious about a girl and settle down. He was such a fun-loving guy, but he had a heart of gold. At least he hadn't fallen into the clutches of Becky Zook. Of course, Sam spent most of his free time with Emma. Malinda expected them to be published any Sunday now.

By September's end, trees already blazed gold, orange, and red. They'd turned early this year. Evening's chill spread into the morning and midday. Even afternoons no longer warmed up so much. Winter might try to sneak in early, but Malinda hoped not. She loved the fall best of all the seasons.

Shortly after tidying up the kitchen following the noon meal on a cool Thursday afternoon, Malinda slipped outside to sweep the front porch. She lifted the broom high to knock down intricate, zigzagging spiderwebs stretched across corners of the ceiling. The feathery webs, some empty and some holding fat, dark spiders, seemed to fill nearly every nook and cranny. Malinda liked studying the various patterns and designs and almost hated to knock them down. Nobody liked walking face-first into a spiderweb, though, and Mamm nearly screamed in terror whenever a spider crawled into the house, especially one of the big, ugly ones with hairy legs. There wasn't much Mamm was afraid of, but she couldn't abide spiders of any shape, size, or color. Most likely the webs would be rebuilt by tomorrow.

Malinda had been inside nearly all week helping Mamm put up the last of the apples, so getting outside in the nippy air provided a pleasant change. They'd made three apple pies and several dozen apple cinnamon muffins in addition to all the preserving. The rest of the apples would be stored for eating. Malinda liked apples, but didn't care to see another one for a while. All the peeling and slicing had made her thumbs grow stiff and her hands ache. She would enjoy all the apple butter and applesauce this winter, though.

Wedding season was upon them, and several couples had already been published. Of course, weddings could occur throughout the year, but most couples still waited until fall, when the harvesting and canning had been completed. Sam and Emma had yet to be published, but Malinda had a strong hunch the announcement would be forthcoming at the next church service. Something about Sam's sly smile led her to believe he was up to something. She wondered if Sam and Emma would live with her parents or if they had their eye on some place of their own.

Land had become more and more scarce in these parts, especially with the *Englischers* trying to snatch up every piece of farmland they could to build housing developments. Houses on top of houses. Malinda would not like to live in a house where she could lean out her window and touch her neighbor's house. She liked space. Thinking of space, surely Emma wouldn't want to live here cooped up with all these rowdy *buwe*. Personally, she thought it might be fun to have another girl around. A girl to talk to—besides Mamm, of course—would be rather nice. But Emma and Sam should have some time for the two of them before *kinner* started arriving.

The crunch of tires on the gravel interrupted Malinda's battle with the spiderwebs. It was probably some *Englischer* turning around or maybe looking for fresh produce. It never ceased to amaze her how many people thought green beans and peas and strawberries grew all year long on Amish farms. Crops grew at the same time on Amish soil as on *Englisch* soil, except many Amish had greenhouses to extend the growing season a bit. Of course, they did still have broccoli, cabbage, greens, squash, and pumpkins, but they usually sold them at the market now, not at road-side stands.

Malinda turned to glance over her shoulder at the approaching vehicle, broom still raised in attack mode. She gasped and nearly lost her hold on the broom as the shiny red car drew closer. It wasn't as if she'd never seen a sports car before. *Englischers* in the area drove all sorts of vehicles, from trucks to long vans with three or more seats to cars so tiny they could almost fit inside the trunks of the larger cars. And she had seen all sorts of vehicles pulled on trailers to the nearby racetrack. But something about this gleaming car screamed, *Look at me. I'm special!* The tinted windows prevented Malinda from seeing the occupants.

Suddenly aware she'd been staring with her mouth hanging open and the broom raised as if she planned to use it for a weapon, Malinda clamped her mouth closed and lowered her broom-wielding arm. She didn't know if she should keep looking toward the car or scoot inside the house. Since the car had driven so close now, it would appear rude to vanish into the safety of the house. Maybe she could offer directions and send the person on his or her way.

Before she could form another thought, the driver's door opened. Music so loud it must have rendered any occupants of the car completely deaf blasted out. The music died abruptly just before a man unfolded himself and stepped out into the brisk afternoon sunshine.

"Malinda?" he called. "Malinda Stauffer?"

How did this *Englischer* know her name? She knew

very few *Englischers* besides a few of their neighbors, their regular produce customers, their *Englisch* drivers, and Dr. Nelson and his *fraa*. Who could this man be? If he moved out of the direct sunlight that was blinding her, she might obtain a better look.

The man straightened his shoulders and stood quite tall, though not as tall as Timothy. He stepped forward a few paces, putting him in a small patch of shade. A lock of sandy hair fell over his forehead, and he quickly brushed it back with a swipe of one hand. Malinda gasped. The broom clattered to the cement porch floor, striking her shoulder on its descent. She flinched but didn't cry out in pain. "Dr. McWilliams?"

"Malinda! It is you. I hoped I made it to the right house. And it's Todd. Remember?"

"H-how did you find me?"

"I've got my handy dandy GPS. I plugged in the address I got from your hospital records, and voilà! I must admit, the GPS wasn't as helpful once I reached this last road." He nodded toward the paved road he had just left. "But I persevered and made it to the right place."

"Wh-what are you doing here?"

"Didn't you get my letter a few months ago?"

Malinda nodded. Her brain couldn't form a single coherent thought to convey to her mouth.

"You didn't answer it."

"I-I didn't think a response was necessary."

"Ah, Malinda, you wound me!" He slapped a hand over his heart.

At first Malinda thought the man was serious, and she prepared to apologize. Then she caught the gleam in his eyes and knew he had spoken in jest. "What are you doing here?"

"Am I not welcome?"

"I, uh, of course. I guess so."

"Don't you remember in my letter I said I had a conference to attend in Baltimore in the fall? You did read my letter, didn't you?"

She nodded.

"Well, it's fall, and here I am."

"Baltimore is not exactly close by."

"No, but what's an hour or two to drive?" The doctor gave Malinda a broad smile and a wink.

Malinda considered an hour or two a long trip—much too far to travel by horse and buggy. Baltimore had to be at least seventy-five miles away, but that shiny red car could probably make the trip in record time. She self-consciously shifted her weight from one black sneaker–shod foot to the other.

"Aren't you going to invite me in?" Todd McWilliams strode toward the front porch.

This was definitely a man accustomed to being obeyed, to getting his way. But Malinda couldn't invite him inside. Mamm had left right after the noon meal to take a casserole to an ailing neighbor. Daed and her older *bruders* were working, and her younger *bruders* were in school. It wouldn't be at all appropriate for her to entertain a male guest in the home alone.

"Uh, we can sit here on the porch." Malinda bent to retrieve the broom and propped it in the corner beneath the spiderweb she'd been battling. She resisted the urge to rub her throbbing shoulder for fear the doctor would want to check it out. She turned back to face Dr. McWilliams, who stood watching her every move, threatening the composure she was struggling to maintain. "Please, have a seat. Would you like some iced tea or water?"

"No, thanks. Come sit with me, Malinda." He dropped onto the porch swing and patted the space beside him. That errant lock of hair fell over his forehead again, lending a boyish look to his handsome face.

Ignoring the doctor's gesture, Malinda inched over to the wooden rocking chair and perched on the edge. There was no way she would squeeze into the space next to him and be pressed so closely against his thigh. Just the thought of such nearness, such familiarity, sent a flush clear up to the roots of her hair, she was sure. She primly arranged her dress and tucked her hands beneath her legs to stop their quaking. Whyever did the man show up here?

"So tell me how you've been." Todd sat back in the swing and set it gently swaying with the toe of one foot.

"I-I've been fine. I haven't had any major issues." Did he drive all the way here to inquire about her health? Did he follow up so thoroughly with all his patients?

"I'm glad to hear that. Of course I'm interested in your physical health, but I wondered if you'd given any thought to what we discussed."

"What we discussed?" Malinda gulped down the lump of dread that clawed its way up her throat.

"You surely remember our discussion about your remaining in Ohio."

"But I am here, as you see." Malinda stalled for time and searched desperately for a way to change the topic. If willing would make it so, Mamm would be trotting up the driveway to rescue her from this uncomfortable situation. *Uncomfortable?* She almost chuckled. How about disturbing or impossible or maybe even frightening?

"I do see, but that doesn't make me very happy. I've missed you. Have you missed me even a tiny bit?" He gave Malinda a crooked little grin and, to illustrate his point, held a thumb and forefinger up, separated by a tiny space.

What should she say? Should she admit her life had been pretty busy and she hadn't given the doctor much thought except for the qualms she had experienced at the arrival of his letter? If she hadn't been sitting on her hands, she'd surely be wringing them. Could she possibly be in a more awkward position? "I-I've been very busy since I returned home."

Todd quirked an eyebrow. "Oh?"

Apparently he thought Amish women sat around all day and watched the grass grow. "*Jah*. There is much to do with a large family." Malinda lowered her gaze to her lap.

"I believe you did mention you have a lot of brothers."

"*Jah*."

"So you have lots of cooking and cleaning and things?" At Malinda's nod, he continued. "And I guess you have to take all that laundry down to a stream and beat it on a rock."

Malinda's head snapped up. "We aren't exactly that primitive, Dr. McWilliams."

"I'm only teasing, Malinda. I know a little more about the Amish than that. I have had other Amish patients before."

Did you pursue those women in such earnest, too? Malinda swallowed her question and tried to breathe normally. Where was Mamm?

"Wouldn't you like a little break from all this?" With a sweep of his hand, he indicated the house and yard. "You could spend a couple of days in Baltimore with me."

"With you?" Now she knew for certain that a flush was staining her cheeks. How could he even suggest such a thing?

"Sure. My conference is just one day—tomorrow. Then I would have the two weekend days before returning to Ohio. We could visit the aquarium, some museums, the Lexington Market. Who knows? Maybe I can talk you into returning to Ohio with me. You already know some people there. We could live near the hospital—"

"Wait!" Malinda jumped to her feet and set the rocking chair thumping crazily. The nerve of the man! He had everything all planned out and expected her to follow docilely along. "That is all preposterous!"

"Oh, Malinda. Sit down and calm yourself. We can talk about this and come to an agreement, I'm sure."

"You don't understand. This is my home." She ignored his order to sit.

"Homes can change. Some people move around often."

"Not me. This is where I intend to stay. I just got baptized and joined the church."

"A mere triviality. You can go to church anywhere. I told you. I would attend a Mennonite church with you—when I'm not working, of course."

"I have no intention of leaving my church, my home, my family."

"Well, come visit Baltimore with me. After a couple days together, I believe you'll change your mind."

"I wouldn't, and I won't be going to Baltimore or anywhere else with you, either."

"Be sensible, Malinda. Who better to help you stay well and to see you through flare-ups besides me?"

"I have a doctor here. Dr. Nelson is very capable."

"For a country doctor, perhaps, but I have all the latest advances and treatments right at my fingertips."

"I have Gott and the support of my family and community. To me, that's even better."

Todd McWilliams rose and took a few steps closer to Malinda. Too close, as far as she was concerned. She couldn't back up any more without falling over the rocking chair. The doctor towered over her. Malinda didn't feel sheltered by his large presence, as she did with Timothy. Instead, she felt threatened and more than a little frightened. Her heart thundered, creating a roar in her ears. She scarcely realized her hands were clutching fistfuls of her dress at her sides.

Malinda gasped when Todd bent and kissed her cheek. "You're a sweet girl, Malinda. Think about what I said. Think about me." He reached into his pocket and produced a small card. He yanked one of her hands free, placed the card on her palm, and folded her fingers around it. "Here's my number. I know you can use a phone when you need to. As soon as I hear from you, I'll be back to get you before you can bat one of those beautiful brown eyes."

Malinda jerked her head sideways when Todd leaned as if to kiss her again. He laughed and squeezed her arm. "I'll see you soon." He winked before turning and jumping down the steps. Once he reached the fancy red car, he gave her an arrogant salute.

"I won't be calling."

Todd gave no indication he heard her.

Anger mingled with fear. The man had really crossed the boundaries of proper doctor behavior. Malinda crumpled the card in her hand. The stove was the perfect place for it, as soon as she finished ripping it into itty bitty pieces.

Chapter Twenty

"Are you feeling all right?" Saloma asked.

Malinda stopped the haphazard rearranging of the beet slices and green beans on her plate and gave her *mamm* a cursory glance. "I'm fine, Mamm. I'm just not very hungry."

"You need to eat, dear, so you don't lose any weight. You haven't yet regained what you lost the last time you were sick."

Malinda silently counted to ten and backward to zero. She was well aware of her weight, or lack thereof. She didn't need her *mamm* to harp at her. It was bad enough Atlee never hesitated to tell her a slight puff of wind would send her airborne. She truly had been trying to eat. If Mamm knew about her afternoon visitor, she probably wouldn't feel like eating, either. She blew out the breath she'd been holding. "I know, Mamm. I'm trying."

"Of course you are, Dochder. You just eat what you can," Rufus said soothingly.

Dear Daed. Ever the peacemaker. Malinda shot him a grateful look but couldn't miss the frown her *mamm* sent his way. Malinda nodded. She speared a pickled beet slice and popped it into her mouth despite her stomach's protest.

Maybe the tanginess of the beet would awaken her taste buds and her appetite.

Should she tell Mamm and Daed about Todd McWilliams's visit? What if he came back? He'd said he would see her soon. Daed would be furious if he knew what the doctor had said to her. Mamm would probably chase the man away with a cast-iron skillet in her hand, though she'd never actually use it as a weapon. Malinda nearly giggled at the image.

She managed to choke down a few vegetables, but her stomach threatened to completely betray her when Mamm urged her to eat the noodles and gravy. Thankfully, Daed started asking Mamm about the neighbor she had visited. Now if she could hurry and clean the kitchen and escape to her room, she might be able to appease the monster residing in her stomach. She would feel much better when the weekend had passed and she knew Dr. McWilliams had left Maryland. *Please, Lord Gott, don't let him* kumm *back here.*

The little bit of excitement she had experienced at the doctor's flattery in the hospital had given way to anger and fear. Malinda got the impression Todd McWilliams expected her to fall at his feet in adoration and gratitude. He seemed to expect her to willingly and eagerly jump at the chance to be with him. The scariest part was he apparently didn't want to take *nee* for an answer.

Malinda didn't need a mirror Friday morning to know her dark-rimmed eyes and puffy lids made her resemble a sick raccoon. Sleep had merely teased her all night. Every time she had begun to fall down that well of utter exhaustion, her fidgety brain had jerked her back up to consciousness. She splashed cold water on her face again and again but didn't believe the effort helped at all. Mamm would take one look at her and be ready to haul her off to Dr. Nelson's office. This would be one time the *Englischers*' makeup would come in handy.

She would simply have to avert her gaze as much as possible. At least getting her little *bruders* off to school should provide plenty of distraction for a short time. It was later, when she and Mamm would be working side by side, that concerned her. Maybe she could invent a cough and plead an oncoming cold. *Nee*. That would certainly warrant a trip to the doctor's office. If only Mamm didn't consider her so fragile. Malinda spent a lot of energy working to dispel that notion. Her appearance today would not help her case.

Continued dawdling would accomplish nothing. If she didn't hurry to the kitchen, Mamm would question that, too. She might as well get the initial encounter over with. At least Todd McWilliams should be tied up with his conference all day and wouldn't be able to visit. She should be able to function normally today, whatever normal was.

"Did you have a bad night? Are you feeling all right? You didn't call for me."

Malinda didn't even get both feet onto the kitchen floor before Saloma started in on her. Whoever made up the notion that cold water relieved puffy, dark eyes? Saloma banged the big metal spoon against the side of the pot of oatmeal she was stirring before laying the spoon on the counter. She whisked across the room to press the back of her hand to Malinda's forehead.

"I'm fine, Mamm." Malinda gently pulled Saloma's hand down. "I just had one of those nights where I couldn't sleep well. You get those sometimes, ain't so?"

"Sure. But you're young. You shouldn't have worries keeping you awake unless . . ."

Unless I'm sick. Malinda could fill in the blank. "I'm feeling fine, Mamm. I'll get the lunches together." Malinda darted out of her *mamm*'s grasp and away from her scrutiny. How she wished there was no such thing as Crohn's disease. Then Mamm wouldn't have to fret over her so much. All her prayers for healing had gone unanswered. Obviously healing was not the Lord Gott's plan. She tried hard to accept that.

Some days Malinda did accept her illness and prayed for strength to face whatever came. Yet, once in a while, she wanted to throw herself to the ground and flail her limbs like a two-year-old throwing a tantrum in protest of the unfairness of her situation. Mamm would definitely be worried if Malinda succumbed to that urge. She hadn't felt like doing that in quite a while, so maybe her faith had been growing.

The sound of stomping feet and masculine voices put an end to Malinda's ponderings. She set Aden's and Ray's lunches near the edge of the kitchen counter so they could grab them on the way out the door. She tossed plastic baggies filled with peanut butter cookies into Sam's and Atlee's lunches and set them aside. Daed and Roman would be working at home and would *kumm* inside to eat at noon.

Malinda spooned thickened oatmeal into bowls and carried them to the table while Saloma filled the plates with scrambled eggs and bacon slices. It was a blessing their hens were *gut* layers. The family must go through at least a dozen eggs at a time. She left her own bowl on the counter so she could add a splash of milk to thin it a bit. Otherwise it would sit like a lead ball in her stomach all day.

"Mamm, can I stay home today?"

"*May* I," Mamm automatically corrected. "Are you sick, Aden?" Once again, Mamm stopped what she was doing to feel a forehead. "No fever."

"Aw, he probably didn't study for the spelling test today."

Ray bumped the table as he settled into his chair, causing *kaffi* to slosh around in the cups.

"Aden, you know your words. When I called them off to you yesterday, you didn't miss a single one," Malinda said, hoping to allay any fears he might have.

"That ain't it, Ray." Aden frowned at his older *bruder*.

"Well, what is it, then?" Saloma stopped dishing up food to stare at the *bu*.

Aden stared at the floor. After a few seconds, he mumbled, "I'm not so *gut* at softball, and Teacher said if everyone worked hard today, we'd have a game this afternoon."

"You're improving." Sam ruffled Aden's dark hair before pulling out his chair. "We'll practice this weekend, *jah?*"

Malinda could have hugged Sam. He was always so thoughtful and sensitive to others' needs. He would make Emma a *gut* husband.

"Do you promise?" Aden asked.

"You can count on it."

"Okay. Maybe I won't even get up to bat today."

With all the males out of the house, Malinda and Saloma settled into their daily routine. Malinda attacked her chores with a vigor she really didn't feel in order to keep her *mamm* from further questioning her about her health or lack of sleep. Besides, Malinda always believed if she expended energy, she received energy. She definitely needed energy today.

As the morning stretched toward noon, Malinda relaxed more and more and began to feel like her old self. A visit from Dr. McWilliams would be very unlikely. Tomorrow might be another matter entirely, but she wouldn't worry about that today. Didn't the Scriptures say something about each day having its own concerns? In other words, don't go borrowing trouble, as Mamm would say. She'd have to remember to search her Bible later for the verse that was hanging at the edge of her memory.

After the disorder from the noon meal had been cleared away, Malinda pulled out the overflowing mending basket. With the canning and preserving over for the season, she could begin to tackle some other duties that had been piling up. Malinda sank into the thick cushion covering the seat of the old oak rocker that had been in the family forever. Mamm had rocked all seven of her *kinner* in this chair and claimed her own *grossmammi* rocked her *kinner* in it as well. Every creak and squeak of the old chair was well deserved.

Malinda pulled the basket and sewing box closer to her and reached for the garment on top. Aden's pants. Not a surprise. Aden didn't walk if he could run. Falling, crawling, or rolling on the ground were everyday occurrences for him. Malinda smiled. How she loved her little *bruder*! She wouldn't mind having a little *bu* exactly like him one day. She sighed. That would probably never happen.

"Mighty deep sigh, Dochder."

Malinda hadn't even heard Saloma enter the living room. Before her *mamm* could ask what was wrong—again—Malinda smiled. "I'm just thinking of all Aden gets into, but he's still a *gut bu*."

"That is true, but he can wear his clothes to threads quicker than all the others did."

"I hope his softball game went okay."

"All life is a learning experience." Saloma picked up the next item from the basket.

The women worked in companionable silence for a while, the creak of the rocking chair providing the only sound. Malinda could be content working alongside Mamm the rest of her life if she never married. She kept telling herself that, but her heart had its doubts. "Take one day at a time." That's what Mamm always said. Malinda had been feeling well, for the most part, since returning from Ohio. Maybe a complete remission could happen. How she prayed for healing—but she tried to be accepting of whatever the Lord Gott might have planned for her.

Chapter Twenty-One

Saturday dawned bright but brisk. Winter definitely whispered for fall to get out of the way. The shadows beneath Malinda's eyes had no doubt deepened after another fitful night's sleep. She need only get through today. Surely Dr. McWilliams knew Sundays were days for church or visiting. After all, he lived in Ohio's Amish country, so he certainly would respect their ways and not intrude, wouldn't he?

Saturdays were very busy days for Amish shops. *Englischers* off from work usually shopped on Saturdays and often brought out-of-town guests to see the farms and shops, so Malinda's *daed* and older *bruders* needed to be out the door the same time as or even earlier than on weekdays.

When Malinda entered the kitchen, Saloma was already standing at the counter cracking eggs into a big glass bowl. Malinda cut slices of the zucchini bread she'd baked yesterday and arranged them on a plate before stirring the oatmeal in the pot on the back of the stove. "*Gut mariye*, Mamm." She avoided looking directly at Saloma. No use starting the morning off with the health questions Mamm would surely ask after taking one look at Malinda's puffy eyes.

"Did you sleep better?"

"Mmmm." Malinda gave a noncommittal sound in answer. She turned her attention to the oatmeal.

"I need you to take the fall produce to the market today, and some of the homemade jams and jellies, too."

Malinda grabbed for the spoon she almost dropped into the thick, bubbling oatmeal. "I thought you planned to go." Malinda debated whether blending into the crowd at the market would be better than lying low at home. A bright, sunny day was bound to bring out a lot of shoppers. The market might be the perfect way to avoid seeing Todd McWilliams if he made *gut* on his promise to see her soon. But what if he came to the house looking for her when she wasn't home? What would Mamm think? What if he mentioned he'd been there expressly to see her on Thursday? She hadn't breathed a word of that to anyone. Maybe she should tell Mamm about that now.

"I had thought to go," Saloma explained, "but Franny is still ailing. I'm going to go help her out a bit. Since Ray and Roman are helping Daed today, I'll take Aden with me to entertain Franny's two little ones." Saloma shoved her silver wire-rimmed glasses back into place.

"Oh." Malinda couldn't think of a single excuse to offer to get out of going to the market. At least the house would be empty if the pushy doctor did show up. Maybe she wouldn't mention anything just yet.

"Ray and Roman are loading up for you. They'll hitch the horse so you'll be all ready to go after you eat. I'll clean up the kitchen so you can get an early start."

With much reluctance and trepidation, Malinda clucked to Chestnut and set off for the farmers' market. Thankfully, at this early hour on a Saturday, traffic was lighter than on weekdays, when cars and tractor trailers flew by at top speed. The bright sun would soon tame the morning's crispness, but Malinda didn't mind the little nip in the air.

When she drove into the parking lot, Malinda saw other buggies and carts loaded with items to sell, as well as *Englisch* farmers' pickup trucks. Spying a familiar face, she called out. "Phoebe!"

The pretty young woman with the unusual strawberry blonde hair stopped in her tracks. She squinted into the sun's brilliance. "Malinda Stauffer. Is that you?"

"*Jah*."

"I'll wait for you to unhitch. We can set up together and share a space, if you like."

"That would be fine. Just give me a minute or two." Malinda heaved a huge sigh of relief. She wouldn't have to man a booth alone. Plus, it would be fun to spend a little time with Phoebe. She hadn't spent much time with *freinden*, except Timothy, since she and Mamm had been so busy with the bumper crop of apples.

"It's *gut* to see you," Phoebe said when Malinda shuffled closer. The weight of her load slowed her down. "Do you need help?"

Malinda noted the concern in Phoebe's blue-green eyes. Inwardly she cringed, fearing another inquiry about her health. Would she always be thought of as sickly? "I've got it. It's more awkward than heavy. You've got a load yourself."

"I'll have to go back for the rest of mine."

"Me too, but we can cover each other. Mamm was supposed to be here today, but she needed to help Franny, who still isn't feeling well." Malinda grunted as she plunked her big box down on the display stand.

"That box is almost as big as you." Phoebe chuckled as she set down her own heavy load and flexed her fingers. "My fingers went numb on me." She shook her hands vigorously.

Malinda smiled. "I know what you mean." She shook her own hands before rubbing her aching upper arms. "I'm glad

I'll have someone to work beside." *And someone to hide behind.*

"Me too," Phoebe agreed. "I wasn't too crazy about setting up here today, but I need to get over my fears. That's what Mamm says, anyway. I haven't been here much since . . ."

Malinda squeezed Phoebe's arm. "That wasn't your fault. No one blamed you."

"I blamed me. It's taken me ever so long to forgive myself."

"Have you?"

"Finally. Ben's *grossmammi* helped a lot."

Malinda would have to be blind not to see the light in Phoebe's eyes at the mention of Ben Miller's name. She was happy Phoebe had made peace with herself and happy she had found Ben. "Naomi is fine, ain't so?"

"She's finally let go of Mamm's skirts and is back to her normal curious little self. She's such a sweet little girl." Phoebe emptied her box. "I'm ready to go back for the rest of my things while you finish setting up. Then you can go. Is that okay with you?"

"That makes sense." Malinda pulled jars of jams and jellies from her box and arranged them so the labels would face the customers. Phoebe certainly appeared to have overcome her self-blame over Naomi's kidnapping from this very market. But Malinda certainly undersood why Phoebe had qualms about being here today. Malinda would feel the same way. She knew Phoebe had counted herself responsible for the little girl's disappearance, since she and her sister Martha had been in charge of their little *schweschders* that day. Malinda gave her head a shake, sending her *kapp* strings swaying. Thank the Lord Naomi had been returned home and Phoebe had absolved herself of all recrimination. No one else, not even Phoebe's parents, had blamed her for the abduction, but Phoebe hadn't been able to forgive herself.

That was in the past. Now Phoebe glowed with happiness. Malinda expected to attend a wedding very soon. A tiny, wistful sigh escaped. It must be so nice to be healthy and happy and to plan a wedding.

"Ugh!" Phoebe nearly stumbled before she could lower another huge box to the ground.

Malinda quickly took hold of one end of the box so they could ease it down together. "What do you have in here, cinder blocks?"

"It sure seems like it. Who would ever have thought squash and gourds could weigh so much?" Phoebe tucked a few loose strands of hair beneath her *kapp*.

"Maybe it's the pumpkins on the bottom."

"Pumpkins? That Aaron! He packed the box. He was supposed to bring pumpkins later when Ephraim came here. *Bruders*!"

Malinda laughed. "I know what you mean."

"I'm sure you do. You have one more *bruder* than I have."

"*Jah*. At least you have some *schweschders*."

"Even though they are quite a bit younger, I am glad to have them." Phoebe pulled vegetables from the box. "I'm glad Aaron didn't load me down with all the pumpkins. These are actually the smaller ones. We had some huge ones this year. Aaron and Ephraim were going to sell at the little market for a while before meeting me here. Hey, do you want to go ahead and get the rest of your things?"

"I guess I'd better." Actually, Malinda would rather stay hidden here, away from the traffic and parking areas. But she was glad Mamm had sent her to this market if she had to go to one at all. Both *Englisch* and Amish sold things here, and the place was more crowded than the small market at the library, where only Plain vendors set up.

Malinda wove her way in and out of vendors arranging their wares in an effort to remain hidden. Surely it was much too early for a person to get here from Baltimore. Just the same, Malinda skirted the fringes of the parking area and kept her eyes pealed for any fancy, red cars. Dr. McWilliams wouldn't think to look for her at the market, anyway, would he? Hopefully, he wouldn't even glance to his left and notice the market if he did choose to travel to St. Mary's County again. *Please, Lord, let him go home to Ohio where he belongs.*

Once she was back at the booth, Malinda tried to fade into the background as much as possible, but scores of people were roaming the market this fine fall day and stopped to make purchases. She nearly leaped from her black sneakers every time a tall, sandy-haired man approached or whenever she glimpsed a flash of red from the distant parking lot.

"Is everything okay?" Phoebe asked during a brief lull.

"Sure. Why?"

"You seem sort of jumpy. Are you looking for someone?"

"*N-nee*. I-I guess I'm a little flustered with all the people. I haven't worked here in a while." The excuse wasn't untrue. It just wasn't the reason her every nerve stood at attention. She had hoped Phoebe hadn't noticed her shifting glances or her trembling hands, but evidently she had.

"I haven't either, to tell the truth."

Yet you are as calm as the wind on a hot mid-July day. If anyone had reason to be nervous at the market, it was Phoebe, after her little *schweschder* was snatched from here. Malinda made an effort to calm herself.

"I thought you were searching the crowd for a special fellow." Phoebe's eyes sparkled with mischief.

Malinda wished searching for a special fellow was her concern right now instead of searching for an *Englisch* man who frightened her.

Phoebe squeezed Malinda's hand. "I'm teasing. I hope I didn't upset you. I think it would be great if you had a special person in your life."

"I'm not upset."

"I guess I want everyone to be as happy as I am."

"I'm glad you're happy. Ben is such a nice *bu*."

"That he is! I thought maybe you and Timothy Brenneman . . ." Phoebe's voice trailed off.

Malinda knew her cheeks must have turned scarlet. "I, uh, Timothy is a nice *bu*, too."

Phoebe elbowed Malinda. "That's it?"

"He is a special person, but I'm not sure if, well, you know . . . I have health issues."

"Lots of people have all sorts of health issues, and they get married and lead normal lives."

"I never know when I'll have a flare-up."

"People never know when they'll get pneumonia or fall and break a leg, either."

"I have to take medications that cost a lot of money."

"Lots of people have diabetes and need to buy insulin and all sorts of equipment they need every day, not just for a flare-up."

"You have an answer for everything." Malinda sighed. "But it's not so cut and dried."

"I don't mean to be a know-it-all. I just want you to see that lots of people have health issues, but they still have relationships."

"I suppose so, but I can't ask someone else to pay out all that money for my medicine and doctor appointments. And what if I end up in the hospital again?"

"We all work together. Remember?"

"*Jah*, but what man would want to do his *fraa*'s work on top of his own? I can't always do all my chores when I'm sick."

"There's no shame in asking for help. Part of love is working together and helping each other. Your parents help each other, ain't so?"

"Sure, but they're both healthy. They can do their own work and then help each other, too."

"Don't borrow trouble, Malinda. You have more healthy days than sick days."

"For right now, I do."

"No one knows what the future holds. We have to trust in Gott's grace. Believe me, I know how hard that can be sometimes."

Malinda simply nodded. To her surprise, tears welled in her eyes, and her nose burned. She bit the inside of her cheek to keep from bursting out into full-fledged sobs. Just in the nick of time, an *Englisch* man and woman approached and drew Phoebe's attention away from her. She had a sinking feeling Phoebe hadn't finished with the conversation, though. Phoebe's penchant for helping people would eventually lead her back to the same topic unless Malinda could permanently divert her attention.

The market became more and more crowded, which kept both girls busy and Malinda's mind occupied. It didn't keep her eyes from darting here and there in between customers, though. Phoebe's *bruders* arrived with a load of pumpkins, and she promptly scolded them for sneaking heavy pumpkins into her box.

"I thought they were going to stay and sell the pumpkins," Malinda said after Ephraim and Aaron left.

"Daed needs them this afternoon, so I get the pleasure of selling them."

"They must have sold quite a bit this morning, since you don't have as many as I thought you'd have."

"It looks like they had a lot of customers. I hope the rest of them sell so I don't have to lug them back home."

Malinda and Phoebe took turns breaking for a quick lunch. As Malinda nibbled on a peanut butter and strawberry jam sandwich, she had a better chance to survey the crowd. Once or twice her heart nearly stalled at the glimpse of a tall, sandy-haired man. She tried to scan as much of the roadway and parking lot as she could. She considered taking a little walk to better check out the cars, but realized that would make *her* more visible as well.

Despite the sweet jam oozing from her sandwich, the peanut butter and bread stuck in Malinda's throat and refused to slide down. She grabbed her water bottle and took a huge gulp to get the mass moving. She rewrapped the sandwich and pushed it back into her lunch bag. Maybe she'd feel more like eating later. She cast a final nervous glance around the market before returning to stand beside Phoebe.

"Are you finished eating already?"

"I wasn't very hungry after all. I saved the rest of my lunch for later."

Phoebe nodded and turned to help a customer select pumpkins. "What's wrong?" she asked when the customer had paid and moved on.

"What makes you think anything is wrong?"

"It could be the frown on your face or the way you keep looking around the market. Or it could be your lack of appetite after we've been working steadily for hours. My own stomach is threatening to eat itself." Phoebe smiled and laid a hand on Malinda's arm. "If you're worried about something, it might help to talk about it. I'm a great listener."

"I'm okay, Phoebe." Malinda deliberately smoothed her furrowed brow. She forced a smile. "You go ahead and eat. We don't want to make your stomach any angrier."

"Are you sure?"

"Positive. Enjoy your lunch. I'll take care of things here."

"I won't be long." Phoebe retreated to a back corner of the booth and rummaged around for her lunch bag.

Malinda expelled a long, pent-up breath. That was close. She had almost spilled her concerns to Phoebe to determine if an outside, unbiased opinion would help her see things in a different light. It could be that she had read too much into Todd McWilliams's words, and a different perspective might clear up her misgivings. She'd have to think about that later.

A mob of *Englisch kinner* descended on the pumpkin display. They tried to yank the larger pumpkins from the bottom of the stack. Malinda rushed over to steady the pile before the whole load of pumpkins tumbled to the ground and smashed little toes.

"Here, I can help," a deep voice called out.

Startled, Malinda jumped, nearly toppling the pumpkins herself. From the corner of her eye, she caught sight of pale blond hair attached to a head much higher than the others around her. In a couple of long strides, he reached the gawking youngsters and their mothers, who clutched jars of jam or handfuls of yellow squash and zucchini. "You tell me which one you want, and I'll pull it out for you," he offered as he smiled into the excited little faces around him.

"*Ach*, Timothy! What are you doing here?"

"I just happened to be in the neighborhood." He smiled at Malinda and then grunted as he freed a pumpkin much too large for the tiny girl who was reaching for it.

"I thought you'd be working today? Sam went in to work."

"I am working. I had to meet a customer here with a cabinet he'd purchased. It looks like I finished my business just in the nick of time." He nodded at the children, most of whom still wore orange team shirts and soccer cleats. "Their game must have just finished."

It took a good twenty minutes to accommodate all the customers. Tim worked alongside Malinda the entire time. When the last parent ushered the last little one away, Malinda swiped her hand across her moist brow. "Whew! That was quite a crowd. *Danki* for your help, Tim."

"*Jah, danki*," Phoebe echoed. "I tried to gulp down my sandwich so I could get up here to help you, Malinda, but then help magically appeared. It looked like you two had everything under control, so I figured I'd stay out of the way."

Phoebe's double meaning was not lost on Malinda. She knew Phoebe really meant she was giving Malinda and Timothy time together. She hoped Timothy hadn't picked up on Phoebe's ulterior motive.

"I'm glad I showed up at the right time to help you out. But I'd better get back to the shop now. See you, Phoebe. See you soon, Malinda." Timothy loped off in the direction of his wagon.

"He'll see me any old time, but he'll see you soon," Phoebe teased.

Malinda elbowed Phoebe. "You're incorrigible."

"I try!"

At least the diversion had kept Malinda's mind off a fancy, red car and its driver.

Chapter Twenty-Two

If Malinda didn't know better, she'd have believed she'd been dragged behind the buggy by the time Chestnut trotted up the long, gravel driveway. The big brown horse must have been as eager as Malinda to arrive home, if his increased speed served as any indication. Malinda yawned and stifled a groan as she climbed from the buggy. She practically fell onto Roman, who suddenly appeared to unhitch the horse. "*Ach*! Sorry, Roman. I must be more tired than I thought. Did Mamm send you out here to help me?" For once Malinda wasn't miffed at Saloma's overprotectiveness. She didn't think she could easily perform one more chore right now.

"She told me to keep an eye out for you in case you needed help unloading."

"I sold almost everything, so I can get the few things I brought back if you'll see to Chestnut."

"Sure."

"*Danki*, Roman." Malinda gently squeezed his arm. When did Roman become so muscular? Her little *bruder* had become a tall, strong, young man.

Malinda paused to drag in a few deep breaths before pulling open the back door. It would never do for Mamm to see her so bedraggled. Even though it had been Mamm's idea for Malinda to work at the market today, she'd surely scold Malinda for working too hard.

"Hey, Roman," Malinda called over her shoulder as softly as she could and still be heard.

Roman stopped talking to the horse and gave Malinda a questioning glance.

"Were there any visitors today?"

Roman's expression said Malinda must have taken leave of her senses. If Mamm had been off visiting and he and his younger *bruders* had been busy with Daed, who would have been around to entertain visitors? "Not that I know of. Why?"

"Just curious." Malinda turned back to the door. She straightened her shoulders and forced her feet to move more briskly. Somehow she had to infuse her body with a bit more energy to get through the meal preparation and cleanup. Then she could take a hot bath and sink blissfully into her bed. "I'll wash up and be right there to help you, Mamm." She forced as much enthusiasm into her voice as she could muster.

"Hey, Malinda." Aden slid around the corner and greeted her with a hug.

"How's my favorite eight-year-old?" She bent to return his hug. It would be a sad day indeed when Aden grew too old to want to hug her. "What are you doing inside already?"

"Daed said I helped enough today and could *kumm* inside."

Malinda bit her tongue to keep from laughing. Translation: Daed had had enough of Aden's questions and constant chatter. "I'm sure you were a big help."

"I was." Aden snatched Malinda's hand and tugged her toward the kitchen. "You got a letter!"

A letter? Who would write to her? "Let me wash up so I can help Mamm." She slid her hand from Aden's grasp. "It's probably from Aenti Mary."

Apparently afraid he'd miss something important, Aden stuck to Malinda's side like bubblegum on the bottom of her shoe. She rushed into the kitchen, with Aden dogging her every move. "What would you like me to do first, Mamm?" She stumbled over Aden and grabbed the counter to keep from falling. "Oops! Sorry, Aden."

"Aden, go find something to do!" Mamm pointed to the door.

Poor Aden. He was being shooed away again. "Here." Malinda held out a stack of paper napkins. "If your hands are clean, you can put napkins and silverware on the table at everyone's place."

Aden looked at his hands, wiped them on his pants, and looked back at Malinda. "They're clean enough."

"Go wash your hands!" Saloma ordered. "I don't want dirty hands with who knows what under the fingernails in my silverware drawer."

"All right." Aden hung his head and shuffled away to scrub his hands.

"I'll leave the napkins right here for you."

Saloma turned her attention to Malinda. "How were sales at the market?"

"I sold nearly everything. There were a lot of people at the market today. How is Franny?"

"She's slowly getting better. She needs to listen to Dr. Nelson and not try to do too much too soon. She had a bad case of bronchitis."

"I'm ready!" Aden sang out. He held up his hands for Saloma's inspection before reaching for the napkins. "Aren't you going to open your letter? It says it's from Ohio."

"I'll get it later. I told you it was probably from Aenti Mary."

"Don't you want to know what she says?"

"She probably wants to know how I'm feeling and to let us know how she's getting along."

"Not everyone is as curious as you," Saloma said. "You know what they say about curiosity . . ."

"What?" Aden asked.

"They say curiosity killed the cat."

"It's a *gut* thing I'm not a cat, then," Aden replied in all seriousness.

Malinda couldn't resist laughing. Even Saloma chuckled and reached out to hug her son. Malinda wondered if she dared remind her *mamm* of the old curiosity saying when Saloma grilled her about the letter later. She'd better not. Mamm most likely wouldn't see the humor in the comparison.

Malinda's fatigue had nearly overwhelmed her by the time she slid onto her chair at the big dinner table. She tried her best to keep up with the conversations floating around her and managed to utter an occasional comment or two. Mainly she focused on keeping her head from dropping into her full plate of food. She wouldn't have thought a day at the market would wear her out so completely. It had been four months since her hospitalization. She should have her energy back. Maybe the emotional strain of the past few days had chipped away at her stamina.

Mamm kept up a steady prattle, detailing her day with Franny and any news she'd gleaned through the grapevine as she and Malinda tidied the kitchen. Malinda saw her *mamm*'s gaze wander several times to the counter where the still-unopened letter lay. Malinda kept right on working, pretending not to notice. She'd read the letter later, and probably even let Mamm read it, unless Aenti Mary had some worrisome health news she didn't want Mamm and Daed to know about. She most likely wanted to catch them up with news in her neck of the woods.

Malinda slipped the letter into her pocket on her way out of the kitchen. Thankfully, Daed chose a short passage for the evening Bible reading. He probably felt sorry for her, if she looked as tired as she felt. Whatever the reason, a short passage meant Malinda could escape upstairs sooner.

The chill in her bedroom now that the sun was no longer streaming through the window sent Malinda diving beneath the blanket and quilt. She stayed warm while submerged in the hot bathwater, but once she stepped out and toweled off, an unpleasant iciness seeped into her bones. When she warmed enough to remove her hands from beneath the covers, she reached for the letter on the nightstand. Funny. There wasn't any return address, and the handwriting didn't look like Aenti Mary's scrawl. The postmark read *Ohio*, though.

Malinda pushed the covers back farther and pulled herself upright. Did one of the girls she sometimes talked to after church in Ohio get her address from Aenti Mary? Surely she would have written her return address so Malinda could send a reply. Even circle letters sent from person to person had return addresses on the envelopes.

There was only one way to solve this mystery. Malinda picked at the corner of the envelope until she could slip a finger inside to tear it all the way open. She pulled out a single sheet of paper folded in half and shook it open. She gasped as she skimmed the words. She went back and read more slowly.

Malinda,

Dr. Todd McWilliams may try to contact you when he goes to Baltimore for a conference. Don't get your hopes up that he wants to see you for romantic reasons. To the doctor, you are a puzzle to be solved. Your medical condition and your culture are a challenge to him, and he always likes a good challenge. If you know what is good for you, you will promptly send the doctor on his way if he shows up at your house. Or better yet, don't even talk to him at all.

I saw the way he looked at you in the hospital, and I'm sure the attention he gave you was flattering. Don't think for a minute that an important, sophisticated doctor could be interested in a simple girl like yourself. He needs a woman of his caliber by his side—an equally sophisticated, educated woman—so in other words, keep your paws off!

Malinda dropped the paper as if it had bitten her. The letter had no signature, but it didn't need one. It could only have been written by Nurse Trudy. Malinda hadn't failed to notice the daggers the blonde, curly-haired nurse had shot at her when Dr. McWilliams wasn't looking in her direction. Trudy had provided adequate nursing care but had seemed possessive of Dr. McWilliams. If he and Trudy had a relationship, why did he say all those things to her about staying in Ohio with him? Why did he track her down at her home to again try to persuade her to live in Ohio? Was she an experiment, a goal to be achieved?

Malinda shuddered and pulled the covers back up to her neck. She never had any intention of taking the doctor up on his offer, but it still hurt to be considered a challenge. She prayed the man was on his way back to Ohio and wouldn't try to contact her ever again. She reached to extinguish the lamp. It seemed that Trudy and Todd McWilliams were two peas in a pod. It also seemed she would be short on sleep again tonight.

Chapter Twenty-Three

Throughout the three-hour church service, Malinda stole occasional glances at the door to assure herself no strangers entered the Hertzlers' big barn. When Phoebe nudged her and raised questioning eyebrows, Malinda figured she'd better keep her eyes front and center—if she could keep them open at all. This day couldn't end fast enough to suit her. She would be able to breathe easier once the weekend was over and there was no additional appearance by Dr. McWilliams.

With fall's crisp weather, the common meal after church would be inside rather than under the shade trees, as it was in summer. Leaves had already begun to blaze with deep red, bright orange, and golden yellow hues that painted a glorious picture against the blue sky. As the men ate, Malinda kept busy by shuttling here and there replacing food and drinks until Phoebe cornered her. "Slow down, Malinda. What's got you so jittery?"

"I, uh, I'm not jittery."

"You could have fooled me. Grab a plate. It's time for us to eat. You remind me of a little hummingbird flapping its wings so fast you can't see them."

Malinda forced a strained smile before filling a plate

with food she had no desire to eat. She dropped to the bench beside Phoebe. A wad of fear filled her stomach, sending distress signals loud and clear. Mary Stoltzfus plunked down on Phoebe's other side and kept up a steady stream of chatter, relieving Malinda of any obligation to converse. Malinda tore off a small chunk of bread to nibble at, but ended up balling it up in her napkin.

"It's a little chilly out, but would you like to go for a short walk?" Timothy spoke close to Malinda's ear shortly after she left the table.

"Uh, sure, Timothy. A short walk would be fine."

Some of the young folks had started a game of volleyball and called out for Tim and Malinda to join them. Timothy glanced at Malinda. "Do you want to play?" At the shake of her head, he hollered back, "Not right now." Younger *kinner* raced around the yard enjoying their own games. "Are you too cold?

"I'm fine for now." *He's always so considerate.*

"Do you want to see how the Hertzlers' lambs are doing? They should be pretty big by now."

"Sure. I saw them shortly after they were born but haven't seen them since." Malinda always liked stopping to watch the woolly black-faced sheep whenever she passed the Hertzlers' farm. Something about their sweet expressions tugged at her heart.

Malinda and Timothy chatted about the sheep, Timothy's work, and Malinda's day at the market as they strolled toward the back pasture. The sound of a car's engine and then the crunch of tires on gravel caused Malinda to freeze in her tracks.

"Who could that be?" Timothy looked toward the driveway. "All the local *Englischers* know we don't do business on Sundays."

Malinda craned her neck to peer around Timothy. She gasped. All the joy of walking with Timothy drained out the soles of her feet, only to be replaced by conflicting emotions. Surprise. Anger. Fear. How dare he interrupt their Sunday?

"Malinda, are you all right? You're so pale, and you're trembling."

"I-I guess I'm getting a little cold." Her gaze stayed fastened on the red car that kicked up dust as it rolled up the driveway a little too fast. Suddenly she wanted to run. It took every ounce of willpower to keep her feet planted where they were. The car had scarcely lurched to a stop when the driver's door sprang open.

"Do you still want to see the sheep, or would you rather go back?" Timothy rubbed one of her cold hands between his large warm ones.

"We can go on." Actually, she wanted to tug Timothy out of sight of the man approaching the volleyball players.

Before they reached the sheep, they heard a voice shouting out to them. Again they stopped to look behind them.

"Malinda!"

"It's Roman." That arrogant man must have sent Roman to fetch her. "*Was ist letz*?" she called when Roman got closer.

"That man," Roman panted. "He wants to see you."

Timothy looked at Malinda. His face was one big question mark. Malinda stared at Roman, who had paused to catch his breath.

"That man says he was your doctor in Ohio," Roman panted.

"Why has he come here?" Timothy's face now exhibited concern. "You're all right, aren't you, Malinda?"

"I'm fine." She didn't feel so fine at this very moment, though. *Please, Gott, don't let him have told anyone about his visit on Thursday or mention any of that conversation to anyone.*

"We'd better see what he wants," Timothy said, deciding for them.

"I'll tell him you're on your way." Roman sprinted back in the direction of the yard.

"I wonder what he wants," Timothy said.

"*Gut* question." Dread tugged at Malinda's soul. The image of a sheep being led to slaughter filled her mind. Timothy must have sensed her reluctance to move. How could he not?

"Would you rather not see the doctor?" Timothy stopped abruptly, causing Malinda to bump into him.

"It's, uh, I don't have any need to see him. I'm not sick." Yet.

"*Englisch* doctors don't usually make social calls." Timothy spoke mainly to himself. When Malinda did not move forward, he asked, "Don't you think you should see what he wants?"

"I suppose I have to." Malinda let Timothy lead her forward again.

The volleyball players and young *kinner* played as before. Adults were still gathered in clumps to talk. The world spun on. Only Malinda's world screeched to a halt.

"Hello, Malinda. How are you?" Todd McWilliams flashed a wide, bright smile.

I was a whole lot better before you drove that fancy car up the driveway. "I'm fine."

"Could I talk to you for a minute?"

From her periphery, Malinda watched her parents approach, worry etched on her *mamm*'s face. "Here are my parents," she said and made the introductions.

"*Danki* for taking care of our *dochder* when she was so sick," Rufus said as Saloma nodded.

"I'm glad I was there and could help." Todd flashed that brilliant smile again

"Is there any problem?" Concern filled Saloma's voice.

"I mean, Malinda is okay, isn't she? You didn't drive all the way here to tell us about some test results or something? It's been several months, and . . ."

"Oh, no, no. It's nothing like that at all. We wouldn't have released Malinda from the hospital if we suspected something was wrong. I had a conference to attend in Baltimore, and I thought it was a pleasant day to take a drive. When I remembered Malinda lived in Southern Maryland, I headed south to see the area and check in on Malinda while I was here."

"That is very kind of you." Saloma's relief was palpable. "Would you like something to eat? We still have plenty of food left."

Nee, Mamm. I want him to leave. Don't encourage him to linger.

"No, thank you. I ate along the way. I would like to talk to Malinda for a few moments, if that's all right."

"Sure. *Danki* again, Dr. McWilliams." Rufus backed away.

Malinda gazed up into Timothy's eyes, willing him to stay by her side.

"I'll check on the volleyball game." Timothy patted Malinda's arm.

All hope of rescue vanished. She'd have to face the man alone. At least he hadn't said anything about his real purpose for being here. Malinda stood like a statue, her heart pounding so hard she feared it would explode. All she could do was stare at the man in front of her.

"It's good to see you again, Malinda. You're looking well." Todd spoke loud enough for anyone still within earshot to hear. When he reached to touch her arm, Malinda jerked free from her inert state and leaped out of reach. "I wouldn't hurt you, Malinda." His voice dropped low so only she could hear him.

"I didn't think you would." Malinda finally found her voice. "I just don't want you to touch me."

"I've touched you before."

"As a doctor. I was your patient. I'm not now." She felt her face heat nearly to the boiling point. Surely the man had not touched her inappropriately when she'd been heavily medicated and not aware of her surroundings. "What are you doing here? You've lived around the Amish. You know Sundays are church and family days."

"I told you I would see you soon."

"And I told you I would not change my mind."

"Is he your boyfriend?" Todd tilted his head in the direction Timothy had taken.

"That isn't any of your business."

"Of course it is. You know how I feel about you. You know I want you to come to Ohio with me. I can give you a good life."

"My life here is fine. I'm happy here and don't intend to leave."

"Will that young fellow be able to take care of you when you're sick? Will he even stay around, or will he run off in fear?"

"You make it sound like I have some horrible contagious disease. Most people here know I have flare-ups of Crohn's. We are used to helping one another. Besides, I've been quite well the past few months."

"But you won't always feel well."

"Who says? Are you able to predict the future?" Malinda found her fear morphing into anger. Dr. Todd McWilliams acted so sure of himself.

"I know the shape of your intestines. Flare-ups are inevitable. Surgery may very well be in your not-too-distant future. How will you manage that?"

"We do have doctors and hospitals here. My family will help me. That's what we do. So you don't have to worry about my medical condition."

"What if I profess my undying love for you? Then would you come with me?"

"Then you would be telling a great untruth."

"How can you think that?"

"Dr. McWilliams . . ."

"Todd."

"*Dr. McWilliams*, we are totally different. I am grateful for your help when I was sick. Truly I am. But that's all there is to it, and that's all there will ever be. Go home to Nurse Trudy. I believe she cares about you and would definitely be more suitable for you."

"Trudy? I don't think so."

"I need to return to my family now."

"Your boyfriend, you mean?" The doctor's voice turned suddenly gruff, harsh.

"Have a safe trip home, Dr. McWilliams." Malinda willed her feet not to run, though all she wanted to do was hide behind her *mamm*'s skirt as she had done as a *boppli*.

Chapter Twenty-Four

Timothy didn't need to shade his eyes from the sun to see the stormy expression on Malinda's usually serene face. What could the doctor have said to upset her? Fear shot through his heart and stole his breath. Surely the doctor didn't have some sort of bad news after all this time. He thought Malinda had been feeling well these last few months. Timothy shifted his gaze slightly to catch the doctor stomping off toward the little red car. His expression definitely displayed anger. He wished he'd stayed a little closer so he could have heard the conversation between Malinda and the man, but that would have been rude. Now he had to decide whether or not to intercept Malinda's journey toward her *mamm*.

"Malinda?"

She whirled around. Timothy could see her struggle to gain control over her emotions. She blinked hard several times, probably to hold back tears. Timothy saw and heard her drag in a deep breath and let it out slowly, taking the furrows across her forehead with it.

"*Jah?*" Her voice came out soft, low.

"Are you all right? Did the doctor say something to upset you?"

"I-I'm fine, Tim."

"You looked so upset, and the doctor sure left in a huff."

"H-he probably has to hurry back to Ohio. It's a long drive, you know."

"*Jah*. He went out of his way to drive down here from Baltimore before heading to Ohio."

"I suppose so."

"That was nice of him to check on you."

Malinda shrugged her slim shoulders but didn't comment. She also didn't answer his question about the doctor saying something to upset her. Timothy decided to let that slide for the moment. "Did you still want to see the lambs?"

"I'd like to see them, but not now."

Timothy watched Malinda's face as her eyes followed the red car speeding down the driveway in a cloud of dust. Her jaw relaxed when no trace of red was visible. Glancing down, he saw Malinda's fingers uncurl from the tight fists they'd been clutched in against her blue dress.

"I hope he slows down when he reaches the road, or he'll kill someone. Are you sure you're okay, Malinda?"

"I'm sure."

Timothy trotted along beside Malinda, not willing to leave her when, despite her protests, he knew she was shaken.

"*Ach*, Malinda, is the doctor gone already?" Saloma scurried away from the women she'd been chatting with.

"He just left," Timothy answered when Malinda didn't immediately respond to her *mamm*'s inquiry. Tim pointed to the driveway, but the doctor had sped away so quickly not even a fleck of dust still swirled in the air. He dropped his arm when he realized he was pointing at nothing.

"I was going to send some food with him for his long drive. It was awfully *gut* of him to drive all the way down here to check on you, ain't so, Malinda?"

"I suppose," Malinda mumbled. "Are you and Daed about ready to go home?"

Timothy saw the concern jump into Saloma's face. For sure and for certain, Malinda wasn't acting quite right, and the color had drained right off her face, leaving her as pale as a white sheet flapping in a snowstorm.

"Are you feeling all right?" Saloma walked closer, her eyes focused on Malinda's face.

"I'm fine. I'm just a little tired. I can sit and wait for you if you aren't ready to leave." The slump of Malinda's shoulders told Timothy Malinda would rather not wait around the Hertzlers' place any longer.

"I was going to let the *buwe* finish their game, but I can round them up." Saloma took in a deep breath as if ready to holler for one of her sons.

"Wait, Saloma. If it's okay with you, Malinda, I'll take you home. Aden looks pretty tired. Maybe he'd want to *kumm* along with us." Timothy nodded to where Aden lay sprawled in a patch of clover. Even though he was a *kinner*, Timothy figured the *bu* would serve as some sort of chaperone so he and Malinda wouldn't be at her house alone.

"He does look pretty beat," Saloma agreed. She turned back to Malinda. "Is that plan okay with you?"

"Sure."

"I'll tell Aden to get moving. We'll be along real soon."

Malinda nodded and headed toward the buggies. She waved to Phoebe and Mary as she passed by. Timothy caught up in two long strides. "I'm sure Aden will be here in a minute. I'll get the horse hitched so we're all set to go."

Malinda mumbled affirmatively but offered no other comment. Timothy's concern mounted. Malinda had seemed fine when they'd set out on their walk. In fact, she had seemed excited about seeing the lambs. He knew her fondness for animals and was surprised she'd changed her mind about seeing them after the doctor talked to her. What did that man say? Would Timothy be able to find out?

Aden panted to a stop beside the buggy.

"You found the energy to run over here?" Malinda playfully punched her little *bruder*.

"*Jah*." Aden paused and gasped for breath. "I was going to play some more, but everyone else was too tired."

"Everyone else? It was you I saw flat out on the ground."

"I guess I'm tired, too."

"Hop in and we'll be on our way." Timothy helped Malinda climb into the buggy.

They made the short drive to the Stauffers' house in relative silence. Timothy's attempts at conversation were met mostly with one-word responses. Aden chattered intermittently, but mostly to himself.

"*Danki*, Tim." Malinda jumped down from the buggy as soon as it stopped, as if she couldn't wait to escape. That happened too often. Every time he thought they'd taken one step forward, she dragged him two steps back. Aden hopped down after her and ran toward the barn.

"The barn cat had kittens." Malinda answered Tim's unasked question. "Four of them."

"Did you want to check on them?"

"I will in a few minutes."

"I'll walk out with you."

Malinda shrugged as if to say, *Suit yourself*, but headed toward the barn.

Timothy stopped her with a hand on her arm. "What happened, Malinda? Please tell me what's wrong."

Malinda slid her arm from beneath Timothy's hand. "I've already told you. Nothing is wrong." She set off for the barn at a brisk pace.

"I'm no mind reader, Malinda, but I believe I know you well enough to tell when something is not right. Did the doctor do or say something that upset you?"

"Of course not."

Malinda's reply came too snappy for Tim to believe the sincerity of it. He'd never believe Malinda would out-and-out lie, but there was definitely something she didn't want to share, something that had put her out of sorts. She turned around and walked the few steps back to where Timothy was still standing. She looked up at him with those dark, doe-like eyes and smiled slightly. "Dr. McWilliams just reminded me of a very unpleasant time that I've tried to put behind me."

"I can understand that, but Malinda, we all get sick sometimes. These human bodies don't always operate as we want them to or expect them to."

"I know that, Tim. I'm trying very hard to accept that I have a chronic disease the Lord Gott has not seen fit to take away. It seems this is a cross He wants me to bear."

"The Lord's ways are often mysterious to us, but I'm sure He has a purpose and a plan."

"I suppose. Let's go see the kittens."

Malinda proceeded slightly ahead of Timothy toward the barn. Had she convinced him that everything was all right? She doubted it. Somehow Timothy seemed more in tune with her mood and feelings than anyone else she knew, except maybe her *mamm*. With any luck, the kittens would provide enough distraction to make Timothy abandon his inquisition.

"Are the kittens with their *mamm*, Aden?" The brightness in her voice sounded phony even to Malinda's own ears. Over her shoulder, she said to Tim, "They've just started wandering around a bit away from their *mamm*."

"Here's the little tiger," Aden announced, holding the little ball of fuzz beneath his chin.

"We have a tiger-striped kitten like the *mamm*, two

black-and-white kittens, and one kind of tortoiseshell kitten. Aren't they all adorable?" Malinda bent to lift the tiny tortoiseshell kitten and raised it to her cheek. "I think this one is my favorite." She knew she was babbling, but couldn't seem to stop. Sometimes when she was nervous, her mouth ran away with itself.

Timothy reached out to stroke the kitten Malinda was cuddling and inadvertently touched her cheek. An electric current shot from her face down to her toes, and her heart thumped in double time. Her eyes flew to Timothy's face and were held captive by his blue gaze. No more prattle issued from her lips. He stared back at her as if he was equally captivated.

The crunch of gravel beneath buggy wheels broke the spell binding Timothy and Malinda. She gently set the kitten by its *mamm* and instructed Aden to return his kitten. "They probably need to eat now. See, the other two are nursing."

Aden settled the tiger-striped kitten with its siblings and raced toward the barn door. "Maybe Ray will play with me."

Malinda smiled. "I thought you were tired." Malinda shook her head. Perhaps now that her family had arrived home, Timothy would be distracted and forget all about Dr. McWilliams's visit. She wished she could forget it, too.

Chapter Twenty-Five

Fall marched on toward winter. The magnificent crimson, gold, and orange leaves had trickled from the trees like raindrops from a big, black cloud. Each gust of wind sent a new cascade tumbling to the ground. Before long, naked branches would stretch out and scratch the winter sky.

Malinda hopped from her bed to the throw rug most mornings now to avoid placing her bare feet on the cold wood floor. Most of the canning and preserving had been completed for the season, and an extra-thorough fall cleaning had been under way. Since Sam and Emma had finally been published, their upcoming wedding meant an extra flurry of activity. Several couples had already married, but Sam and Emma would be married later in November. No doubt out-of-town guests would stay with them, so Mamm would want everything in the house to be shipshape.

Half-frozen fingers made getting dressed and pinning up her hair difficult tasks. Malinda wiggled her fingers a few times to erase the stiffness. If she could put on a few more pounds, she might have some insulation from the cold, but lately her appetite had waned even more. Stress wreaked havoc with her sensitive intestines. She'd had no further correspondence from Todd McWilliams or Nurse Trudy, but somewhere deep inside, Malinda knew she hadn't heard the last from them.

Malinda hurried downstairs to help Mamm get breakfast on the table and lunches packed, and to get warm. She cracked one egg after another into the big ceramic bowl and thought of Timothy as she whisked them with salt, pepper, and milk. The mixture hissed when it hit the hot cast-iron skillet coated with bacon grease. She stirred briskly to keep the eggs from sticking.

Timothy had been so patient and understanding. She knew he wanted their relationship to move forward at a faster pace, but he didn't try to rush her. Her heart wanted to follow Timothy's lead with a quickness, but her head continued to apply the brakes. Thankfully, he had not returned to the subject of Todd McWilliams, and she had done her best not to appear distracted or worried. In truth, though, she was both.

The intestinal discomfort she'd been feeling for the past two days blossomed into a sharp pain. She snatched the skillet from the heat and plunked it down on a hot pad lying on the counter. She felt hot and cold at the same time. With a groan, she clutched her midsection and bolted from the room.

"Malinda? Are you all right?" Saloma called after her.

Malinda didn't dare stop to answer. Another flare-up! And she'd taken her medication as prescribed and always chose her foods carefully. Still the ugly monster returned. Unbidden tears coursed down her cheeks. Tears of pain, tears of frustration, tears of hopelessness. *Please, Lord Gott, if You won't take this sickness away, help me bear it. And please don't let this time be as bad as the last one.*

Weak and exhausted, Malinda knew she had to try to remedy her red, puffy eyes before she returned to the kitchen. She splashed cold water on her face over and over and patted her face dry. That was the best she could do. No amount of pinching or rubbing her cheeks would remove her pallor. She wobbled back to the kitchen and tried to paste a pleasant expression on her face.

"Malinda?" Saloma wiped her hands on a dish towel and took a step toward her *dochder*.

"I'll be all right." She grabbed Saloma's hand before it reached her forehead to check for a fever.

"Go lie down, dear. I can handle this." Saloma had, in fact, finished preparing breakfast and had begun filling the lunch boxes.

"I want to keep busy." Malinda shuffled to the counter and tossed shiny, red apples into each box. She filled small plastic bags with homemade peanut butter cookies. Saloma wrapped thick meat-and-cheese sandwiches in wax paper and laid them on top of the other lunch items. At the sound of clomping feet, Malinda carried plates of food to the table. She tried not to inhale too deeply. Smells sometimes triggered nausea, and she didn't want to race from the room again. She didn't set a plate for herself.

"Can't you try to eat something?" That worried frown ran across Saloma's forehead again.

"Maybe later. I'll drink something, though." She had to make herself drink. She couldn't let herself get dehydrated and end up in the hospital.

The day had been longer than long. Malinda had done her best to stay busy and out from under her *mamm*'s watchful eye. She knew Saloma counted each of Malinda's many flights down the hall to the bathroom. Malinda forced down fluids all day but could not coax solid food past her lips. She managed to sit through the evening meal only pretending to eat, sure she wasn't fooling anyone. She felt weaker than a newborn kitten, but refused to complain or shirk her duties.

A tap at the door as she carried her plate to the kitchen

made Malinda want to weep. She prayed the visitor would be someone for her *daed* or one of her *bruders*. She didn't see how she could possibly endure an evening sitting with guests, yet she couldn't be rude and disappear into her room, no matter how much she yearned to do just that.

"Hello, Malinda. How are you feeling?"

Malinda turned from scraping her plate into the scrap bucket to face the owner of that deep voice she knew so well. Sam stood slightly behind Timothy, unable to conceal the sheepish look that had spread across his face. "Hi, Tim. I'm okay."

"Sam mentioned you weren't feeling well at lunchtime today, so . . ."

"Did you take an ad out in the *Budget*, too, Sam?" Malinda plunked the plate on the kitchen counter none too gently and, with fists on her hips, glared at her *bruder*.

"I just mentioned it in passing." Sam attempted to defend himself.

"I'm sorry if I upset you by stopping by, Malinda. I only wanted to make sure you were all right."

Malinda blew out the breath she'd been holding and let her anger ride out on the air. She didn't want to make Tim or Sam feel bad for caring about her. She simply hated being the focus of attention. She hated being a bother to anyone. She hated having a disease that made life miserable. But she had no right taking her frustration out on others and making them miserable as well.

"I'm sorry for snapping at you." Malinda laid a hand on Timothy's arm. "And you, too, Sam. I appreciate your concern, but I don't want to be a bother."

"You are never a bother." Timothy's blue eyes bore into Malinda's. He took a tiny step closer. Sam used the opportunity to slip from the room. He must have asked Mamm to wait to clean up, since no one else entered the kitchen.

"If I cause you concern, then I'm a bother." Malinda

whirled around, not wanting Timothy to glimpse the tears that sprang into her eyes. She reached out to pick up the plate she had been scraping when a hand clamped down, fingers completely encircling her wrist. She gasped and looked over her shoulder.

"*Kumm* outside with me," Timothy urged.

"I-I need to clean up."

"It can wait a few minutes. Please?"

Malinda nodded her head. She grabbed a shawl from the peg near the door and let Timothy lead her down the back steps and away from the house. If he hadn't kept a hand on her arm to steady her, she wasn't sure she'd have had the strength to put one foot in front of the other.

Her breath was coming out in little huffs and puffs by the time Timothy stopped walking halfway between the house and barn. Surely no one would overhear them now, except for any deer that ventured toward the few remaining plants in the garden. As chilly as the evenings had become, frost would soon claim the broccoli, greens, and pumpkins. A little shiver washed over her body, leaving goose bumps in its wake.

"*Ach*, you're cold. I'm sorry, Malinda. I wasn't thinking about how cool the evenings are now. Maybe we should go back inside." He tugged on her arm to lead her back to the house.

"I'll be okay. It was hot in the kitchen anyway." She pulled her arm from Timothy's grasp so he wouldn't feel her trembling when what she really wanted to do was throw herself into his arms and have him reassure her everything would be all right. But Timothy couldn't make that promise.

He cleared his throat. Malinda heard his pensive sigh. He seemed to be grappling with his thoughts. Gently he tilted her chin so she had to look at him in the waning light of dusk. "I have told you before, Malinda. You could never be a burden or a bother. Please don't think of yourself that way."

"Look at me, Timothy. I'm sick. I'm having another flare-up. I never know what will happen. I try so hard to do everything right, but I still get sick." Malinda faced Timothy as if in a showdown, hands curled into fists, fingernails digging into her palms. She barely kept from stomping a foot, more in frustration than in anger.

"I'm guessing you still did all or most of your chores today, ain't so?"

Confused, Malinda's brow wrinkled. "Well, *jah*, but what does . . ."

Timothy held up a hand as if stopping a runaway horse. "Even though you didn't feel well, you weren't—as you seem to think—useless. I'm sure you did a lot."

Malinda considered her day. "I guess I did most of my usual chores, but Timothy, sometimes I feel worse and can't do much more than lie in bed." And run to the bathroom.

"So what if a few chores don't get done? They will be there when you feel better or someone else can pick up the slack."

"That's just it. I don't want someone else to have to do my work or to take care of me."

"Then you don't give someone else the chance to serve the Lord Gott by helping you."

"Huh?"

"Doesn't Gott want us to serve Him and to help others?"

"That's what I've always believed."

"Don't you try to help others?"

"Of course. Whenever I can."

"Maybe it is Gott's will for someone to help you at the times you're feeling poorly. Maybe that someone is unable to serve Gott because you won't allow him or her to help."

"That doesn't make . . ."

Timothy held up his hand again and interrupted before Malinda could complete her sentence. "Before you say that doesn't make sense, think about it. Really think."

Malinda nodded. She allowed Timothy to take her cold hands and rub them between his, a simple gesture that warmed her body and soul.

"When people care about others, they want to help them." Timothy's voice was whisper-soft.

"I can understand that, but I'm sure it gets to be a nuisance after a while. Even the most generous caregivers get tired and aggravated with the disruption in their lives and routines."

"They may get tired, but not tired of helping or caring." Timothy gave her hands a gentle squeeze.

"I-I better go inside." Malinda felt on the verge of tears, and the pain in her gut threatened to cut her in half. She tried to pull her hand away, but Timothy held fast.

"I'll walk with you."

Malinda used every ounce of strength and willpower she possessed to walk upright rather than hunched over in pain.

"You're hurting now, ain't so?"

Malinda nodded.

Timothy slowed his steps and wrapped an arm around Malinda to lend support.

Malinda resisted at first but then acquiesced and leaned into Timothy's strength. *Please, Lord, take this pain away, or at least let me get inside before the situation gets worse and I embarrass myself or Timothy.*

Lamplight spilled out of the windows as they drew near the house. When they reached the back door, Timothy leaned down to whisper, "Think about what I said, Malinda. And remember, I care and I really want to help." His warm breath tickled her ear and raised a new crop of goose bumps. She nearly forgot her pain when Timothy pressed his lips to her forehead in a feathery kiss.

By the next afternoon, Saloma had raced to the nearest phone to call Dr. Nelson. Malinda had crawled from her bed at her usual early hour and had helped get everyone else fed and out the door. Once again, she simply sipped hot herbal tea and skipped solid food. She'd begun to tackle her morning chores, but weakness caused her to drop onto a living room chair. At Saloma's insistence, she returned to her room and curled up in her bed. Tears leaked from her eyes as she prayed Dr. Nelson wouldn't ask her to go to his office or, worse yet, the hospital. "See, Timothy," she whispered to the empty room. "I'm not fit for anything."

In her head, she knew the flare-up wouldn't last forever, but right now she couldn't see any end in sight. She would never be able to manage a household like this. She could barely take care of her own needs. Frustration washed over her, and she allowed herself to wallow in self-pity. *How could I take care of a home and* kinner *like this? How could I cook and clean and garden and do all the other things I'd need to do to run my own home? Will I always have to rely on Mamm to take care of me like a* boppli*?*

Malinda uncurled from the fetal position she'd assumed and sat straight up on her bed. Dizziness assailed her at her quick change in position. She would have to start eating or she would continually grow weaker. She also needed to stop feeling sorry for herself. There were a lot of people much sicker than she was. Some suffered every single day, with no respite from pain. She had to calm down and stop worrying that Todd McWilliams would contact her again. Stress did not help her condition one little bit. It may have even triggered this flare-up.

She closed her eyes and conjured up a picture of the

Wicomico River on a lazy summer Sunday. Sometimes several families would pack buggies with a picnic lunch and head for the river. She inhaled to a count of three and slowly exhaled, imagining her stress floating out with her breath.

Malinda shuffled to the bathroom to splash water on her face. She tucked loose tendrils of hair into place and straightened her clothes. She tried to keep the picture of the river in the forefront of her mind as she made her way to the stairs. With one hand on her midsection and the other grasping the handrail, she cautiously descended the steps.

"I thought you were staying in bed."

Malinda gasped. The hand on the banister flew to her chest to pat her thumping heart.

"You scared me half to death, Mamm. When did you get back?"

"Just now. I thought you were resting."

"I need to be doing something. What did Dr. Nelson say?"

"I wrote down some adjustments to your medicines. He said to try that and the usual remedies you've already tried. He said if you can't eat or drink, you will have to go to the hospital for fluids."

"*Nee*. Not the hospital. I have been drinking. I'm going to try to eat right now."

"What do you feel like trying?" Saloma started for the kitchen.

"I can get it, Mamm. You go ahead with whatever you need to do. You've wasted enough of your day tracking Dr. Nelson down for me."

"I haven't wasted my day, Malinda. And it's no trouble to fix you something to eat. Do you need help getting to the kitchen?"

Malinda bristled at the idea of being considered an invalid, but she told herself Mamm was only concerned and wanted to help. "I can get it, Mamm. Really."

"If you say so. Holler if you need me."

Malinda nodded and slowly made her way to the kitchen. Now to find some food her irritable insides would accept with a minimal amount of protest. She wandered around the kitchen weighing her options. What she really wanted was to go back to bed, as her *mamm* had urged her to do, but she would not give in. She had no desire to wind up in another hospital.

Bread. She should be able to handle a small slice of Mamm's homemade whole wheat bread. If that was accepted by her belligerent gut, she'd try some applesauce or something else light. She at least wanted to have the strength and energy to work on the mending or her quilting.

Chapter Twenty-Six

By the end of the week, Malinda felt more like her normal self. She'd been eating a little more each day, and her strength gradually returned. Her pain had lessened, and she'd taken little walks outside whenever she felt worried or stressed. And time spent talking to Gott among His creation did wonders for the mind, body, and spirit.

The long white envelope she pulled from the mailbox on Friday afternoon nearly sent Malinda into a tailspin. Her breath came in short, quick pants, and her heart pounded with such force she felt sure the earth was shifting beneath her feet. She didn't have to look at the letter twice to know who sent it. She considered tearing it to bits without opening the offensive thing, but she needed to read it to learn of any possible impending propositions or visits. Malinda had been truly glad to help Aenti Mary, but she certainly wished she'd never set foot in Ohio. She should have stayed in Maryland and let someone else tend to her *aenti*.

Malinda tucked the other letters and advertisements under one arm and slid a forefinger beneath the loosened flap of the envelope addressed to her. She withdrew a single sheet of white paper that had been folded in thirds to fit inside the envelope. She sucked in a deep breath before shaking the paper open. The words, written in a neat, bold script, were few and to the point.

> *I've missed you, my angel, and will be back to get you as soon as you give the word. Maybe I'll come anyway. I'm sure I can persuade you to join me.*
>
> *Yours,*
> *TM*

Oooh! How could he write such a thing? She had told him in no uncertain terms she would not even consider returning to Ohio with him. Why was the man so obsessed with her? There were plenty of women right under his own nose at that huge hospital or the nearby university who would be far better suited for him than she was. Could he be that determined to prove a point? Did he find it an irresistible challenge when someone refused to share his opinion and ideas or to blindly follow whatever he demanded? And a demand was what this had all seemed like to Malinda. Or maybe a threat veiled as an invitation.

Malinda shivered, although the day was merely crisp, not cold. Maybe Todd McWilliams was a stalker obsessed with his prey. Maybe she should be afraid instead of angry. She stomped a sneakered foot on the gravel driveway. She would march straight up to her room and write Dr. Todd McWilliams a letter telling him to leave her alone. She'd run right back out so the letter would go out in tomorrow's mail. That should take care of this ridiculous problem once and for all.

Determination provided the energy that allowed Malinda to quicken her pace on her return trip to the house. So much for the peacefulness of nature! She slipped inside the house, grateful her *mamm* was nowhere in sight. She dropped the rest of the mail on the kitchen counter and tiptoed through the house and up the stairs. She wanted to complete her mission while anger fueled her. If fear set in, she might not get the necessary words written.

Malinda entered her room and carefully closed the door so it would latch softly. She needed a few minutes to herself. That's all it would take. She opened the drawer of her nightstand and pulled out a sheet of writing paper, an envelope, and a black ink pen. She knelt on the floor and slid the lamp aside to use the top of the nightstand for a table. With no hesitation, she scrawled her message. There. That should do it. She sat on the floor to read the words she had written.

Dr. McWilliams,

I do NOT plan to move to Ohio as you wish, not now or in the future. My life is in Maryland, where I intend to stay with my family and community. I am grateful for your help when I was in the hospital, but that is all. There is no possibility of any other relationship. I am happy with my life here. Please do not write or visit or otherwise contact me again.

Malinda Stauffer

Short and to the point. She'd made her stand clear, she hoped. The doctor was a smart man. Surely there would be no other interpretation of her words. She didn't want to be rude and write *Leave me alone*, but maybe she should have.

She folded the sheet of paper in half and slid it into the envelope. She licked the gummy edges and pressed the flap closed before she could change her mind or add any other words. She pulled out the doctor's crumpled letter so she could copy his address on her envelope. At least he had written a return address on his envelope. She tossed the crumpled letter and the pen into the drawer before creeping down the stairs to retrieve a stamp.

This time she race-walked down the driveway, adrenaline still pumping. She set the letter inside the mailbox, closed the metal door tightly, and raised the red flag on the side of the box so the mail carrier would be sure to stop tomorrow. She wanted that letter on its way to Ohio with a quickness.

"Malinda, was that you going out twice?" Saloma called from wherever it was in the house she'd busied herself.

Malinda sighed. Nothing ever escaped Mamm's notice. Here she thought she'd been so quiet. "*Jah*, Mamm. It's me." Even if Mamm was deaf and blind, Malinda had no doubt she'd still know exactly what was going on in her house.

"Is everything all right?"

"Fine. Where are you?"

"I'm upstairs cleaning your *bruders*' room."

She must mean the room Roman, Ray, and Aden shared. It's a wonder Mamm didn't waylay her when she was upstairs a few minutes ago.

Malinda climbed the stairs and paused in the doorway of her *bruders*' room. Mamm was on her knees, reaching under the bed for some unidentifiable object. She jerked back with a little yelp. Malinda dashed across the room. "*Ach*, Mamm! What is it? It's nothing alive, I hope."

"I'm not sure. It's something kind of prickly in a box. That *bu* is going to make every last strand of my hair go gray."

"I'll check." Malinda dropped to her knees beside her *mamm*. "At least we don't have any porcupines around here, so it can't be a family of those critters." Malinda felt around under the bed until her fingers found the edge of a fairly large box. Slowly she dragged it out.

"Whew!" Saloma blew out her breath. "Pinecones. At least it's not something I have to chase out with a broom."

Malinda rummaged through the box. There were large,

fat pinecones, long, skinny pinecones, and perfectly formed pinecones shaped like little trees. Even pieces of pinecones and dilapidated pinecones littered the bottom of the box.

"Why in the world is he collecting these?"

"They are kind of pretty, Mamm. The intact ones are, anyway." Malinda picked up a few of the pinecones and turned them over in her hands. Some had sharp points that bit into her fingers. "They are all slightly different, like snowflakes."

"I'm just glad it isn't a box full of worms or spiders or something equally as bad." Saloma shuddered.

"He probably shoved them under the bed so Ray and Roman wouldn't squash them with their big feet. Do you want me to push the box back under, Mamm?"

"I think I'll tell him to keep his collection in the barn. When these things rot and fall apart, we'll have a big mess."

"I think I felt another box under there." Malinda flattened herself on the floor to stretch her arm out as far as possible. With a little grunt, she grasped the edge of the box and slid it toward her. Something inside the box rolled and clacked against something else.

"It sounds like marbles," Saloma said.

Malinda slithered out from her position halfway under the bed. "Rocks." She sat up and rummaged through the box, which was filled with every kind of rock imaginable. "Do you want these in the barn, too?"

"They won't make a mess. We'll leave some of his treasures inside."

"I'll take the pinecones downstairs for you." Malinda scooted the box of rocks back under the bed.

"*Danki*, dear. Why were you outside twice?"

"I've been trying to go for walks lately, you know."

"Two times so close together?"

"I went back the second time to mail a letter." Malinda hoped a simple explanation would satisfy her *mamm*.

"Did you get a new circle letter?"

So much for wishful thinking. "*Nee*. The letter was to someone I met in Ohio."

"It's *gut* you made some new *freinden* there."

This person definitely did not fit into that category. Should she say as much to Mamm, or keep silent and let the matter drop? Malinda chose the latter. She pushed to her feet, brushed off her dress, and reached for the box of pinecones.

"You don't have to take them all the way to the barn," Saloma said. "You can leave them by the back door, and Aden can tote them out later."

"I don't mind. That way I can peek at the new kittens."

"You're as bad as Aden as far as animals are concerned."

"I know. Those kittens are so adorable, though. Can we keep them? There are only four." Malinda hated the thought of separating them and giving them away.

"Four more cats!"

"They're so little."

"They won't stay little for long."

"They'll probably grow up to be *gut* mousers like their *mamm*."

"We'll have to see what your *daed* says."

At least Mamm hadn't refused outright. She and Aden together could probably convince Daed to let the kittens stay. Malinda shuffled toward the hallway with the box of pinecones. She had successfully drawn the conversation away from the letter. Maybe during supper preparations she could get Mamm talking about Sam's upcoming wedding.

Chapter Twenty-Seven

Winter was definitely only a whisper away. Malinda gazed around the Swareys' big barn, set up to hold all of Emma's and Sam's wedding guests. She wouldn't be surprised to see snowflakes flying through the frosty air by Thanksgiving next week. The joy lighting Emma's face almost brought tears to Malinda's eyes. To know such happiness must be truly amazing.

Emma and Sam had exchanged vows in strong, confident voices near the end of the three-hour service. The Swareys had relatives visiting from three states. All the neighbors and relatives practically filled the barn to overflowing. With so many bodies in close proximity, along with her duties as a table server, Malinda should be wiping perspiration from her brow. Instead she rubbed her arms in an attempt to chase the chill away as she checked the laden food tables. If the bagginess of her blue dress served as any indication, her latest flare-up had left her another few pounds lighter. If she lost any more weight, Atlee's prediction may very well prove accurate. She might blow clear into Charles County with a fair-sized puff of wind.

"Are you okay?" Phoebe paused in her duties as a server to whisper to Malinda.

"I'm fine. Don't worry about me. I'm just a little chilly."

"You're chilly, and I could use a breath of fresh air."

"I think being so scrawny makes me cold. Atlee says I'm going to dry up and blow away." Malinda chuckled.

"That Atlee! Don't you pay any attention to that rascal! You look just fine. And we definitely won't let you blow away. There's one person here who can't take his eyes off of you. He will definitely not let you get away."

"Go on with you." Malinda playfully slapped Phoebe's arm. Now she felt warm. Her face must be glowing.

Phoebe leaned closer and whispered, "I hope things work out between you and Timothy. You'll give him a chance, won't you?"

Malinda shrugged.

"Don't let your fears push him away, Malinda. He's a great guy."

Malinda nodded. "I'd better refill some dishes. There are a lot of people here with healthy appetites." Malinda sped off before Phoebe could sing any more of Tim's praises. She knew Phoebe cared and wanted Malinda to know the same happiness she'd found with Ben Miller, but Phoebe didn't have health concerns weighing her down. A little tingle racing up her spine forced her to glance around until her eyes connected with sky blue eyes that had been observing her every move.

Tim smiled when Malinda's chocolate eyes connected with his own. He wondered what Phoebe had been saying to Malinda. Too bad he hadn't been close enough to hear. He saw Malinda's face flush and the little punch she gave Phoebe. He wished with all his heart Phoebe, or someone, would talk some sense into Malinda. Someone needed to help her see that her illness didn't define her, and it did not make her unattractive or undesirable. So far, he had not been successful in getting through to her.

Timothy winked at Malinda and smiled more broadly when her lovely face flushed an even brighter shade of red. She quickly broke eye contact and scurried about her duties. Tim felt the smile slide from his face. His best *freind* had gotten married today. Would he and Malinda ever get married? He knew his own feelings, but sometimes he wasn't so sure of Malinda's. His gaze swung to the newlyweds, seated at the *eck*. Their special table had been set up in the corner. Their heads were tilted toward each other, and huge smiles lit their faces. Would he ever be seated at such a table and smiling down at his bride? Timothy sighed.

"Mighty deep thoughts on a festive occasion." A jab to the ribs accompanied the comment.

"Hey, Atlee. I'm just taking a little break." Tim and Atlee were both table servers, too. "It's hard to believe Sam got married."

"So when are you getting married?" Atlee nodded in the direction Malinda had just taken.

"When are *you* getting married?" Tim turned the tables on Sam's younger *bruder*.

"Me? I'm not ready for that. I'm not even courting anyone."

"That could change in a hurry. I'm sure you've been looking." Timothy couldn't resist teasing the fellow who was always so quick to tease everyone else.

"Looking, maybe. Acting, not at all."

"I've seen a few girls staring in your direction."

"*Jah?* Who?" Atlee's eyes roved the crowd.

"I thought you weren't interested."

"Interested, but not ready to settle down. You, on the

other hand, are the same age as Sam. From the looks you give my *schweschder* and your visits to our house, I'd say you were ready to tie the knot yourself. Right?"

"Both people have to be ready."

"She'll be ready soon, if she isn't now." Atlee folded his arms across his chest and nodded knowingly.

"How can you be so sure?"

"I know my *schweschder*."

"I'm not so sure, Atlee." Timothy frowned. He thought he knew Malinda pretty well after all the years he'd hung around the Stauffer house. He'd watched her grow from a spindly little girl to a lovely young woman. Sometimes he felt secure in the knowledge that she cared for him. Other times she pulled away and dashed his hopes. "Whenever she has any kind of setback, she pulls inside her shell like a scared box turtle and shuts me out."

"Malinda has always been determined. You might not remember because she was behind us in school, but she always wanted to be perfect. She had to spell all her words correctly. She had to add all her sums right and have the neatest handwriting. She had to be the best she could be. Well, she can't control her illness. She can't make everything all right when she has a flare-up, no matter how hard she tries. So it's been hard on her physically, for sure, but it's also hard up here." Atlee tapped the side of his head. "She has to accept she is powerless over this disease."

"That makes sense. You're pretty smart after all, Atlee." Timothy nudged the younger man.

"I'm not just a pretty face."

Timothy chuckled. Atlee could find—or invent—humor for any situation.

"So which girls did you see watching me?"

"We'd better get back to our duties, Atlee."

Tim continued to covertly observe Malinda every chance

he got. She began to look tired as she helped clear the last tables, but he could plainly see the determination etched on her face. Atlee's words had given him much to think about. He could see things a bit more clearly now. Malinda needed to feel in control over this disease by forcing herself to accomplish her usual activities.

For some reason, she seemed to want to fight the illness on her own without accepting help, except possibly from her *mamm*. She wrestled with accepting any limitations, and maybe with accepting Gott's grace to sustain her. He closed his eyes for a moment to offer a brief prayer for the girl he cared for so deeply.

By the time most wedding guests had departed, except for the young unmarried folks, who would sing and socialize, Malinda's weariness had seeped all the way down to her bones. Fatigue rapidly gobbled up the joy she'd experienced all day.

"*Kumm* sit with me."

Malinda leaned into Timothy and let him lead her to a seat. His hand wrapped around her upper arm, giving her the strength to place one foot in front of the other. She silently prayed the exhaustion wouldn't trigger another flare-up. She'd barely recovered from the last one.

"If you're as tired as I am, a rest is long overdue." Tim tugged Malinda down onto the bench beside him.

"It does feel *gut* to sit. It has been a nice day. I'm so happy for Sam and Emma."

"They make a great couple. I wonder who Atlee will end up with."

Malinda's gaze wandered to where her *bruder* was laughing with the fellows around him. She couldn't help but smile. "Atlee is Atlee. There is no other way to describe him." Malinda laughed aloud. "Sometimes I think he'll never grow up and settle down, and sometimes he seems wise beyond his years."

"I'm sure there is someone just right for him."

"I wonder who? She'd have to be awfully tolerant of Atlee's silliness. She'd have to be awfully special."

"You're very close to Atlee, ain't so?"

"All my *bruders* are dear to me. Sam has always been my protector—whether I needed one or not. Atlee has always cheered me up. He can brighten the gloomiest of days."

"Laughter is healing for the body and the soul."

"It certainly is."

Malinda and Timothy sat in companionable silence and watched the other young folks mingle and talk . When Timothy cleared his throat twice, Malinda braced herself. She knew his mannerisms well enough to recognize that the throat clearing meant he had something important to say or something he wasn't sure she would want to hear. She kept still, waiting for Tim to speak his mind.

"Malinda?"

"Hmmm?"

"I don't know if this is the best time, but what about us?"

"What exactly do you mean?" Malinda realized she was hedging. She really didn't want to have this conversation right now.

"I guess I want to know where we stand. Sam and Emma look so happy. Don't you think we can be happy together, too?" Timothy gave Malinda's hand a little squeeze and then kept her hand in his.

Timothy's clasp was strong, but not so tight that it was uncomfortable. Just like Timothy. Strong but gentle. Malinda drew strength from his strength. A blanket of peace and security wrapped itself around her whenever she was with Timothy. At the same time, her heart sang and danced at the sight of him and a tingle shot up her spine at his touch, like it did right now. But she couldn't let him throw his life away on her. What kind of life would it be for him if he was always worried about her health?

"Malinda?"

"Maybe we shouldn't talk about this here." She nodded toward all the young people close by.

"They're all too busy to pay any attention to us." Timothy paused for a few seconds. "How did you feel watching Sam and Emma promise to care for each other?"

How could Malinda explain it? She'd felt happy and sad at the same time. She'd wanted to smile, but tears filled her eyes. She'd pictured herself making the same promises to Tim, but . . . "But neither of them is sick," she blurted.

"Don't let your illness define you, Malinda. You are not your disease. You are a caring, beautiful person who happens to have a medical condition. When I look at you, I don't see a disease. I see you, Malinda Stauffer, a woman I'd like to spend my life with."

Malinda gulped down a sob. Timothy had to be the sweetest man ever. "Wh-what if this illness makes it hard for me to, uh, have *kinner*?" She sniffed hard.

Timothy looked at her with beams of love flashing from his blue eyes. "No couple knows if the Lord will bless them with *kinner*. If He does, that's great. If He doesn't, they have each other to love and cherish. Sam and Emma are healthy and happy. I pray they stay that way, but they don't know if illness will strike or if Gott will give them *kinner*. They love each other and want to share their lives—no matter what."

No matter what. Could Timothy love her no matter what? No matter if she had pain and weakness that prevented her from doing her daily chores? No matter if he had to pick up some of the slack after putting in a hard day's work of his own? No matter if her condition worsened and she had to be hospitalized or have surgery? No matter if her illness caused huge medical bills? No matter if she couldn't give him a houseful of little ones?

Malinda choked back a sob. She loved *kinner* and very much wanted to cuddle her own *bopplin* in her arms. The gentle pressure of Timothy's hand squeezing hers halted her journey down that road of depressing thoughts. She squeezed his hand back.

"You know I care for you, Malinda, and have cared for a long time. I'm not going anywhere. I can wait for you to be ready, as long as it's me you're ready for." Timothy smiled down at her.

"If I'm going to be ready for anyone, it will be for you." She wished she could say the words he wanted to hear, but she couldn't. Not yet. She had some issues to resolve. She had to see if she would get well or could stay in remission or could accept that she'd do neither. *Please, Gott, heal me of this disease. I want to live a normal life and be able to do the things a* fraa *and* mamm *would need to do each day. You said if we ask, You will answer. I'm asking—again.*

Even though it felt so right to be with Tim, she couldn't give him false hope. She looked across the room at Phoebe Yoder and Ben Miller. They gazed at each other so tenderly. Phoebe had overcome obstacles and allowed Ben into her life. Maybe, just maybe, Malinda would be as fortunate.

Timothy gently nudged Malinda and nodded in the opposite direction from where Malinda had been staring. There stood Atlee, talking and laughing with several other young men. He wasn't with a girl at all! "He didn't even pair up with anyone!"

"Maybe he couldn't decide which girl to approach."

"Or maybe they all turned him down if he acted silly. I

should get Daed to have a talk with him. At the rate he's going, he'll never settle down and get married."

"I wouldn't worry about Atlee."

"Why? Did he say something to you? Did he tell you someone he's interested in? Tell me, Tim." Malinda squeezed Tim's hand a little harder.

"Now you know we fellows don't discuss such things like you girls do."

"How do you know we girls share such things if you all don't do the same?"

Timothy shook his head. "I'm trying to make sense of that."

"You're trying to avoid my questions. You know perfectly well what I mean."

Timothy chuckled. "Even if Atlee did tell me anything—and I'm not saying he did—I couldn't betray a confidence."

"He did tell you something!" Malinda fought to keep her voice low.

"I didn't say that. I said 'if.'"

"Oooh!" Malinda pulled her hand from Timothy's, crossed her arms over her chest, and pretended to pout.

Tim laughed. "You sure look pretty when you're pouting with your bottom lip poked out. I imagine as a little girl you were easily able to get your way with that pout."

"Don't change the subject, Timothy Brenneman."

Tim tugged at the arm closest to him and captured Malinda's hand again. "Your *bruder* did not reveal any secret to me, but I did get the impression he is more serious about finding someone than he lets on."

"Well, that's *gut* to hear. It's about time. He's twenty-one, for Pete's sake."

"Practically ancient!"

Malinda elbowed Timothy. "And you like to tease almost as much as Atlee does."

"Maybe. But I am ready to settle down with a special someone, and I know who that special someone is."

Malinda's cheeks grew feverishly warm. She truly cared for Tim, but she didn't want to delve into that discussion again. "Let's grab a snack!"

Chapter Twenty-Eight

Malinda had barely caught her breath after Sam's wedding when it was time to make Thanksgiving preparations. She had tried to take it a bit easier for a few days to ward off another flare-up. Sometimes just a little extra stress or a little change in eating or sleeping habits sent her into a relapse. She'd been careful to follow the diet that usually worked for her and had tried to get extra rest. Now she felt up to the challenge of baking pies and treats to serve when family and neighbors gathered.

Malinda counted her blessings often. Despite her disappointment at her unanswered prayers for healing, she was thankful she'd come through the last flare-up and had been feeling stronger. She gave thanks for her loving, supportive family and *freinden* and for Timothy. He'd been visiting regularly, but as promised, he hadn't pushed her to make any decisions. She sometimes feared his patience would eventually wear thin and he would give up on her, but she still didn't want to tie him to a sickly *fraa*.

It would be best to get her hands busy and trust her mind to follow. She didn't need to dwell on what she couldn't have. Yet, whenever she saw Sam and Emma together, she could hardly bear the longing to know such joy herself.

"Apple pies first, Mamm?" Something about baking soothed her. The spicy scents of cinnamon and apples lifted her spirits. "I love to smell apple pies baking. It's the perfect holiday fragrance."

"Apple pies will be fine, Dochder."

"This is the best time of year. The air outside is so crisp and clean, with just a hint of wood smoke. The kitchen is always cozy and smelling of pies and pastries."

"This always was your favorite time. You've helped me bake Thanksgiving pies and Christmas cookies ever since you were able to stand on a chair and stir the ingredients. I used to put my hand over yours to help you mix the dough when it became too stiff for you to stir."

"I remember." Malinda smiled at all the happy memories of working in the kitchen beside her *mamm*. She'd probably continue the traditions with Mamm for the remainder of her life.

"Someday you'll be stirring up ingredients with your own little girl." Saloma smiled as if picturing the scene.

A plume of flour fanned out around Malinda as she set the canister on the table harder than she'd intended. *Not likely,* she wanted to say, but she held that thought. She didn't want to spoil the day with a lecture from Mamm about her gloomy outlook.

Malinda gradually relaxed as she rolled out dough for pies. It helped that Mamm had moved on to a new topic of discussion. She knew Mamm meant well and only wanted to see her happy, but the lectures grew tiresome. "Do you think we'll have snow for Christmas this year?"

"It's hard to tell. We have had more snow than usual the last few years. Weather here is quite unpredictable."

"I don't want a blizzard or a foot of snow, but a little snow at Christmas is always so pretty." Malinda bit her lip as she crisscrossed strips of dough over the apple pie filling. She and Mamm would bake as much as possible today.

They'd have tomorrow to prepare other food and to clean for Thanksgiving the following day. Sam and Emma would be there for dinner, and most likely other folks would drop in later in the day, so they would need plenty of food to serve.

Malinda and Saloma set aside their last pies to cool just in time to ladle hearty stew into bowls and cut thick slices of wheat bread for supper. Malinda still missed having Sam at the table with them but knew he was happy with Emma. Roman and Ray talked almost nonstop throughout the meal. Every now and then, Aden butted in to make his presence known. Malinda smiled at Aden. Her youngest *bruder* held a special place in her heart. He was so sensitive and kind to all people and animals.

When Atlee cleared his throat, Malinda cut her eyes over to him. "Before I forget"—he looked straight at Malinda—"that fancy Dr. McWilliams left a message at the cheese factory. He said he wasn't sure if he'd be able to reach you by phone, but somehow he found out about the factory. We don't usually get calls, so that was a little strange. Anyway, he wants you to call him, Malinda."

Malinda's spoon clattered to her bowl, ricocheted off the edge, and bounced to the floor, splashing stew onto the tablecloth and floor. She sucked in a sharp breath.

"I'll get your spoon for you." Aden shook the whole table as he scrambled off his chair and crawled around between seven pairs of feet.

"Here's his number." Atlee pulled a scrap of paper from his pocket and slid it across the table to Malinda.

Shocked by the doctor's brazenness, Malinda stared at the wrinkled paper. Feeling all eyes on her, she slowly reached across the table and snagged the message. She crumpled the paper in her hand without looking at it. "*Danki*," she whispered to Aden, who produced the wayward spoon and laid it beside her bowl.

"You won't be able to read it if you keep crinkling it."

Roman shoved a chunk of bread into his mouth and chomped. "Atlee's handwriting is bad enough without all the wrinkles." He swallowed, but coughed when Atlee elbowed him.

"Huh?" Malinda looked down at her hand. She hadn't been aware that she had balled the paper up into a tight little wad.

"You can go call him tomorrow." Mamm dabbed at her mouth with a napkin.

"That's okay. We have a lot to do tomorrow."

"You can surely take a few minutes to return a phone call." Daed gave her a stern look.

"He was just here. He knows I'm fine. I don't think there is a need to contact him. Besides, I have Dr. Nelson to take care of me when I need it."

"If he took the time to call, you should be polite and return the call." Daed's tone left no room for argument.

If only he knew what Dr. Todd McWilliams was really up to, he'd probably jump up from the table and seek a phone right now to call the man himself. And he probably wouldn't be very polite about it, either! Malinda kept silent but nodded in acquiescence. Since Dr. McWilliams obviously didn't comprehend or accept her written request to leave her alone, maybe she could make him understand over the phone. At any rate, she wanted to head off any notion he might have to make another visit.

Malinda swallowed her sigh. Here she'd been looking forward to the holidays and feeling well despite the flurry of activity. Now that fist of fear punched her in the stomach. Mamm's tasty stew churned. Malinda grabbed her glass and chugged down a huge gulp of water, hoping it would wash the stew back down where it belonged. No more supper for her! Would this meal ever end? Would the nightmare with Todd McWilliams ever end?

* * *

Malinda ignored the cold seeping into her bones a short while later as she ran to the barn, following the zigzagging beam of her flashlight. She needed to calm herself before attempting to go to bed. She slipped into the barn and stole over to the far corner, where the cat was snuggling with her kittens. Malinda dropped to her knees in the straw and crooned to the kittens. She stroked the protective *mamm* first and then each of the kittens. Carefully she lifted the tiny tortoiseshell kitten and nuzzled it with her chin.

"You're such a pretty kitty with your speckled fur and little orange patch on your foot. I need to think of a special name for you. I hope Daed will let me keep you."

"I'm sure he will."

Malinda stifled a scream and juggled the kitten to keep from dropping it when she jumped in fear. She cuddled the kitten close as her eyes roamed the shadows in the barn. Each one loomed unnaturally large in the thin beam of the flashlight. One shadow detached itself from the others and stepped forward.

"I didn't mean to scare you."

"A-Atlee?"

"*Jah*."

"What are you doing out here?"

"I saw you sneaking toward the door and figured you were headed for the kittens."

"I wasn't sneaking—exactly. Why did you follow me?" Malinda had been accustomed to Sam championing her causes and listening to her woes. She didn't think Atlee would be interested.

"Why do I get the feeling something isn't quite right?"

Maybe Atlee was more perceptive than she gave him

credit for. Maybe he really had grown up. Still she kept silent.

"So?"

"So?" she echoed.

"So tell me what's wrong."

"Can't I visit the kittens without there being something wrong?"

"Sure, but late at night when everyone is ready to go to bed?"

"Did Mamm or Daed see me leave the house? Do they know you followed me?"

"*Nee* to both. They think you headed for the stairs, not the door. And they're used to me wandering about before I go to bed."

"I'm just trying to clear my head after a long day. Seeing the kittens calms me."

"What are you clearing from your head?"

"Just because I don't go out to a job doesn't mean I don't work hard all day!"

"Whoa! Don't get all defensive. I know you and Mamm work hard taking care of all of us." Atlee reached down to pick up a mewing black-and-white kitten, which fit in the palm of his big, rough hand. He stroked the kitten with his free hand. "Does Dr. McWilliams have something to do with the troubles you need to clear from your mind?"

"Why would he?" Malinda tried hard not to squirm. At least the flashlight cast too little light for Atlee to observe any expressions on her face. She'd always been told her face gave her away. That certainly made it hard to have any secrets.

"Your reaction at the table makes me think there's some sort of problem."

"All I said was I didn't see a need to call the man. He took care of me in Ohio. I'm in Maryland now and plan to stay here. I trust Dr. Nelson to take care of me when I need help." Malinda's voice rose as she spoke. She continued to stroke the fuzzy little kitten.

"That makes sense. Why did you wad up the paper?"

"I didn't plan to call, so why keep the paper?" Malinda leaned over to replace the kitten with the others so it could nurse. "I need to get inside." She pushed herself to a standing position.

"Wait!" Atlee returned the kitten he was holding and snagged Malinda's arm. "Tell me what's wrong, Malinda. I'd like to help."

Could Atlee help? "I already told—"

"I heard what you said, but tell me what's really going on."

"Nothing is 'going on,' Atlee! How could you think such a thing?"

"I didn't mean anything like, uh, like what you're thinking. I just sense something is not right here. You seem, I don't know, afraid or upset."

"I-I'm not . . ." To her horror, Malinda burst into tears. Just before she dropped the flashlight, she caught the look of surprise on Atlee's face. She stooped down and fumbled around for the flashlight so she could escape, but Atlee pulled her into his arms and patted her back. With Sam married and gone, Atlee must feel compelled to take on the protective role Sam had always played. It took Malinda a moment to relax against her *bruder*.

"Shhh." Atlee patted her back. "Let me help you, if I can. That's what big *bruders* are for."

Malinda sniffed and dragged in a ragged breath. "D-Dr. McWilliams wants me to move to Ohio," she whispered against Atlee's broad chest.

"Does he want you to be part of some kind of study?"

"*N-nee*." Malinda sniffed again.

"Does he think you need some kind of medical treatment you can't get here?"

"*Nee*. Lots of people have Crohn's disease. My case isn't

special, except . . ." Malinda wasn't sure she should tell Atlee the whole ugly story. Would he run to Daed? She didn't want a big fuss. The situation was stressful enough as it was.

"Except?" Atlee gave Malinda a little shake.

"Except t-to him."

"Do you mean personally, not medically?"

"*Jah*." More tears leaked from her eyes. "I've told him over and over that I have no intention of going to Ohio. I thanked him for taking care of me in the hospital, but that was it."

"That's the real reason he came here? To get you to go back to Ohio with him?"

"I believe he really had a conference in Baltimore, but that is why he came here."

"And you . . ."

"I told him then and in a letter that I was not interested and to leave me alone."

"He's written letters, too?"

"One telling me he would try to visit. I didn't have enough time to reply to that one. The other letter came recently. I answered right away. Maybe I wasn't forceful enough."

"I can be forceful. Give me that paper. I will call the man. Who does he think he is that he doesn't have to accept *nee* for an answer?"

"I-I'll call him, Atlee. I appreciate your concern."

"Concern? I'm furious. He can't treat you that way. You *kumm* to the cheese factory tomorrow. We'll place that call together. Okay?"

"Okay. Atlee, uh, Mamm and Daed don't know about this."

"Why haven't you told them?"

"I thought I could handle things. I am an adult, you know. I had no idea Dr. McWilliams would be so persistent. He most likely isn't used to being rebuffed. The nurses sure seemed interested in him, especially . . ." Malinda stopped. No use getting into that.

"Especially?"

"One nurse seemed possessive of him. She, uh, wrote me a note, too."

"*Kumm*." Atlee wrapped a hand around her upper arm and led her to a hay bale. "Sit. I think you'd better start this story over again from the beginning. Then we'll decide what to tell Mamm and Daed."

Chapter Twenty-Nine

Malinda had planned to head to the cheese factory early in the morning to make her phone call with Atlee hovering nearby, but the morning chores and baking ate up the hours. Before she knew it, she was setting the table for the midday meal. She didn't feel too upset delaying the dreaded call. If she could, she'd avoid making the call altogether, but she certainly didn't want Dr. McWilliams showing up here again to stir up trouble. She prayed this phone call would be the last contact she ever had with the man.

"Have you made your phone call yet, Dochder?" Rufus asked as soon as he raised his head after the silent prayer.

"I got busy and lost track of time this morning. I'm going right after I clean up here."

"See that you do."

"I can clean up so you can go as soon as you are finished eating."

"*Danki*, Mamm." Once again, Malinda's appetite fled, and that iron fist of dread punched her in the stomach. Now she wished she had made time this morning to place that call. Then it would already be over with.

As promised, Malinda hitched Chestnut to the gray buggy as soon as she'd removed her plate from the table.

Mamm had frowned at the food shoveled into little mounds around the perimeter of the white plate, but she made no comment. At her raised eyebrows, Malinda gave a slight shrug and headed for the scrap container. At least she hadn't piled her plate too full, so she didn't have a huge amount of food to discard. Nothing went to waste, anyway. Table scraps either went to the animals or the compost pile.

The late November air had a definite bite that caused Malinda to shiver whenever a breeze blew. She stopped at the end of the driveway and jumped out to pull the mail from the big metal mailbox. She quickly closed herself back in the buggy and shook the reins to get Chestnut trotting at a brisk pace. Dark gray clouds swirled across a blue backdrop, foretelling an upcoming change in the weather pattern. Most of the oak, maple, gum, and elm trees had lost their colorful foliage. Spotty clumps of withered brown leaves clung to branches here and there. Fuzzy-looking loblolly pines, white pines, and fragrant cedar trees danced in the wind.

Malinda pulled the fleecy blanket across her lap, grateful for its warmth. She slowed Chestnut to make the turn onto the narrow side road leading to the cheese factory. She rehearsed possible dialogues so she'd be prepared when Atlee handed her the phone. She only had a few minutes left to plan her strategy. When she plunged one hand into the pocket of her heavy black cloak to feel for the crumpled slip of paper, the stack of mail slid off the seat and onto the floor. Familiar handwriting peeked out at her from the letters and junk mail littering the floor. All her planned conversations deserted her. Her pounding heart roared in her ears, drowning out even the horse's clip-clopping on the blacktopped road.

Chestnut found his own way to the cheese factory without any guidance from the human sitting trancelike inside the buggy. An irrational fear washed over Malinda. She warily regarded the white envelope with black curlicues as if it was a copperhead poised to attack. She'd rather face a copperhead. She could take a rake to it and destroy it. Nothing seemed to obliterate the nightmare she found herself in. If only she hadn't gone to Ohio, none of this would have ever happened.

The buggy jerked to a stop when Chestnut decided they had reached their destination. Malinda looked up to discover the horse had stopped close to the hitching post. Automobiles occupied nearly every parking spot. People must be planning cheese dishes for their Thanksgiving meals. Atlee might be too busy to add his two cents to her phone call. That might be a *gut* thing. Malinda reached down to scoop up the scattered mail and set the stack on the seat beside her, all except for the one letter addressed to her.

Malinda tore open the envelope and pulled out the single sheet of paper. She may as well read the letter before making her call. There was no polite greeting at the top. The writer plunged right in with the content.

I thought I warned you to stay away from Dr. McWilliams. How hard is it to understand you are not his kind? I know you people are backward, but are you really that dense? If you think he would ever really care about you, you are more delusional than I thought. Surely there is one of your own people you could set your sights on. I really don't want to have to come there to make this clear to you. Stay away from Todd McWilliams.

As before, this note was unsigned, but Malinda had no doubt whatsoever who the author was. How could she make it clear to Nurse Trudy that she had no interest in Todd McWilliams? Malinda stuffed the letter in her pocket.

Atlee would be even more furious when he read the newest correspondence.

Malinda hopped out of the buggy, looped the reins around the rail, and scurried toward the building. She held on to her black bonnet, since the wind threatened to snatch it off her head and send it soaring through the air. The heavy wooden door caught Malinda's heel as a gust of air slammed it closed behind her. She yelped and jumped aside, thankful that customers and workers were too preoccupied to notice her embarrassing entrance. She kept to the back of the store and scanned the faces in search of Atlee.

"Looking for someone?"

"Atlee! You scared me." Malinda patted her pounding chest. "I thought you'd be too busy . . ."

"I'm never too busy for my little *schweschder*, especially when she has something important to take care of."

"It looks like you don't have time right now. I can wait."

"No use putting off until later what you can do now, ain't so?"

Malinda gulped. She'd like to put this particular task off forever. "It's pretty noisy in here and busy up by the counter where the phone is."

"I'll go find a cell phone, or we can go back to the office."

"Won't there be too many people around?"

"I think all employees are out here in the shop or in the processing area. Don't you want to get this over with?"

"I don't want to do it at all."

"I know. Do you have the number?"

Malinda reached into her pocket. The folded letter she'd just received flew out of her pocket and landed on Atlee's foot.

"What's this?" He bent to retrieve the letter before Malinda could snatch it away.

"Is this another letter from him?"

"Not from him."

"Then who?" Without asking permission, Atlee yanked the letter from the envelope and scanned the words. "It isn't signed. Do you know who wrote it?"

"Probably Trudy."

"The nurse? She's threatening you? Let's go." Atlee tugged at Malinda's arm. "The *gut* doctor will have to get things straight with Nurse Trudy, or we'll have to make more than one call."

Malinda hung her head. How did this horrible situation keep getting worse?

"What's wrong?"

"I'm so ashamed. This should not be happening."

"You did nothing wrong, so you have no reason to feel ashamed. These people"—Atlee shook the paper so hard he stirred up a breeze—"are the ones with a problem. We need to straighten this mess out right now."

Malinda prayed the problem would be solved as easily as Atlee thought. He hadn't heard Dr. McWilliams's tone or seen his smug self-assurance. She might have to let Atlee talk to the man if she couldn't convince him once and for all to leave her alone. She allowed Atlee to lead her toward the office. Why did she feel like a naughty scholar about to be reprimanded by the teacher?

Atlee pushed the squeaky door closed after nudging Malinda into the office. He guided her to the desk and pulled out the chair for her to sit. He pressed a little button on the phone with the word "speaker" printed below it.

"What does that do?"

"It puts the call on speaker so I can hear the conversation, too."

"Won't everyone else around be able to hear it?"

"We're the only ones here."

"But someone could walk in, ain't so?"

"I guess, but I want to hear what this man has to say. I'll have to stand close, then."

"You know, Atlee, he's probably not going to answer. He's a busy person and is most likely seeing patients or doing something important at the hospital. I'll probably have to leave a message. *Ach*, I don't know what to say!"

"Dial!" Atlee handed her the phone.

Malinda laid the crumpled scrap of paper on the desk and squinted at the numbers through the tears that suddenly clouded her vision. Her fingers trembled so violently she could hardly push the correct buttons.

"Here." Atlee pulled the phone from her hand. "I'll dial. We want to reach the right person." He punched in the numbers. "It's ringing." Atlee thrust the phone back into Malinda's hand and leaned close. Only the phone kept their heads from slamming together.

"I don't think he's going to answer." Malinda sucked in a sharp breath. "D-Dr. McWilliams?" She cleared her throat and tried again. "Is this Dr. Todd McWilliams?"

"Malinda? Wow! Is this really my little Malinda from Southern Maryland? I didn't dare hope you'd call me."

"I-I'm not your little Malinda." She knew she had spoken too softly when Atlee nudged her.

"What did you say, dear?"

That did it! One simple little word was enough to raise her ire. "I said I am not your Malinda. I am calling to ask, *nee*, to tell you to stop calling me and writing to me."

"Aw, come on, Malinda. How about if I take a little road trip down that way over the weekend? I won't interrupt your family's Thanksgiving. I'll come on Saturday. We can go someplace and talk . . ."

He talked so fast that Malinda had no choice other than be rude and interrupt. "Didn't you hear me? I've told you over and over I am not interested in a relationship with you.

I'm Amish and plan to stay Amish. I live in Maryland and plan to stay in Maryland." Malinda paused to inhale.

"People's plans change all the time, Malinda dear. Even if you moved to Ohio, you could visit your family often."

"You are not listening." Malinda stomped her foot beneath the desk and fought tears of frustration. She felt Atlee's agitation beside her. She expected him to snatch the phone away from her at any moment. "Dr. McWilliams . . ."

"Todd. I've told you over and over to call me Todd."

"And I've told you over and over to give up on me. I am not going to change my mind."

"I can be pretty persuasive."

Malinda bit her trembling lower lip. How did she get through to someone with such a one-track mind? "All the persuasion in the world won't change my mind."

"I can take care of you when you get sick. I'll know what to do."

"Dr. Nelson is perfectly capable of taking care of me."

"But I'm a specialist."

And not used to not getting your way. She silently considered another tactic.

"We'll talk on Saturday."

"*Nee*!"

"Dr. McWilliams, Malinda has very politely explained her position," Atlee broke in.

"Who's there with you, Malinda?"

"This is Malinda's *bruder*. She has asked you not to contact her anymore. No phone calls. No visits. No letters. And you can tell Nurse Trudy the same thing."

"Nurse Trudy? What on earth does Trudy have to do with any of this?"

"She's been writing my *schweschder* threatening notes."

"I think she'd be happy for your attention," Malinda interrupted. "She is far more suitable for you than I am.

My *bruder* is right. I do not wish to have any further contact with you or Trudy. Please."

Silence on the other end surprised Malinda. Could she and Atlee finally have gotten through to the man?

"Oops! Sorry!" A gangly young employee stuck his head in the door and instantly retreated, clicking the door shut again.

Great! Malinda wondered how much he might have overheard. She didn't relish being the weekly topic on the grapevine.

"Is that your final word?" Todd said, finally breaking the silence.

Malinda jumped. She'd thought they'd been disconnected or that the doctor had hung up. "Absolutely. I will not change my mind. Ever."

"I see." A soft click followed those two words. This time he did hang up.

"Do you think he really does see?" Malinda looked into Atlee's green eyes.

"I hope so. Should we place a call to the nurse now?"

"I don't know a number for her."

"We could call her later at the hospital if we need to. You still have your papers from there, don't you?"

"*Jah*, but let's pray we won't need to do that."

Chapter Thirty

Thanksgiving passed in a blur of activity. Malinda had stayed busy from before sunup until just past sundown. She peeled, chopped, stirred, or served food most of the day when she wasn't washing or drying dishes, wiping the table, or scrubbing kitchen counters. There were times—and this was one of them—when being the only girl in the family was a definite disadvantage. Of course, Emma helped after she and Sam arrived, but most of the preparation for the huge meal had already been completed by that time.

Malinda had been ever so grateful to sink onto her chair at the big, heavily laden oak table. She'd been almost too tired to actually eat, but she did manage to get down a few bites of roasted turkey, mashed potatoes, and green beans. She made sure she avoided gravy, butter, stuffing, and anything else she feared could possibly trigger a flare-up.

Even though the morning had been stressful, it wasn't a bad kind of stressful. She'd enjoyed working alongside Mamm in the kitchen. Staying so busy kept her mind off of what caused real, damaging stress. Whenever the slightest thought of Todd McWilliams tried to sneak into her mind, she quickly banished it. So far, Atlee had kept quiet about their phone conversation with the man, and she certainly hadn't mentioned it.

It was only as slices of pumpkin and apple pie were passed around that Daed suddenly remembered their supper conversation from Tuesday evening. "Did you ever make that phone call? I forgot to check yesterday."

All plate scraping and chewing ceased as eight pairs of eyes flew to Malinda's face. "*Jah*, Daed. It's all taken care of." *Please let that be true, Lord.*

"*Gut*." Rufus forked a big bite of pie into his mouth, and everyone else resumed eating as well.

Whew! Daed didn't appear to be interested in pursuing the topic any further. Malinda hoped the nightmare Todd McWilliams had caused had ended. She returned the smile Atlee shot her from across the table and listened to the various conversations humming about her.

By the time the kitchen had been cleaned yet again and evening devotions were finished, Malinda wanted nothing more than to retreat to her waiting bed. She didn't even have the strength to sit beside the stove and knit. She only wanted to sleep and sleep some more. Tomorrow would be another busy day of household chores, and then she'd have a weekend of jumping at every sound to get through.

Midafternoon Saturday, Malinda swept crinkly brown leaves off the front porch with vigorous flicks of the straw broom. Although a breath of fresh air brought relief from the stuffy kitchen, the wind had more of a bite than a nip. If the wind kept up, sweeping leaves would be a losing battle. If Mamm sensed her jumpiness, it would only be a matter of time before questions flew. Malinda breathed deeply, taking in the smoky smell from the belching chimney. There was something comforting about the scent of wood smoke. She exhaled slowly, imagining her tension and fear flowing out with her breath.

The crunch of tires—automobile tires, not buggy tires—on the gravel driveway brought Malinda's fears back full force. She relaxed only a little when she determined the car was silver rather than red. A successful *Englisch* doctor may have more than one vehicle, though. She fought the urge to run inside and slam the door behind her. The car sped up the driveway. Malinda inched to the opposite side of the porch. Maybe she would be out of the visitor's line of vision. She glanced down. Purple dress pressed against a white house. Not exactly inconspicuous.

The silver car screeched to a stop. A woman emerged before the engine even stopped thrumming, a woman with short, curly, blonde hair. Malinda tried to shrink back into the shadows.

"Malinda Stauffer, is that you?"

So much for hiding. Malinda stepped out into the sunlight. "*Jah*." She forced her feet to carry her forward, all the while praying she could get the woman to leave before Mamm realized they had a visitor. "Wh-what are you doing here?" She cringed at her lack of manners. Guests were always treated with respect. Mamm would be ashamed of her.

"I've been looking for you. It looks like I've been successful at last."

Malinda quickly crossed the porch and ran down the steps to meet the visitor in the middle of the walkway.

"Apparently you haven't been receiving your mail, or you've been disregarding it. You are literate, if I remember correctly." The kind, caring smile from the hospital had changed into an ugly, twisted sneer.

"I can read. And I can write, too. In fact, I mailed you a letter a few days ago."

"Really?"

"I thought about trying to call you, but I didn't have a phone number."

"Do you have a phone?"

"*Nee*, but I used one at a local business to call Dr. McWilliams right before Thanksgiving."

"Aha! So you have been in touch with him even after I, uh, *encouraged* you to stay away from him."

"'Encouraged'? It sounded more like a threat."

"Yet you still had the nerve to call Todd, uh, Dr. McWilliams?"

"I called him because he left a message for me to call him."

"Why couldn't you leave him alone like I said?"

"I want *him* to leave *me* alone. I wrote to him asking him to stop contacting me. I told him the same thing when I spoke to him."

"Did you now? It seems to me if that's what you really told him, he wouldn't keep contacting you. Maybe you gave him some indication you liked his attention."

The blonde woman fixed Malinda with a hard stare, making Malinda want to cringe. The nurse reminded Malinda of a curly-haired poodle, but her manner was more akin to that of a Doberman. As the woman took one step forward, Malinda took one step backward. The woman was a nurse. Surely she couldn't be prone to physical violence, could she? "I did not give Dr. McWilliams any mixed messages. My words should have been totally clear to him."

"Do you really think a highly educated man could misinterpret what a simple girl said to him?" She jabbed one index finger with a brightly polished nail toward Malinda's chest.

Malinda shrank back a bit farther. "I may be simple in that I am not so highly educated, but I am not stupid, Nurse Trudy. I am able to speak my mind clearly."

"I can vouch for that." The deep voice startled both

women, who had been too intent on their discussion to notice anyone's approach.

Malinda gasped. Her heart pounded harder than she thought could possibly be compatible with life. "Atlee, I thought you were at work."

"I got off early. I was in the barn. It looks like I came out at just the right time." Atlee didn't remove his black felt hat. His green eyes darted from Malinda to the woman staring at her in an accusatory manner.

"Who are you, and how is this your business?" Trudy's face grew bright red, and she puffed up like a hen plumped up its feathers to guard its baby chicks.

"This is my *bruder* Atlee."

"And my *schweschder* is my business. I was with her when she made the phone call. I heard every word she said and every word Dr. McWilliams said." Atlee moved closer to Malinda and crossed his arms over his chest. He stared hard at the curly-haired woman, as if daring her to question him.

"Hmpf!"

"I also read this last letter you sent my *schweschder*."

"What letter?"

"I know you wrote the letter warning me to stay away from Dr. McWilliams. The handwriting was the same as on the first letter you sent and even matches the writing on my hospital discharge papers." With Atlee's support, Malinda's courage returned.

"You could have saved yourself a trip if you'd talked to Dr. McWilliams or waited for your mail," Atlee pointed out.

"Trust me, Nurse Trudy. I have no wish to return to Ohio. I am not interested in Dr. McWilliams. This is my home, and this is where I will stay. You are totally free to pursue your own relationship with Dr. McWilliams. I pose no threat to your plans."

"Plans!" Trudy muttered half under her breath. "The man

scarcely knows I exist other than to fetch things for him. He's been spellbound by a little Amish girl and thinks she should be groveling at his feet like every other woman he meets."

"Not this Amish girl," Malinda said, breaking into the nurse's ramblings. "I am not groveling at anyone's feet. I only want to be left alone. I hope Dr. McWilliams got the message once and for all."

"I'll see that he does." Trudy spun on her heel and stomped off toward the silver car.

Malinda raised a questioning look to Atlee, who shrugged his broad shoulders in response. Together they watched the silver car whip around and speed down the driveway, scattering pebbles in all directions.

"Who was that?" Saloma called from the back door.

Malinda looked at Atlee. Neither spoke for a moment. Mamm missed nothing.

"Was it just someone looking for something?"

"I guess you could say that." Atlee nudged Malinda and winked.

"Malinda, you'd better get a cloak if you're going to stay outside."

Malinda smiled. Mamm was ever the worrier. "I'll finish sweeping the porch and be right inside." She wiggled her cold fingers to restore their circulation. She'd sweep fast.

"Okay. Did you point that person in the right direction?"

"I hope so."

"*Gut*." Saloma withdrew into the house, closing the door firmly behind her.

"Do you think we got through to Nurse Trudy?" Malinda desperately wanted to permanently close that chapter of her life.

"If we didn't, nothing will convince her. The way she tore out of here makes me think she is heading straight for

Ohio and a confrontation with the doctor. You know, those two seem a perfect match."

"Whatever they do, I hope they stay in Ohio." Malinda rubbed her arms before reaching for the broom. "*Danki*, Atlee."

"Just doing my duty."

Chapter Thirty-One

One week after Thanksgiving, Malinda watched Phoebe Yoder and Ben Miller exchange wedding vows. Again Malinda bustled about serving at a wedding dinner. Would she ever sit at the *eck* with her groom, or was she destined to be a server until she got too old and became the community's old *maedel*?

But she would not be gloomy today. She was too happy for Phoebe. After all the Yoder family—and especially Phoebe—had been through with little Naomi's kidnapping, this wedding served as an extra-special blessing. Malinda could be content with sharing the joy of her *freinden* and *bruders* as they married and spoiling her *bruders*' little ones when they came along. Couldn't she?

Malinda had caught Timothy staring at her several times during the service. She wiggled like one of Aden's captive frogs trying to escape the little *bu*'s grubby grasp. Timothy made butterflies take flight in her belly when he looked at her with those big, blue eyes. She wasn't quite sure when it had started, but she'd begun to care very deeply for the big, gentle man. Too much. She cared too much to saddle him with a less-than-perfect *fraa*. He deserved the best, and that was not her.

"Will you and Timothy be next?" Mary Stoltzfus nudged Malinda with an elbow.

"Huh?" Malinda hadn't heard Mary's approach.

"You've been staring at Timothy, and I noticed him sneaking peeks at you during the service."

"You did? I was?" Could she be any more flustered? Malinda brushed at imaginary lint on her dress and looked away from Timothy.

"I didn't mean to embarrass you, Malinda. I'm only teasing."

"I know. I guess I was a little distracted."

"A little?" Mary chuckled. "I called your name three times."

"Oops!"

"Tim is a nice fellow."

"He is, for sure."

"You two make a nice couple."

"*Ach*, Mary, I don't know about that."

"It's plain he's crazy about you, and I have a notion you feel the same way."

"Well, there's more to it than that."

"Don't let him get away, Malinda. Count your blessings."

Count your blessings. Mary's words echoed in Malinda's mind as she prepared for bed. She had a loving family and *freinden*, a warm home, plenty of food. Only her health spoiled the picture. Generally she felt strong and energetic, but that rug could be pulled from under her in an instant, sending her crashing to the floor. Timothy could be one of her blessings, if she allowed him to be, but he deserved someone he could depend on. He didn't need to wonder and worry about whether her health would fluctuate from one day to the next, or if it would deteriorate altogether. To be totally fair, she should cut all ties with him. A tear slipped down her cheek as she crawled beneath her quilt.

"Another letter for you, Malinda," Aden announced the next day. His cheeks were rosy from his walk home from school. He had asked at breakfast if he could get the mail this afternoon, since he was expecting some sort of bug book he'd been allowed to order from an ad on the back of the cornflakes box. "My book came today. I just knew it would!"

"Change your clothes and do your chores before you start looking at that book," Saloma admonished.

"I will, Mamm."

"Do I need to hold the book until you finish?"

"*Nee*, Mamm. I'll go change and get started right now." Aden thrust the mail into Malinda's hands and dashed for the stairs.

"Bugs! That's certainly one way to get him to move." Saloma clucked her tongue.

Malinda tried to squirrel the letter away in a pocket. She silently folded the envelope in half and jammed it into her pocket with one hand while the other hand tossed the rest of the mail onto the kitchen counter.

"It seems you've been getting a lot of mail lately."

Malinda merely shrugged.

"A circle letter?"

"I don't know. I didn't look at the return address." She wasn't sure the envelope even had a return address in the corner, but the creator of this missive was probably one of two people. Both were people she had hoped to never hear from again. "I'll read it later." Malinda got busy peeling potatoes. She wished Aden had kept quiet and not made a grand announcement about her mail. She couldn't blame him, though. He thought he was being helpful.

Atlee must have felt Malinda's eyes boring through him as he ate. He shot her questioning looks from time to time. She ever-so-slightly shrugged her shoulders. No doubt he would seek her out later. Atlee seemed to have taken over the role of her protector.

Sure enough, Atlee snagged Malinda before she could escape to her room after prayers. "What's up?"

"Another letter," Malinda mouthed without a sound.

Atlee nodded toward the kitchen. "Is there more pie, Malinda?" He spoke louder than necessary so his voice could be heard in the living room.

"You can't still be hungry."

"I'm a growing *bu*." Atlee patted his trim midsection.

Malinda rolled her eyes. "If Roman and Ray didn't sneak back into the kitchen, there might be a piece of pie or two left." She stomped off toward the kitchen with Atlee at her heels.

"It looks like you're in luck. There's a bit of pumpkin pie and a larger piece of apple pie left."

Atlee caught her hand as she reached toward the pie plates covered with aluminum foil. "I don't really want a piece of pie. I'm stuffed," he whispered, patting his belly.

"Well, you'd better make room for a sliver. I won't be part of any lie."

"Give me a teensy-weensy piece of apple, then."

"I'm going to put it on a paper plate."

"Make it small enough, and I'll hold it in my hand."

"So you only want a bite?"

"If I have to put anything else in my stomach, a bite is all that will fit."

Malinda sliced the tiniest piece of pie she could, trying

to make her cut even despite her shaky fingers. Before she could transfer the sliver to the waiting paper plate, Atlee snatched it and popped it into his mouth.

"There." He gulped down the fat chunk of apple wrapped in flaky, golden crust. He pressed his finger to the counter and popped his finger into his mouth. "*Nee* crumbs, either."

Malinda turned on the water to rinse the knife. Under cover of the running water, Atlee asked, "Who is the letter from?"

"I don't know. I haven't read it yet."

"Where is it?"

"My pocket." Malinda re-covered the pie, pressing the foil around the edges of the plate. She heard the light tapping of Atlee's foot on the linoleum floor and knew his patience was wearing thin. She quickly rinsed and dried the knife and replaced it in the drawer. She hung the dish towel on a hook and reached into her pocket.

"I can't believe you haven't read it yet. If it's just one of your circle letters, I'll—"

"I haven't had time to read it. Aden brought it in while Mamm and I were fixing supper. And it's not a circle letter. There wasn't a return address."

Atlee yanked the letter from Malinda's hand and ripped open the envelope.

"Hey! That's my mail!"

"You're moving too slow." Atlee shook the letter open. Huddled close together, they read the few lines scrawled across the single sheet of plain white paper.

"Is everything all right in there?" Saloma called.

Atlee scrunched the paper in his hand as Malinda slipped the envelope into her pocket. "Everything's fine, Mamm. Malinda is cutting me some pie."

"All right. Your *daed* and I are heading up to bed."

"*Gut nacht*," Malinda called. She held her breath until she knew Mamm wouldn't enter the kitchen.

Atlee waited until there were no more shuffling sounds from the other room. "Whew! That was close." He used both hands to smooth the wrinkles from the paper. Malinda scooted closer to read along with him.

My Dearest Malinda,

I understand your position. I know your family and community are important to you. I had hoped I would be important enough for you to alter your plans a bit. Ohio truly is a good place to live. I will honor your wishes and not contact you again. If you change your mind, all you have to do is give me the word, and I'll drive nonstop to Maryland to get you. You will always have my devotion.

Yours,
Todd McWilliams

P.S. I will speak to Trudy and tell her to leave you alone. I believe she will listen to me.

"Of all the nerve! I'm not his dearest, and I gave him no reason to hope I would change my mind. I can't believe . . ."

Atlee's hand on her arm calmed her. "He seems a rather conceited fellow, but I always knew you wouldn't fall for someone like that."

"Not in a million years! I wouldn't dream of leaving my home and family." Malinda paused for breath. "Do you think this whole mess is truly over? Do you think he will keep his word and leave me alone?"

"If we can believe his letter, it sounds like he will wait to hear from you." Atlee elbowed her and snickered.

"Well, he will have a very long wait, then!"

"Maybe Nurse Trudy will get her wish at last."

"I hope she does. She certainly has much more in common with the man than I ever would." Malinda pulled the envelope from her pocket and snatched the paper from Atlee's grasp. She slid the door of the woodstove open and tossed in the papers. "All gone!"

"Good riddance, I say."

"*Danki*, Atlee, for your help."

"I keep telling you, that's what big *bruders* are for."

Chapter Thirty-Two

Timothy whistled a tune from the Ausbund as he dusted the fancy little curlicues on the china cabinet he'd finished constructing just this morning. The tall, heavy cabinet was solid cherry wood with a dark cherry stain. Sam had helped him move it to a safe corner in the front room of the shop. Even used to heavy lifting as they were, their muscles strained with the effort of relocating it.

It was actually more ornate than his usual pieces, but the *Englisch* customer had definite ideas for decorating the cabinet. She had liked his sketches and had visited the shop weekly, oohing and aahing over his progress. It had turned out nicely, if he did say so himself, and it would probably bring in more customers to Swarey's Furniture Shop. The woman's husband and some helpers were due to pick it up this afternoon, and Timothy wanted to remove any specks of dust. He even sprayed the window cleaner on the glass sections and vigorously wiped away any smudges or fingerprints. He threw an old quilt over the cabinet to protect it before heading back to the work area, where the noise of air tools and hammering drowned out his whistling.

The shop had been busy for weeks now and would only

grow busier with the arrival of the holiday season. He and Sam and the Swareys had been putting in long days to fill their many orders. Thankfully, most customers did not want something as elaborate as the china cabinet. His next order was a child's oak dresser that would not be nearly as heavy or showy. It was a solid, functional piece of furniture that he would like to make for his own *kinner*—if he ever had any.

If Timothy had his way, he and Malinda would be published and married the next week. He had promised to give her time, but he hadn't expected it would take this long. He had hoped her *bruder*'s marriage or Phoebe's would have turned her thoughts to her own wedding. He believed Malinda cared for him, but she hadn't yet been able to overcome her misgivings. Maybe he hadn't done a *gut* enough job convincing her the Crohn's disease or any other medical condition didn't matter to him. He scratched his head. He'd convince her yet. Somehow. He picked up the hardware the customer had selected and got to work on the dresser.

Timothy could no longer hear his own whistling as the noise level rose in the work area. He never heard Sam holler for him, but he did see Sam flapping his arms. From Sam's gestures, Tim gathered his china cabinet customer had arrived. He sure hoped she liked the finished product. He'd be glad to have the cabinet safely moved to its home. He brushed his hands against his dusty pants and headed for the front of the shop.

He emerged from the workroom just in time to see his customer tug off her woolen mitten and rub her hand over the uncovered cherry cabinet. "This is absolutely amazing. It's the most wonderful present from the most wonderful husband." She stood on tiptoe to kiss the tall man's cheek. Longing replaced Timothy's initial embarrassment. Would Malinda ever reach up to kiss him? Not in public, of course, but in the privacy of their own home? His cheeks burned hotter than the embers in the bottom of the woodstove. Timothy cleared his throat.

Instantly the woman jumped away from her husband. Her cheeks flushed, but she continued to gaze lovingly at him. A twinge of envy shot through Timothy's core. He needed to curb these yearnings and concentrate on his work.

"This cabinet is absolutely beautiful, Mr. Brenneman. It's even better than I envisioned. You certainly did a magnificent job."

"I'm glad you are happy with it." Timothy felt more than a little awkward at the woman's high praise. "We can help you load it into your truck when you're ready."

"My brother came to help, too," the woman answered. "I've brought some old blankets to wrap around it for protection. Will that work?"

"That should be fine." Timothy riffled through the orders in a brown accordion-style folder on the counter. He plucked out the right one as the woman's husband extracted his wallet from a back pocket.

"We've told everyone about your shop and referred them here for high-quality furniture, right, hon?" The woman latched onto her husband's arm and batted her eyes at him.

"We sure have." The man stopped pawing through his wallet long enough to pat his wife's hand.

They must be newlyweds, Timothy thought. Aloud, he said, "We appreciate that." After completing the cash transaction, Timothy motioned to Sam to help them move the bulky piece of furniture.

"Call Jonathan to come help," the *Englisch* man told his wife. Immediately, she ran to the door and hollered for her brother.

"I think we can get it," Timothy said. He and Sam were accustomed to lifting heavy furniture. They'd moved this very cabinet several times. Lifting it onto a truck would be a bit more challenging, but nothing out of the ordinary for Tim and Sam.

"Wait, Cassie! Tell . . . oops, too late," the customer began, but stopped when a young, gangly man of about eighteen stepped into the shop. "I was going to say Jonathan could back the truck to the door, and I'd help lift."

"I can't drive stick shift anyway," the boy mumbled.

Timothy wasn't sure how much help the fellow would be lifting such a heavy piece of furniture, either, unless those spindly arms were stronger than they looked. Maybe Tim could convince him to spread the blankets in the bed of the truck so he'd be helping but out of the way. He didn't want anyone to be injured.

"Let me back the truck a little closer. Did you leave the keys in the truck?" The customer turned to look at the younger man.

"Yeah. I didn't think any of the horses or cows would steal anything."

The woman rolled her eyes and punched her brother's upper arm. "Don't mind him. He got up on the wrong side of the bed."

"Got up too early, you mean," he grumbled.

Timothy glanced at Sam and suppressed a smile. At nearly midday, they had been up and working for hours.

"Okay. He got the truck as close as possible. I can't wait to get the cabinet home!"

The boy pulled open the front door of the shop, admitting diesel fumes from the truck's idling engine. "Let's get this done."

"How about if you jump up there and spread out a couple of the blankets first?" Timothy hoped that would occupy the younger man while he and Sam got a grip on the cabinet and hoisted it up to carry out the door.

The boy grunted and shrugged his bony shoulders, but shuffled to the door to do as Timothy suggested. Timothy nodded at Sam. On the count of three, they grasped opposite edges of the cabinet and lifted it with relative ease. They sidestepped to the door the *Englisch* lady braced herself against to keep the wind from blowing it closed on them.

"They dragged me here to help, you know." The whiny voice came from somewhere behind Timothy, but he couldn't see over the cabinet to tell exactly where the surly fellow stood.

"Stop, Jonathan!"

Timothy heard the shout the same instant the cabinet swayed in his direction. He couldn't let the cabinet fall and get scratched or even worse. He grunted as he struggled against the momentum of the tilting cabinet.

"It's out of my grasp, Tim. Let it go!"

Sam's voice sounded miles away. "I-I can't." Timothy's muscles shook and strained to bear the entire weight of the monstrous piece of furniture. Somehow the thing struck him on the head. He slid but didn't fall to the ground. Something kept him there with the cabinet, but he couldn't figure out what it was before blackness overtook him. A scream was his last conscious memory.

A jostling movement brought on a series of soft moans that Timothy gradually realized came from his own lips. He tried to turn his head and push himself upright but could do neither. He squinted to try to bring something into focus. Pain clouded his thoughts, and a strange voice floating above him admonished him to stay still. "Wh-what . . ." A gasp took the place of words.

"Tim! Tim! Are you okay?"

"Step back please, sir," the strange voice called out.

"S-Sam?" Timothy tried to turn again.

"*Jah*. I'm here, Tim."

"Lie still, Mr. Brenneman. I'm Russ, a paramedic. We have you immobilized on a backboard in case you have a spinal injury. How are you doing?"

"Pain." Tim struggled not to moan again. "M-My hand."

"I'm sure that hurts. We're going to get you to the hospital right now and get that checked out."

"The hos . . ." Talking took too much effort. Timothy clenched his teeth against the pain that threatened to consume him. He was only barely aware of the stretcher moving toward the flashing lights on the ambulance.

"I'll tell your folks," Sam called.

Timothy couldn't formulate even a simple reply. Pain flashed in his brain like the red lights flashing before his eyes. He felt the stretcher being raised toward the gaping back door of the ambulance. As the vehicle swallowed the stretcher, Timothy allowed the lurking blackness to engulf him and give him blessed relief from the excruciating pain.

Chapter Thirty-Three

Malinda picked at her fingernails as she paced back and forth across the waiting area of St. Mary's Hospital's emergency room. Every now and then one of her black sneakers squeaked on the gray and white tile floor. One of their *Englisch* drivers had raced to the hospital with Timothy's parents, Sam, Emma, Atlee, and Malinda stuffed inside her van. Malinda couldn't see from her seat all the way in the back, but she was pretty sure they'd exceeded the speed limit most of the way.

Tim's parents, Melvin and Fannie, sat side by side in matching plastic chairs, whispering to each other. Sam and Emma occupied two nearby chairs. Malinda couldn't sit still, hence her pacing. As she passed by Sam and Emma, she overheard snippets of their conversation.

"I should have been able to hold that cabinet."

"You couldn't have held it, Sam, if that *Englisch* fellow tugged on it. Once he made it move, there was no way you could have controlled it." Emma squeezed Sam's hand.

"This is crazy. It shouldn't have happened." Sam rubbed the dark whiskers that had been growing since his marriage.

Malinda paced on. What was taking them so long? Shouldn't someone be able to tell them how Tim was doing?

Didn't they know the extent of his injuries by now? She jerked to a stop when Atlee grabbed her arm. She'd forgotten he was leaning against the wall observing the comings and goings in the waiting room.

"Be still," Atlee whispered. "You're wearing a hole in the floor."

"I can't. I'm too nervous to sit still. What is taking so long?" From experience, she knew hospital visits were rarely quick. Assorted people poked and prodded and then poked some more. *Please, Lord Gott, let Timothy be all right. Please don't let him be badly hurt. Let them bring us* gut *news soon. Let us be able to take him home.*

"You know they have to do X-rays and who knows what other tests."

"I know. It's just so hard to wait." Malinda prepared to resume her pacing, but the double doors leading to the patient care area swung open. A tall, lanky, middle-aged man in light green scrubs topped by a white lab coat strode across the waiting room. He stopped in front of Timothy's parents. Malinda rushed over to hear the man's report, with Atlee at her heels.

"Mr. and Mrs. Brenneman?"

"*Jah*."

Malinda gripped the back of a chair and braced herself for the news.

"I'm Dr. Allan." He held out a hand to Melvin. "We're going to admit Timothy. He had a pretty nasty bump on the head and may have a mild concussion. There is no brain bleed or brain injury that we can see on the reports, but we want to watch him."

"*Nee* brain injury. That's *gut*," Fannie whispered.

"But his hand is another story." The doctor's expression became more serious. His bushy brown eyebrows drew together, and a deep frown creased his forehead. "We've called in an orthopedic doctor to take a look. That hand got pretty mangled. There appear to be several broken bones. The orthopedist will have to assess the damage and decide if surgery will be necessary."

Melvin nodded. Fannie grasped her husband's arm. "How bad is it?"

"The hand is very swollen and bruised. I'm not the expert, you understand, but I'm hoping with therapy he will be able to regain some use of that hand."

"Some?" Malinda gasped. Timothy needed that hand. His livelihood depended on being able to bend his fingers to craft furniture. He needed strength in his hand to lift and use tools and move furniture about. He might be able to get by with limited use of one hand with another type of job, but a furniture maker relied on both hands.

"The orthopedist will be able to tell you much more. With all the swelling, he may not be able to tell the extent of the injuries right away."

"Can we see him?" Malinda asked.

"We've medicated him. He's been in a lot of pain. He may be a bit groggy, but yes you can come back. We're waiting to transfer him to a room. There won't be enough space for all of you to come back, though." Dr. Allan's gaze roved over the six Amish people in front of him. "Maybe two or three of you."

Timothy's parents stood to follow the doctor. "*Kumm* with us, Malinda," Fannie said. "I know Timothy will want to see you."

Malinda stood rooted to the spot. Even though she was the one who had asked to see Timothy, she hesitated. Atlee's little nudge to her ribs propelled her forward. What would she say to Timothy? She hated to see him in pain. She could not cry in front of him, even though her nose burned and her eyes watered. She hung back behind the Brennemans as they crept into the tiny examining room. Dr. Allan was right about there not being much space.

"Timothy?" His eyes were closed, and a deep frown creased his forehead. His eyes fluttered open at his *mamm*'s voice. "How are you feeling?"

"Ugh! I-I've been better."

"You'll be all right, son," Melvin said. "You've always had a hard head."

A tiny flicker of a smile curved the edges of Timothy's lips. "N-not my head I'm worried about." Timothy paused for breath, as if speaking those few words had taxed his strength. "I c-can't move my fingers."

Fannie reached back to grab Malinda's hand and pulled her forward. "Look, Timothy. Malinda is here."

"M-Malinda?"

"I'm here, Tim." Malinda stepped closer to the head of the bed as Timothy's *mamm* scooted back, dabbing at her eyes with a raggedy tissue. Malinda remembered how confusing everything seemed in the hospital. Somehow she had to try to put Timothy's mind at ease. "Your hand is pretty swollen right now, so your fingers are probably too stiff to wiggle. Besides, you have a splint or some sort of contraption on your hand to keep it still."

"The doctor isn't sure how bad it is."

"A specialist will look at it."

"I've got lots of work to do."

Malinda wanted to reassure him, to take away his fears and doubts. "Don't worry about work. Sam and the Swareys will handle things until you return."

"Sam is okay?"

"He's fine. He just feels bad that he couldn't keep the cabinet from falling on you."

"The *Englisch* fellow?"

"He wasn't hurt, either, unless his *schewschder*'s punch on the arm gave him a bruise."

Malinda hoped to make Timothy smile, which he did for a second.

"The cabinet?"

"Sam said it was fine. There was one small scratch that he buffed out. The customers took it home."

"*Gut*." The word came out with a grunt. Timothy's frown deepened.

Malinda forced a slow, calm breath. She could not cry in front of Timothy and his parents. "I know you're hurting, Tim." She touched his uninjured hand. "Try to let the pain medicine work."

"I want to go home now." The words came out a little slurred. "My tongue feels furry and too big for my mouth."

"That's from the medicine. They want to keep you tonight, Tim. They have to make sure your head is all right, and the orthopedic doctor needs to see you."

Timothy tried to nod, but groaned instead.

Not knowing what else to do, Malinda patted Timothy's hand. "Rest now." She wanted to smooth his brow, but didn't dare do so with his parents looking on. Instead she focused on the rise and fall of his chest and prayed—*nee*, begged—for his complete healing. The Brennemans remained silent as though at a loss for words. Maybe they were still in shock. It had been a freak accident, something that never should have occurred. If it hadn't been for that *Englisch bu* . . .

Stop it, Malinda! The *bu* didn't mean to cause the accident. He didn't plan for Timothy to get hurt. He'd probably carry guilt around for a long time. Sam said the *bu* had apologized profusely. She would not hold a grudge. She would not blame. She would forgive. That was their way.

"Well, folks, we have a room ready. Timothy will be transferred in just a few minutes." Dr. Allan stepped into the cubbyhole of an examining room.

Malinda scooted back from the bed to give the doctor room to check his patient. "You are welcome to wait and see him again after he's settled in his room, but I can tell you he will probably sleep pretty soundly for a while."

Until the pain awakens him when the medicine wears off, Malinda almost said. She knew how that worked. She glanced from Dr. Allan to Tim's parents. The decision was theirs, since she was not Timothy's *fraa*.

"We will return in the morning," Melvin decided.

"That's probably the best plan," Dr. Allan agreed. "We'll let Tim rest as much as possible." At the sound of voices at the door, he added, "It sounds like the transporters are here now to move him." He backed up a few steps and shook hands with the Brennemans as they thanked him for caring for their son.

Malinda shuffled closer to the bed again. She lightly stroked Timothy's arm. "I'll be back tomorrow, Tim. You sleep now." She resisted the powerful urge to kiss his cheek. She'd be completely mortified if she gave in to that urge. Timothy's pain medicine must be working. His wrinkled brow was now smooth.

She would gladly sit with him all night if they would let her. She hated for him to wake up alone in an unfamiliar place. She glanced up at the bag of clear fluid hanging on a pole. It dripped down a long plastic tube into the arm she carefully patted. She remembered how uncomfortable the thing felt, especially all the tape securing it in place. Malinda squeezed Timothy's hand before following his parents from the room.

"Will he be able to go home tomorrow?" Fannie asked.

"That will be up to the orthopedist, but you could bring him some clothes." Dr. Allan walked with them to the waiting room door. As if on cue, a nurse rushed forward to hand the Brennemans a plastic bag filled with Timothy's belongings. As soon as they stepped through the door, Sam, Emma, and Atlee jumped from their hard plastic chairs and joined them.

Melvin turned to the doctor before they left. "*Danki,* Dr. Allan. We will be back tomorrow."

Tears of relief and gratitude filled her eyes as Malinda bowed her head to offer a quick prayer of thanksgiving before she crawled into her bed. Timothy's accident could have been so much worse. He could have had a head or back injury. He could have been paralyzed or even killed if that heavy cabinet had struck him just right.

Ach! What would she have done then? She shuddered and sniffed hard. She couldn't imagine that. She didn't even want to try to imagine that because . . . because . . . A tear overflowed its banks. Because she loved him. For sure and for certain, she truly loved Timothy Brenneman. She wasn't sure when or how it all had happened, but beyond the shadow of any doubt, she loved Tim with all her heart.

Malinda wanted to laugh and twirl about. She wanted to shout out to the world that she totally loved Timothy, but one drawback sobered her in an instant. She dropped her head onto her folded arms and sighed. Timothy's hand might be too damaged to create the magnificent pieces of furniture he built. Without exhibiting one single ounce of pride, Timothy had told her of his dreams to design and build furniture to meet the needs and desires of his Plain and *Englisch* customers. How would he do that if he couldn't properly use that hand?

Somehow she already sensed his withdrawal from her, in attitude if not in words. His concern for the other fellows and that cabinet let her know his mind was on work. She could understand that. She could also understand his worries over the use of his hand. That was only natural. But she knew Tim. She knew his thoughts the same as if she lurked inside his brain. If Tim couldn't craft furniture, he'd be unable to earn a living. If he couldn't earn a living, he couldn't provide for a family. If he couldn't provide, he couldn't be a husband or a *daed*. He'd be useless. He would totally push her away to spare her. But Tim didn't know what the future held.

Oh my! Malinda jerked upright. That's the very way she thought. She'd tried to push Timothy away because she believed that her illness limited her, that it would keep her from being a *gut fraa* or *mamm*. She couldn't predict the future, either, but now she was absolutely certain she wanted that future to be with Timothy.

Somehow she would have to get through to him. She needed to tell him how wrong she'd been to live her life according to what-ifs. No one had a guarantee. They could only take one day at a time and pack as much love into each day as they could. She would march right back into that hospital tomorrow and tell Timothy Brenneman she loved him and needed him.

Chapter Thirty-Four

A gray day greeted Malinda when she ran down the steps toward the big, idling van. She greeted the driver before crawling into the backseat so Tim's parents could have the second seat. She prayed it would be a *gut* day with *gut* news. She had, in fact, prayed all night, since sleep had eluded her until just before time to crawl out of her warm bed.

"Did you get any sleep?" The driver's eyes connected with Malinda's in the rearview mirror.

"Not a lot." Malinda rubbed her eyes and pushed a wayward strand of hair beneath her black bonnet.

"I'm sure Timothy will be fine. He's a big, strong guy."

It was a blessing there was no sign Timothy had any brain injury. What concerned Malinda now was Timothy's hand. What would happen if Timothy could no longer perform the job he enjoyed? Somehow, if necessary, she would find a way to help him deal with that.

Timothy's parents must have been watching for the van. As soon as it stopped beside their house, they ran out and climbed inside. One look at Fannie's face told Malinda the older woman had gotten no more sleep than she had. Melvin looked only slightly better. Malinda prayed they would all feel relieved after seeing Timothy today and hearing whatever news the orthopedic doctor could give them.

They tiptoed into Timothy's room in case he was sleeping but found him sitting straight up in the bed with two pillows tucked behind his back. The IV tube still ran from the bag on the pole to Timothy's uninjured arm. Dark circles rimmed his eyes, but he looked more alert. The squiggly lines across his forehead indicated he was stoically enduring the pain. Malinda let Tim's parents enter the room first. Maybe the Brennemans would give her a little time alone with Tim in a while.

"How are you feeling, son?" Fannie rushed to the bedside and pressed a slightly trembling hand against her son's forehead. "Has the specialist been in yet? Can you move your fingers?"

"Let him answer one thing before you ask another." Melvin laid a hand on his *fraa*'s shoulder.

Timothy raised his wrapped hand and dropped it back onto the bed with a grimace. "I don't know much yet. They did more X-rays. The specialist hasn't been in to tell me what she thinks." Timothy's eyes left his parents' faces to shift to Malinda's.

"Hello, Tim."

"You came back?"

"Of course. I told you I would."

"Let's step out for a minute." Melvin gave Fannie's arm a tug.

"He didn't answer how he's feeling," Fannie protested.

"I'm okay, Mamm."

"You don't look okay."

"*Kumm, fraa.*" Melvin tugged again. He lowered his voice. "Let them talk a few minutes."

Fannie's expression softened as if she suddenly realized Malinda was in the room with them. She nodded and followed

Melvin to the door, offering Malinda a little smile on her way out.

Malinda tiptoed closer to the bed. Why she tiptoed she couldn't imagine, since it was plain to see Timothy was wide awake. "You're in pain."

"Um, *nee*, um . . ."

"You are. I see it in your eyes and your scrunched-up forehead." Immediately Tim relaxed his facial muscles. Malinda chuckled. "You can't fool me, Timothy Brenneman. I know you are hurting."

"Maybe, some . . ."

"I'm sure it's more than some. Aren't you taking the pain medicine?"

"I'm trying not to."

"Why? You don't need to suffer with so much pain."

"It's not so bad."

"Is that why you're clenching your teeth—because it's not so bad?"

Timothy's lopsided smile managed to unclench his jaw. "That medicine makes me all woozy and fuzzy-headed. I need to think."

"You need to think about resting and healing."

"I need to think about what I'm going to do if I can't build furniture anymore. That's all I know how to do."

"I'm sure you can do anything you set your mind on. That's just the kind of person you are. Smart. Determined."

"Stubborn, you mean?"

"Hmmm. Maybe a bit, but a *gut* kind of stubborn."

Timothy laughed out loud. "I didn't know there were kinds of stubborn." His mirth died quickly. "A person needs his hands to do most things in life, you know."

"Lucky for you, you have two of them." Malinda wanted to keep Timothy smiling, but she understood his fear and worry.

"One may not work right again."

"Aren't you getting a little ahead of things?"

"I need to figure out what to do." With his good hand, Timothy bunched the stiff white sheet into his fist. The plastic IV tubing jiggled with each jerk of his arm. Malinda reached out to still his movement. "I know we don't have any formal commitment, Malinda, but I want you to know you're, um, free."

"Free?"

"Free to, um, find someone else. Maybe you still have some feelings for Isaac." Timothy stared at Malinda's hand on top of his.

"Timothy Brenneman, you look at me!"

Timothy jumped at Malinda's tone and jerked his eyes up to meet hers. His mouth formed a question, but no sound came out.

"You know *gut* and well I don't have any 'feelings' for Isaac Hostetler." Malinda lowered her voice. "I only have 'feelings' for you."

"If I can't work and support myself, how could I support a *fraa* and a family?"

"It seems to me you're borrowing trouble. You don't even know what the doctor will say."

"I can't move my fingers."

"Look at them, Tim. They have a bandage around them and are very swollen. The accident only happened yesterday. You have to give it some time."

"If the specialist tells me . . ."

"As my *mamm* always tells me, Gott's grace is sufficient. Trust in Him."

"But I don't expect you to take care of a crippled man."

"Didn't you say you were willing to take care of me no matter what? You said even if my disease got worse or I had bad flare-ups or even needed surgery you would help me. Right? You said that didn't matter, that vows were for sickness and health . . ."

"*Jah*, I said those things."

"Didn't you mean what you said?" Malinda's eyes flooded with tears.

"Of course I meant what I said. Please don't cry, Malinda." Timothy wiggled his uninjured hand to thread his fingers through Malinda's.

Malinda sniffed and squeezed her eyes shut in an effort to stanch the flow of unwanted tears. Timothy's strong grip kept her from fleeing the room to cry in private. "W-well if you would stand by me, why wouldn't I stand by you?" Malinda sniffed again. She hated the uncontrollable wobbling of her voice. She prayed the pain in her belly stemmed from the ball of nerves lodged there and not from the Crohn's. She needed to be strong right now.

"It's a little different," Timothy said after a seemingly interminable silence. "I'm supposed to be the breadwinner, the strong one."

"We would be a team, working together." Malinda's voice grew stronger and steadier. She had to get Timothy to listen to reason. "Besides, you will work again."

Timothy grunted as he attempted to lift his injured hand. "Really?"

"I believe you will make furniture for the rest of your life if you want to," Malinda said with all the conviction she could muster. "Have faith, Tim."

"You've prayed for your own healing and that hasn't happened. What makes you think Gott will favor me with healing?"

"I know I've been disappointed and frustrated and sometimes angry that the Lord Gott didn't answer my prayers the way I wanted Him to. But maybe He has other plans for me. Maybe He has been trying to teach me to rely on Him. Or maybe I can use my illness to help someone else. After all this time, I think I finally know deep inside what Mamm and the apostle Paul knew all along. Gott's grace is sufficient for me. Gott's grace is sufficient for us, ain't so?"

"Do you truly believe that?"

"*Jah*. Finally. If the Lord doesn't have healing in store for me, I believe He will see me through any flare-up I may have. I trust Him to give me the strength to get through the hard times."

Timothy squeezed Malinda's hand a little tighter. "Do you believe I would gladly care for you when you are sick and would help you any way I could without any qualms or complaints?"

"*Jah*. Do you believe I would help you and care for you even if you could never make furniture again? You are the same Timothy no matter if you are a farmer, a furniture maker, or a shopkeeper. Who you are inside is what matters."

Tears shimmered in Timothy's blue eyes. He blinked. "And you are the same Malinda whether you are sick or well, weak or strong. I love the Malinda inside and have loved you since you tagged along behind Sam and me. I didn't even mind when you threw rocks in the pond and scared off all the fish."

"You l-loved me since then?"

"Always."

"Why didn't you say anything before?"

"You needed time to find out what you wanted."

"What if Isaac and I . . ."

"I loved you enough to want your happiness even if that was with someone else." Timothy paused as if afraid to ask. "Did you love him?"

"*Nee*! It was flattering to be asked to go for rides, but Isaac was not for me."

"Is there someone else you'd want to consider?"

"Absolutely not."

"Not even a smart, well-to-do *Englisch* doctor?" Timothy offered a crooked little grin.

"Timothy Brenneman! You know better!" Malinda tried to pull her hand from his grasp, but Timothy clung fast.

"I just wanted to make sure."

Malinda poked her tongue out at Timothy, causing him to laugh out loud.

"So even if I have to do some other kind of work and have limited use of my hand, you'll stay, um, interested?"

"More than just interested. Together we can weather whatever storms may *kumm*, ain't so?"

Timothy raised Malinda's hand to his lips and pressed a feathery kiss on the back of it. He smiled his dazzling, heart-stopping smile and looked into Malinda's eyes. "We can."

"Ahem!"

Malinda snatched her hand away and jumped back from the bed. Heat seared her cheeks.

"Sorry to interrupt." Melvin shuffled into the room with Fannie right behind him. "The nurse said the specialist was on her way to talk to you."

Malinda's heartbeat roared in her ears. Its thundering rivaled any saw, drill, or hammer in Swarey's Furniture Shop. What would the doctor say? Would Timothy be able to bear the news? Would he be able to live up to the words he'd just uttered? *Please, Lord, give us strength.*

"Everything will be all right," she whispered. Timothy's wink told her all she needed to know. He would accept and deal with whatever the outcome would be. Together they would face any challenge.

Melvin fiddled with his black felt hat, turning it around and around in his hands until Fannie laid her hand on his arm. "Have you thought what you'll do, Tim, if . . ."

"I've been thinking of all sorts of things, Daed. I'll trust the Lord Gott to lead me." Timothy looked straight into Malinda's eyes. His gaze was so intense Malinda felt he could see into her soul. A strange warmth raced through her veins, warming her from her head to her toes. Was this what people meant by finding a soul mate?

Footsteps sounded in the hallway and stopped outside Timothy's door. Malinda took a deep breath and scooted a little closer to Timothy so she could clasp his hand again.

"Good morning, folks," the tall, thin doctor called out before she even entered the room. Strands of her sandy hair escaped from a big, gold clip and fluttered over her shoulder. She wore street clothes, not hospital scrubs, beneath her white coat. "I'm Dr. Cline." She held out a hand to each of them. "I've been going over your X-rays and scans, Timothy."

Malinda sucked in a breath and held it. She could see that Timothy did the same thing. She prayed the news would be positive.

"From what I can see right now," Dr. Cline continued, "they look like clean breaks here and here." The doctor pointed to bones along the top of Timothy's hand. "These fingers also have simple fractures." She indicated the index and middle fingers.

"What does a simple fracture and a clean break mean?" Fannie asked the question that whirled through Malinda's brain.

"It means the bones should heal just fine without surgery. I'll need to align them properly and cast the hand. I'll also want you to go to physical therapy once the cast comes off."

"So I will be able to use my hand normally?" Timothy's grasp on Malinda's hand tightened.

"You may have some residual pain and stiffness for a little while, but the therapy should help with that. If all goes well—and I'm anticipating it will—you will be building furniture again before you know it."

Malinda blew out the breath she'd been holding. "*Wunderbaar* news, Tim." Her broad smile matched Timothy's. "*Danki*, Gott."

"After you are discharged today, you will need to come

to my office so I can properly cast your hand," Dr. Cline said. "I'll tell my staff to work you in when you get here."

Fannie hugged her son before she and Melvin followed the doctor out of the room.

Timothy tugged on Malinda's hand. "Why the tears?"

Malinda used the back of her free hand to swipe across her damp cheeks. "Tears of happiness. The Lord answered our prayers."

"He did, for sure. He always answers."

"Sometimes the answer isn't what we would like, but He does answer," Malinda agreed.

"Do you feel sad or angry that He answered this way for me, but you still have your disease?"

"I used to feel envious when other people experienced healing or when they seemed to get everything they wanted. But now I know Gott knows best. Of course, I'd like to be well, but I can deal with my illness with His help."

"And my help?"

"And with your help. Gott's grace truly is sufficient. His love and your love are all I need."

Epilogue

Fall nipped at summer's heels before August even ended. Malinda didn't mind one bit. In fact, she scarcely noticed the cool breeze that tickled the little hairs on the back of her neck. Her focus rested entirely on the tall, blond man walking beside her along the wooded path.

She stepped briskly, even though Timothy had shortened his stride so she wouldn't have to run to keep up. But she felt like she could run one of the *Englischers*' marathons. She'd had no severe or even moderate flare-ups in a long while. She felt strong and happy. Of course, the young man beside her had a lot to do with that happiness.

Tim had worked so hard during his weeks of physical therapy, pushing himself harder than the therapists demanded. Once the doctor told Timothy a full recovery was possible with hard work, he threw himself into making that happen. He performed his strengthening and stretching exercises at home daily. Malinda knew he'd set his mind on regaining full use of his hand and would accept nothing less, no matter how many times she assured him her love did not depend on his recovery. But she fully believed Timothy Brenneman could do anything he put his mind to. He'd returned to Swarey's Furniture Shop, working on what he called easy projects, but he said he was ready for more challenging assignments.

Malinda knew she was not supposed to be prideful, but she couldn't help feeling a teensy bit proud of Timothy's progress. The Lord Gott had been so *gut* to them. They'd both made great strides, but not only in their health. Their faith in Gott and in each other had grown tremendously. Weathering their medical storms had drawn them even closer, so that their love had deepened and strengthened.

"It seems like fall wants to move in early this year. Look, Tim, there's another fuzzy caterpillar." Malinda pointed out the light brown furry-looking creature inching its way across the path. "The old folks say they're a sign of a hard winter."

"I don't know about that, but I, for one, am anxious for fall to arrive."

Tim winked at Malinda, causing warmth to creep into her cheeks, even though no one was close enough to see them. He reached for her hand and threaded his fingers through hers.

"Timothy! That's your hurt hand." Malinda stopped in her tracks. She grabbed his other hand. "Squeeze both at the same time."

Timothy squeezed.

"Squeeze harder. I can take it. I'm tough."

Timothy chuckled. "That you are." He squeezed harder.

"It's the same, Timothy! You squeezed equally hard with both hands!" Malinda practically jumped up and down in her excitement. She looked up at his amused expression. "You knew that, ain't so?"

"*Jah*."

"You didn't tell me your strength had completely returned."

"I wanted to surprise you."

"Well, you certainly did that."

"I have another surprise."

"Really? What is it?"

"It wouldn't be a surprise if I told you."

"You tell me right now, Timothy Brenneman." She stomped a foot for emphasis.

"Or what?"

"Or I'll . . . I'll . . ."

Timothy burst out laughing. "You sure are cute when you're mad." He bent to kiss her cheek.

"I'm not mad."

"I know. I'm teasing. But you sure are cute." He held up a hand before she could comment. "Okay. I won't torment you any longer. I've started making our kitchen table. I'm using walnut instead of oak."

"Our table?"

"*Jah*. And I've decided on the style of rocking chair to make for you to rock our *bopplin* in."

Malinda clapped a hand to her fiery cheek. "You have? What if I can't . . ."

Timothy placed an index finger on Malinda's lips. "No more what-ifs. Remember?"

Malinda nodded. Her attention was captured momentarily by a movement in her periphery. She shifted her eyes to take in a plump gray squirrel scampering off with an acorn. "It looks like he's getting ready for fall, too."

"I think fall will be my favorite time of year from now on."

"Why is that?"

"It will always remind me that is when you became my *fraa*. You will marry me in the fall, won't you, Malinda? You aren't still worried about your illness . . ."

This time Malinda stood on tiptoe to press a finger to Timothy's lips. "Our love will be able to mend any rift in my health or overcome any disappointment we may face. *Jah*, Timothy, I will marry you. Hurry up, fall!"

Please turn the page for an exciting sneak peek of
Susan Lantz Simpson's

THE RECONCILIATION,

coming soon!

"Hey, Isaac," Atlee Stauffer called as he closed the door of the Clover Dale Dairy behind him. He took long strides to catch up with Isaac Hostetler. He and Isaac had completed their workday and headed out into a blustery January wind. Darkness would creep in early on this cloudy winter day, so both young men hurried to hitch up and get home to do their outside chores before daylight entirely vanished.

"*Jah?*" Isaac slowed his pace a tad but didn't stop. It seemed to Atlee that Isaac generally tried to steer clear of him. He probably felt embarrassed after the mess he'd made of things with Atlee's sister, Malinda. It was pretty hard to blend into the background, though, in a small community, and hard to avoid each other when they worked at the same place.

"Are you going to the singing on Sunday? I hear the visitors from Oakland may postpone their trip home. There might be some new acquaintances to make." Atlee gave Isaac's arm a playful punch.

Isaac pulled his jacket tighter around his neck as if trying to keep the brutal wind from flying down to numb his torso. He hadn't been to singing in a long while. Atlee sincerely doubted this coming Sunday would be any different—even if there were some pretty girls in the load visiting from another community—but he thought he'd inquire anyway. Isaac gave a noncommittal shrug.

"You aren't still pining away for Becky, are you?"

"Good ol' Atlee. You can't let a subject die a natural death," Isaac muttered, not quite under his breath.

Atlee knew the fiasco with Becky had been ever so much worse than the failed relationship with Malinda, but it was time for Isaac to get over that and move on. That was Atlee's humble opinion, anyway.

"*Nee*." Isaac rubbed a gloved hand across his eyes. "Getting involved with Becky was a mistake from the very beginning. I was too much of a *dummchen* to realize that."

"Don't be so hard on yourself. You weren't the only fellow to fall prey to Becky's charms. Besides, we all make mistakes."

"Some of us make more than others. I was stupid enough to think she really cared. Was I ever wrong! I threw away anything Malinda and I had, but I guess that wasn't right, either. Maybe I'll never get it right."

"You will. That's what *rumspringa* is for—to learn and find out what we want, ain't so?"

"I guess so, but you haven't fallen flat on your face twice."

Atlee chuckled. "Who knows what blunders I'll make? Think about Sunday." Atlee clapped Isaac on the back and hurried to hitch his own horse.

Atlee barely had to cluck at the horse to get him moving. He was as anxious as Atlee to get home and out of the cold. Atlee glanced at the heavy gray sky in front of him as they trotted away from the dairy. If it didn't snow tonight, it was missing a *gut* chance. One thing you could always count on about Southern Maryland weather was that you couldn't count on Southern Maryland weather. In a matter of a few short hours the weather could go from sunny to stormy. Some years they had snowfall after snowfall, and some years they didn't even have a trace of snow.

They'd had a mere dusting at Christmas this year, just enough snow to cover the grass and coat the tree limbs, like cream cheese frosting on Mamm's carrot cake. At mid-January, they weren't out of the woods by any means. They still had plenty of time for snow. Some years, winter seemed to last until almost May.

Atlee rubbed first one hand and then the other on his pants leg to create some warmth. He must have left his gloves at home that morning. He'd have to remember to search for them. Frostbite or cracked and bleeding fingers were no fun, that was for sure and for certain.

Atlee's stomach rumbled louder than the clip-clopping of the horse's hooves. He hoped Mamm or Malinda had cooked a big pot of beef vegetable soup or chicken noodle soup. He could almost feel the hot broth sliding down his throat. Maybe his younger *bruders*, Ray and Roman, would have finished helping Daed with the chores by now.

He still missed Sam. Older by two years, Sam had married Emma Swarey last November. He would probably be a *daed* before too long. Atlee's only sister, Malinda, two years younger, already had a beau. She'd gotten over Isaac in record time. Now she and Sam's best *freind*, Timothy Brenneman, were courting. That was all hush-hush, of course, as was the Amish way, but everyone expected Timothy and Malinda to end up married. That was probably a big part of the reason Atlee held no grudge against Isaac. If his little *schweschder* had been weeping and moping about, forgiving Isaac for hurting her would have been a lot harder.

Maybe Atlee should heed the advice he had offered Isaac earlier. Maybe he should check out the visitors at Sunday's singing. He hadn't felt ready to settle down before, but those settling-down feelings had been stirring more and more of late.

He shook the reins to get the horse moving a little faster. "*Kumm* on, Star. We're almost home." Star—what a name for this big, sleek beast. Too bad Daed had let Malinda name him. Even if he did have that tiny white star-shaped spot above his eyes, he deserved something more powerful. At least Chestnut, their other driving horse, had a slightly more dignified name.

Catching the lights of an approaching vehicle in his side mirror, he slowed Star and tried to scoot horse and buggy over as far as he could toward the edge of the country road that had no shoulder to drive on. Most *Englischers* who regularly traveled this road looked out for buggies and patiently waited to pass them. Every once in a while, though, someone unfamiliar with the area or someone in a big hurry made travel downright scary. Since he was able to see around the curve up ahead, he leaned out of the buggy to signal the driver that it was safe to pass him.

Slowly the van drove up beside him. Before Atlee pulled his head back into the buggy, he returned the driver's wave and locked eyes with the passenger in the backseat. Becky? Of course it was Becky. No one else had hair the color of honey dripping from a hot, flaky biscuit and eyes a brighter green than his own. Had she returned home to stay? He smiled and waved again, but she dropped her eyes and withdrew into the shadows of the van.

"Brrr!" Atlee shivered as he closed up the buggy. He didn't know what was frostier—the air or Becky Zook's attitude. The girl in the van did not act like the flirty, flighty girl of a few months ago. He wondered what had happened to subdue that carefree spirit that was sort of akin to his own. Atlee shrugged and urged Star on again. No doubt, any news about Becky would trickle down the grapevine soon enough.

Gut. It looked like his *bruders* were finishing up the chores. He should be able to get away with simply parking the buggy and caring for the horse.

"Great timing!" Roman, his sixteen-year-old *bruder*, called as he exited the barn with thirteen-year-old Ray on his heels. "You managed to show up right when we're finished."

Atlee shrugged. "It couldn't be helped. I had to work a little later."

"Sure you did." Ray tried to scowl but ended up grinning.

Atlee thought Ray was the sibling most like himself. Both of them loved to tease and laugh. "I'll have you know I did not stop off anyplace but raced right home." Atlee feigned hurt at Ray's remark. "Where's Daed?"

"Still in the barn. He told us to go on inside and wash up," Ray replied. "I'll beat you, Roman."

Atlee chuckled at his *bruders'* playful shoving as they sped toward the house. He had half a notion to run, too. The wind's bite had intensified, and with the increasing clouds, full darkness was almost upon them. Atlee finished up the same time as his *daed*, so the two walked to the house together. "I've got to find my gloves." Atlee blew on his hands.

"I probably have an extra pair somewhere."

"*Danki*. I'll search for mine and let you know."

They clomped up the back steps. Warmth and delicious smells enveloped Atlee the moment he crossed the threshold. "Smells like . . ." Atlee paused to sniff deeply. "Beef stew?"

Daed sniffed the air. "I believe you're right."

"Great. I'm starving and freezing!"

"Then we'd better hurry."

"Hey, my gloves!" Atlee lifted his heavy dark gray gloves off the kitchen counter.

"You must have dropped them in your haste this morning,"

Malinda said. "I found them near the door. I even sewed up the little hole on the right thumb."

"*Danki*. What would I do without you? Tell me that's beef stew I smell."

"It is."

"I knew it." Atlee scooted past Malinda and took his place at the big oak table.

After the silent prayer, a plate piled high with thick slices of golden corn bread was passed around. For a few moments, only the clinking of stainless steel spoons against blue ceramic bowls and slurping sounds broke the silence. Then the chattering and laughing began. The Stauffer house was generally not a quiet one. Atlee kept his strange encounter with Becky to himself. What in the world had been going on in her life?

Shadows felt safe. Maryland felt safe. At least she hoped it would be safe. It had to be safer than New York had turned out to be. Rebecca leaned forward only enough to see black-and-white cows happily chewing their cuds in the wide, open field. A windmill spun in the breeze at the next farm. Across the road, a pickup truck and a sports car sat in an *Englischer*'s driveway. That's the way it was in Southern Maryland. The Amish and *Englisch* lived peacefully side by side with fields of corn or soybeans or hay in between them. Nothing like what she had seen in the city. Was it only a little more than six hours ago that she had woven her way among throngs of pedestrians, trying to get to the bus station without being followed?

Rebecca was beyond tired. Even her eyelashes and toenails were weary. She pulled back into the shadows again and leaned her head against the window, just like she had done on the bus. The vibration rocked her, and the van's